TURQUOISE DREAMS

First published in Great Britain in 2020 by:

Carnelian Heart Publishing Ltd
Suite A
82 James Carter Road
Mildenhall
Suffolk
IP28 7DE
UK

www.carnelianheartpublishing.co.uk

Paperback ISBN 978-1-8380480-6-8

Ebook ISBN 978-1-8380480-7-5

Compiler and Editor:
Samantha Rumbidzai Vazhure

Beta reader and proofreader:
Andrea Leeth

Cover design: Rebecca Covers

Typeset by Carnelian Heart Publishing Ltd
Layout and formatting by DanTs Media

Acknowledgments

I would like to express my heartfelt gratitude to the women who contributed to this anthology. I believe each one of them is talented in a unique and extraordinary way.

To:

Mantate Queeneth Mlotshwa
Nyasha Melissa Chiyanike
Tinatswe Mhaka
Nkosilesisa Kwanele Ncube
Nadia Tafadzwa Mutisi
Sibonginkosi Christabel Netha
Chipo Moreblessing Mawarire
Edith Moreblessings Virima
Gwadamirai Majange
Panashe Mawoneke

Thank you for sharing my values, believing in my vision and entrusting your precious art to me.

I would also like to thank:

Andrea Leeth who beta read and proofread the short stories.

Daniel Mutendi of DanTs Media for the interior design of the book.

Rebecca covers for the beautiful cover design.

 5

"There is no greater agony than bearing an untold story inside you."

Maya Angelou

Contents page

Editor's note

The stories in Turquoise dreams provide a context on day to day life from the perspective of Zimbabwean women.

As part of my advocacy work, I compiled and edited this anthology of short stories by Zimbabwean women who had not been published before. The project gave the contributing writers an opportunity to have their story-telling skills showcased to the world.

The name "Turquoise" was inspired by chromotherapy, a centuries old belief in the healing properties of colours; i.e. vibrations in colours are understood to improve mood and overall health. The colour turquoise is associated with feminine energy, as well as sophisticated calming wisdom, creativity, emotional balance and intuition. Turquoise is believed to induce internal serenity, flush negative emotions from the mind and to support detoxification of the body. "Turquoise" was therefore a befitting name for this women empowerment project.

With contributing writers from Matebeleland, Midlands, Masvingo, Mashonaland and Manicaland, the stories portray post-colonial struggles amidst societal degeneration within a declining economic environment in Zimbabwe and beyond its borders. Each writer's biography is presented immediately before their stories.

As an advocate for mental health I feel obliged to include a trigger warning for this collection written from a place of truth:

Some stories in the collection contain themes of self-harm, suicide, alcoholism, depression and abuse. If you are affected by the issues in these stories, please visit any of the following charity websites for help, or search in Google for similar charities local to your jurisdiction.

Suicide - https://www.samaritans.org
Abuse, Anxiety, Bullying, Depression, Loneliness, Self-harm,
suicide - https://giveusashout.org
Suicide and other mental health challenges - https://
www.thecalmzone.net
Mental health issues - https://www.mind.org.uk

My reflections on each story:

Tinatswe Mhaka

Bloody cloth is an engaging account of a victim of marital abuse,
Mwenje, who is stuck between a rock and a hard place. The story
relentlessly explores the themes of emotional and physical abuse,
exacerbated by an unstable economic and political climate in
Zimbabwe. Mwenje eventually takes matters into her own hands
to free herself. The detailed scenes of gruesome violence are epic,
and dare I say poetic!

Mwanangu is a great story highlighting the struggles of a young
girl who is put in an unfortunate situation when her parents die,
and she is left with only one family member to try and make ends
meet. It is sad to find that once again, women have to do what they
have to do for survival, and it is sickening that it has to be at the
expense of using their bodies to do so. Once again, the
deteriorating economic situation in Zimbabwe fuels the appetite
of predator males, and the patriarchy is seen playing its part to
disadvantage the girl child.

Saving Trymore is an exceptionally enchanting story exploring the
aftermath of Cyclone Idai. It is riddled with constant death, and
sexual and mental abuse.

Mantate Queeneth Mlotshwa

Dear mother is a heart-wrenching suicide letter, showing the difficulties of being a married woman in a culture where it seems the husband can never do any wrong, and the woman is always to blame in some form or fashion. Pertinent themes, from the suffocating patriarchy, to gender-based violence, depression, bereavement, are explored beautifully in this story.

The Evidence is an exceptional account highlighting what women have to go through sometimes when dealing with 'gatekeepers' of institutions, who sometimes abuse their power.

The place of a woman is a captivating story about a female political leader who despite her competence struggles to attain equality within her political party. This account left me thinking, *do men really want to see women in positions of power, ever? Probably not!* And this story highlighted that fact.

Nyasha Melissa Chiyanike

Screwed from birth is a truly raw and beautifully written account of a man in a position of power who then took advantage of it. Abusing a young girl with no remorse or shame and no care of how this abuse would affect her life and mentality. It truly baffles me how someone could be so cruel. The themes of abuse, sexism, adolescent pregnancy, poverty, bereavement and depression are well presented in this story.

Cut off is a gruesome account exploring female genital mutilation. I found it shockingly intense and captivating at the same time. This story highlights the extent of cruelty that society is willing to go to cultivate the ideology of patriarchy.

Regret for dessert is a remarkable page turner exploring the problematic issue of arranged marriages in a patriarchal society.

The story also touches on betrayal and is full of twists and turns that kept me in suspense and surprised with each new reveal of events.

Nadia Mutisi

Of Sunsets and New Dawn is a beautifully written story highlighting relatable issues, such as migration and separation of families driven by the unstable economic and political climate in Zimbabwe. The story also explores a transitional period of a young lady who is becoming an adult, in the absence of her mother.

Sinking Roots is an enthralling and nostalgic story highlighting a privileged girl who is disconnected from her culture due to her circumstances growing up. By attending her first funeral, Rutendo feels uncomfortable being around her family because she cannot perform all the customs that are required. The detailed description of a typical Zimbabwean funeral is very well done.

The Storyteller is a charmingly unique piece in this collection. Narrated by a woman, the focus of the story is an older man and his life experiences involving women. We get to see the burdens he has to deal with now, based on the decisions he made as a younger man.

Chipo Moreblessing Mawarire

Naila is a beautifully written emotive piece exploring the emotions most of us do not dare to explore or talk about. I found it an amazing perspective to write this story in the form of a letter to the narrator's family, expressing thoughts that perhaps she did not feel comfortable to say in person, a common predicament for a lot of people who grow up in a culture of silence to avoid ruffling feathers.

Finally, I cried is an excellent chronicle of how the narrator used her role in a play to be the space where she finally liberated her tears. In this charmingly written piece, which a lot of readers will relate to, the themes of grief and the role of culture in dealing with loss are relentlessly explored. I journeyed with the narrator and felt every word, thinking to myself *sometimes that is all one needs to do to release all the pain that is sitting on top of their shoulders, to truly feel free and unburdened.*

Tombstone unveiling is a captivating account with so many layers, from the culture using women as pawns of the patriarchy, to the ending of a mother-daughter relationship and the spiritual death of her sister at such a young age. The dramatic ending is the climax of the story, which I found exhilarating.

Sibonginkosi Christabel Netha

The Office is refreshingly romantic, and I really enjoyed having the perspective from the two characters, Tendai and Victoria, as they narrated their experiences with each other. The narrative is based in South Africa and explores the themes of migration, xenophobia and separation of families. Both sexes are equally represented in this story and I smiled throughout the read.

The thing with feathers is a delightful story inspired by Emily Dickinson's poem, "Hope is the thing with feathers". The theme of displacement and its impact on mental health is very well handled through vivid descriptions, and I like the fact that for a change a woman saves the day in this story. The men also appreciate what she is doing, rather than ostracise or pressure her into the usual dichotomy of gender-based roles. This is different and a breath of fresh air.

Ukuhlalukelwa explores grief exceptionally well, illustrating the aftermath of a twin sister who decides to take her own life - A really sad situation, but not uncommon, which is truly heartbreaking. I found the description of the funeral amusingly relatable.

Nkosilesisa Kwanele Ncube

Lost is a well-written impassioned piece exploring the themes of love, loss and grief. In this tragic love story, the scene is taking place at a funeral and we are driven to empathise with Azania who has lost the love of her life.

Precious is a powerful story showing the naivety of a small-town girl living in a big city and dealing with the pressure of her peers who look nothing like her. It is a huge adjustment for such a young girl, and certainly a life-lesson. I found this piece beautifully presented, aptly exploring the themes of love, miscarriage, tribalism and culture within marginalised communities in Zimbabwe.

Sins of the father is an excellent story highlighting what someone with a mental health issue deals with on a daily basis. The story navigates the triggers of suicide, however simple they may seem to others. The issues of abuse, alcoholism, depression, challenging relationships with parents are some important themes that a lot of readers will relate to.

Gwadamirai Majange

Her dilemma was a welcomed change up from the stories of men abusing women. In this delicately presented piece, we get to see a woman in power who is killing it at work, but unfortunately her children are suffering with both parents not being home often. It is clear from this account, that the burden only falls on the wife and not the husband, as in most patriarchal societies.

She is not my type is a well-written suspenseful story where the scene is set in an Uber in South Africa. It was refreshing to see that a woman played a role in a man's life that led him to shift his consciousness, from superficial wants and needs, to things that are more valuable in life.

Looking to the spirit is a lovely switch up in the book, with more of a positive outcome after Fari struggles financially and mentally in the middle of her life, due to societal judgement and shaming in a marginalised community. The themes of culture, religion and mental health are refreshingly explored in this story.
Edith Moreblessings Virima

The marriage is a scandalous story set at a *roora* (bride-price ceremony) scene. The story exceptionally highlights the toxicity of family enmeshment, an aspect of life that African society refuses to grasp, because it is not aligned with its culture. Unfortunately, two women are the victims of betrayal and deceit.

The promotion is a story that expertly presents power struggle and gender inequality in the workplace. It is clear from this story that even when women make the effort to attain qualifications and climb the career ladder, they are highly likely to be sidelined for progression opportunities. Other themes, such as mental health, child loss, deception and infidelity are also weaved in this story which ends on a classic cliffhanger.

The secret is a well presented fast-paced short story which reveals an unusual mess at the end. Themes such as the decline of the economy, causing the characters to cross the borders of Zimbabwe into Botswana for basic commodities are subtly explored.

Panashe Mawoneke

Cyclone Idai is a great narrative on the events leading up to the tragic Cyclone Idai. Set in the village of Ngangu in Chimanimani, the mindsets of people who were worried and the ones who seemed unbothered before the cyclone hit are well presented. The aftermath was truly horrific, and the narrator competently painted that picture in this story.

Coronavirus gives a perspective on the impact of the Coronavirus in a marginalised society already suffering the aftermath of Cyclone Idai. People are struggling financially or losing their job due to the lockdowns. The narrator explores the paradoxical situation from which local residents cannot escape. Either keeping people 'safe' by imposing lockdowns in the country, but people cannot earn a living to pay for their day-to-day survival; or keeping everything open, and potentially 'risk' more people getting sick. The story is a candid reflection of the very strange experience of living through consecutive natural disasters.

Mantate Queeneth Mlotshwa

Mantate Queeneth Mlotshwa is a creative passionate about the meaningful participation and representation of women and youth in policy and decision-making processes. In her professional work as the Programme Lead for Art4Change at Magamba Network, Mantate works with young, socially conscious artists who use music and film, and other forms of art to amplify the issues prevalent in their communities. She is a speaker and poet, a blogger on www.radites.com and a social media enthusiast who uses her voice to push for justice, inclusion and the empowerment of marginalised voices. Mantate has been listed in the Gumiguru Incorporated 40 Under 30 Emerging Leaders of 2017, and recently, the 100 Most Influential Zimbabweans Under 40 by Zimbabwe Leadership Institute.

The Evidence

Just like that, university is a wrap. All the four years are done, and I will be a first-generation graduate in my family. My father will be proud. It feels almost impossible that I, a girl who comes from nothing is suddenly becoming something. Well, maybe I should not count my chickens before they hatch. I still have to get my dissertation mark, but it is guaranteed that I will pass. My supervisor confirmed that I will get a distinction even. I should call my father and let him know the good news, but first I need to pass through Dr. Mbali's office. He must want to tell me the outcome of my dissertation. I can feel the chills sprinting through my body. The feeling is unmatched. I am done with my degree!

"Good afternoon Lwazi, you look gorgeous today. Please come in and take a seat."

Oooowkay! The department chairperson just told me I look gorgeous. It is a compliment, but it feels misplaced, like it is not his place to comment on how I look. Maybe I am just being petty, so I tone myself down and say my thank you as I sit across from him in one of the couches in his spacious office. By this time, he is grinning and showing off unevenly shaped yellow teeth. His eyes are disturbingly dark, making him seem somewhat dangerous looking. I think I watch too many movies, which may explain my paranoia. I mean, the man is probably overly 'kind' yet dark, evil-eyed. My mind wanders into thoughts of the weirdness of this man. A soft pat on my shoulder snaps me back to reality. I freeze. Dr. Mbali is sitting on the arm of the couch I am sitting on and has his hand lightly grazing over my right shoulder. I jump off the couch startled and the first thing that jumps out of my mouth is, "What the hell Dr. Mbali, what are you doing?"

"Oh, please Lwazi stop acting innocent. You know you are attractive so just cut this chase. What do you expect from men if you parade yourself in tight dresses and short skirts? We are visual beings and almost always want a slice of what pleases our eyes. It is not rocket science. Besides, you want a pass on that dissertation do you not? It is in your best interests that you come back and sit down here or take a fail. The university will be happy to see you come back to repeat a year. It is your choice, just do not waste my time!"

His hand is pointing at the couch I had jumped off from, signalling for me to sit back down. I stand frozen, like my feet are nailed to the carpeted floor. My entire world dropping down from ecstatic to terrifying in a matter of minutes. The inner me is screaming, throwing weak punches and telling me to run, but my feet remain frozen. Returning to that couch is definitely out of the question, but the one thing I cannot shake off is the reality that this resolve, to not submit to this extortion, is the basis for my failure to pass my dissertation, and therefore to graduate from university. My success, and the dignity of my family, depends on the demands of a man who told us on orientation day four years ago that his job is to make our experience in the humanities department fair and one of equal opportunities. This monster who now stands before me and demands that I understand how it never will be about how smart I am, but about what those with influence think I need to give of myself to progress through the different levels of life. I am disgusted!

"But Dr. Mbali, this is not fair. It violates the principles that govern our learning institution. A student needs to compile her dissertation as guided by her supervisor and whether she gets a pass or a fail has nothing to do with her attractive body. What about those girls you do not view as attractive, do they get straight passes because they do not possess that which you seek to extort from me? Why should I be made to suffer for the way I look, as if it is a crime to be attractive? Why...."

I can see the irritation turning into flames in his eyes. He is now standing and walks over to me with a glare that I suppose is meant to make me feel the weight of his demands. "Spare me the lecture Lwazi, I have no time for this nonsense. I have other students coming in to check on their dissertations and if you think you cannot give me what I want, then step out of my office and I will see you when you come back to repeat your fourth year. Do not try to drag my name with ridiculous claims when you get out of this office. No one will believe that a man of my reputation would hit on a poor, good-for nothing girl like you. If anything, it will get you expelled for threatening to distort my character. Get out."

I almost sprint out of his office, gripped by both fear and the overwhelming need to locate my supervisor. I cannot fail, I have to graduate. It was difficult to pull through the final year and if I do not wrap this up, I may never get to finish my degree, unless I get a job and save enough. That would also take over two years. I also cannot call my dad and cause alarm, and besides, he is most likely to be angry at me for supposedly seducing my department chairperson. Why does there seem to be a lot of things I cannot do, and not so much I can do. Reporting the chairperson to the dean of students would make sense, but I have seen them drink together outside of work, so it is most likely they are friends. Well the entire system of staff in this school looks like they would defend the "respectable" dean over a 24-year old girl who I am sure they think is drama because she supposedly parades her attractive body around so that males in the school can reach out for a slice. That statement still infuriates me. But I will address that later. I have to find the supervisor; he is a good man and has consistently commended my hard work. I am sure he will side with me and help me to fight for my pass. I hope he will!

I heave a sigh as I find his office door open a couple of inches. I guess my entry is a little too loud, too out of the ordinary, because right when I enter, he jumps up and says, "What in the name of the Lord is wrong with you Lwazi, you are pale?" He is not exactly wrong. My face is ghost-white and I am shaking. My bloodshot eyes screaming with anger, hurt and helplessness. In all my struggles with the dissertation, I had never cried or complained to my supervisor, and so seeing me in a broken state must be rattling him, because he stands there unsure of what to do. My brain is instructing me to breathe, deeply, and let out this avalanche of emotions that I am allowing to accumulate inside. I do. Take almost five deep breaths, before bursting, "I will not be graduating. I am not getting that distinction you said my dissertation deserves. I will not be anything in life. Success is not reserved for poor and powerless people like me!"

"Lwazi, slow down. What is going on? What are you rambling on about? Your dissertation is a masterpiece, and all your courses are up to date with above satisfactory credits. What nonsense are you declaring by saying you will not be graduating? What happened?"

For some reason I am relieved by my supervisor's shock. Dr. Mbali's arrogant conviction that the school will never side with me had made me suspect that my supervisor might know his unruly tendencies and actually side with him regardless...because of the stupid bro code! Seeing him almost tear apart at the words he hears surging out of my mouth is all the confirmation I need that this is the man I can trust. If I am going to fight the school for my pass, I need the one person who knows me for the consistent, hardworking student I am. His confidence in me, and his authoritative voice might form the pillar for the allegations I am determined to raise against Dr. Mbali. I want justice, but justice does not come on a silver platter for people like me, who are not connected to anyone. Justice for the poor needs voices that matter to be on our side, otherwise the battle is a guaranteed win for those who perpetuate abuse and injustice. With Dr. Nhlalo on my side, my hopes start to flare. Maybe there is still a chance that I could still graduate.

I narrate my experience in Dr. Mbali's office, and by the time I finish, Dr. Nhlalo is lost for words. When he finally speaks, his words break me. "I will not even lie to you Lwazi, I believe you. What makes this heart wrenching for me is the very possibility that there are so many more students who have been failed for rejecting the advances of the chairperson. I have always been concerned when the best students I have supervised come back to me with a fail on their dissertation. I just never thought Dr. Mbali, in all the reverence and worship his name is dished, could be this selfish and unprincipled. It offends me enough to want to help you in the best way I can."

That is all I need from him. His unwavering support as I prepare myself for a legal battle. Yes, that is the route I am taking. I am taking Dr. Mbali to court. However, the court will want evidence, so I need to find an excuse to go back to his office and document his advances. I also need to make sure he does not suspect I have told anyone in the school. If the man has been doing this for years, he probably knows how to be careful. I just need a bright idea that he will not even suspect to be a trap. Bingo! I know just the thing he will love to hear. If I tell him that I have been thinking about his proposal, and want to talk further, he will want to see me as soon as possible. That is exactly what I type into the text I send him, which as I suspected, gets an instant call back.

"Hello gorgeous, I knew you would come around. I am still in the office if you want our little talk to happen right now. We can finalise everything and see where I will meet with you after school tomorrow for our little exchange. I like how smart you are, choosing your dissertation over some hot-headed rejection of an influential man like me. I cannot imagine anyone would want to cross me."

How naive does he think I am? I need to let him go on thinking he has me wrapped around his little finger. He will not know what hit him. This recording will be the end of this career and position whose influence he flaunts. I will make sure I end him so that no other female student gets extorted by him. How I manage a shift from a serious, matter-of-fact face to a plastic smile on entering Dr. Mbali's office is a mystery. I am just standing there, and he does not waste time. I had left the door open but he walks around me to close it, and then comes back, wraps his hands around my shoulders and starts going on about how I have made a good decision and should be proud of myself. The irony! I had made sure to start running the audio recorder before I entered his office, so I do not flinch as he walks me to the chair next to his desk and tells me to sit and relax. I pretend to be okay with the stench coming out of both his mouth and his body. The nausea I feel is not just about his disgusting odours, but the thought of how much of an animal he is. I want to throw up, but I continue with that pasted smile, because this is not about me, but the precedence of abuse that I have the opportunity to break. Even if it means keeping up with this filthy man.

Again, I am lost in this train of thought and do not see that Dr. Mbali is getting out of his trousers. His shirt is already off, and all this time he has been speaking, but I had shut off completely. My panic levels are shooting off the roof and I am doing my best not to scream. As I snap back into reality, I hear him say, "You think I do not suspect that you might change your mind if I plan this for a different day? I know you sneaky young ones. You think you are clever. Come on get that dress off, I do not have all day!" I stand frozen. I am so terrified that I cannot move a limb. I am sure he notices that, because he rushes to me and starts trying to unbutton my dress. I gather the courage to push him off, but he is strong, and I can't resist him. My best bet at freedom is an ear-splitting scream and that is exactly what I break into. I feel the walls vibrate and in almost a split-second, I hear people beating down the door. This man is so conniving, he had even locked the door. He thought he could force himself on me and I would not scream for help. I came here for an audio recording of a man in authority demanding sex from a student to approve her dissertation. Scared as I am, and risky as this move was, the door bursts open, and the universe gives me just the evidence I need. Dr. Nhlalo is the first to step into the room, his face a mixture of fear and relief that I am okay, but also that the man was caught right in the act. This is where it stops, this is where I stop being afraid of not graduating.

Dear Mother...

It has been well over a year since I wrote to you, and almost three years since I saw you. I cannot say that I miss you, at least I do not see there being a reason for me to do so. Our last conversation did not exactly end in a way that makes a daughter feel her mother can still play a role in her life. It stripped me of the freedom to come back to you for the kind of support and guidance expected of one who gave birth to me. I would like for you to not mistake my writing as a sign that I have forgiven you. I have not forgotten how you chose everything over me and my sanity. Rather, I write to you because I need to be clear about what you did wrong, so that you are not in the grey lines about my decision to stay away from you, and your family. I just addressed you as mother and it feels sour in my mouth, so maybe I should resort to calling you Hlelekile, your first name, because you do not from where I stand, live up to the premises of motherhood. I will get straight to the point. I can imagine that with all the hospital errands you need to do for your sick husband, you barely have time for letters.

In my last letter to you, I mentioned that Nkondlo had on multiple occasions raped me. From the tone of your reply letter, it was not difficult to pick out your disbelief, and much unfortunately, your disappointment in me for supposedly viewing my husband in a way that disgraces you and your family. I am not surprised that as always, the issue jumped from the urgency of my sexual violation to the dignity of the Mdlongwa name. You stated quite authoritatively that there is no rape in marriage! That a husband cannot rape his wife, and that is something I was trying to emphasise in my last letter to you. The idea that a man who loves his wife would not violate her. Well, I did think we were in agreement until I read further and listened to you explain that it was not rape I was enduring, but the fulfilment of my husband's rights to my body, even at the expense of my own. That consent is not something meant for women like me. You mentioned that because he paid my lobola in full, I owed it to myself to give all of myself without reservation to my husband. I still cannot reconcile the reality that an exchange of cows in the name of strengthening family ties is an insignia of relinquishing my rights as a woman, and my submission to be abused by a man who stood in front of a pastor and vowed to love me in a way that honours and respects me. It is not just this realisation that overwhelms me, but hearing it from my mother, and the terrifying possibility that I will be expected to instil the same in my daughter one day. Every other word in your letter felt like a sharp-edged sword being driven right through my heart, and to this day I still bleed. I still bleed!

My hope in opening up to you about the half a decade of rape by Nkondlo, which felt like a lifetime, was that you would read between the lines of my decision to say "no" to him and understand that something was amiss in my marriage. Clearly, I overestimated your willingness to know if my marriage had been a happy one. I am compelled to conclude from the tone of your letter that from the time you received my lobola, you ceased viewing me as your responsibility. I have reason to think I am to you and your family a commodity that you were relieved to get rid of and are annoyed by my reaching out with a truth that may disrupt the comfort of your relations with Nkondlo's family. It is these thoughts that sadden me, that I am that insignificant to you. As I already mentioned at the beginning of this letter, I want to highlight as much of the sources of my resentment for you as I can, so that you gain a thorough understanding of why my relationship with you is in my eyes beyond repair. I do not see myself coming back on this decision to cut ties with you and the Mdlongwa family for life.

In the second year of my marriage to Nkondlo, I sent you a letter with the precious news that I had conceived, and you would be a grandmother. I had hoped you would visit me and share in the joy of my journey to motherhood. I thought because it is something that was hammered in as priority on the list of things I am expected to fulfil as part of my duties to my husband, you would be thrilled. I kept telling myself that you were busy, that you had justifiable reasons for not showing up until I did not have to, because eventually there was no baby to even talk about. I was young and my trauma became my companion. I wanted to write to you and tell you that you would not be a grandmother after all, and that I was so broken. I wanted to tell my mother of how wrecked I was that I never got to carry to full term the child I had hoped would be the source of my consolation and comfort in the otherwise violent marriage. I did not write to you because Nkondlo said he had told you, and you had said I was not the first nor the last woman to suffer a miscarriage.

Cold as those words felt in the already uncaring world of loss, fear and isolation that I was drowning in, I still wrote to you a year later informing you that you would be a grandmother. That the heavens had smiled down on me and allowed me to conceive again. You would think that by that time I had learnt to not expect a joyous response from you, but no. I kept waiting for you to show up and tell me that this time it would work out and I would be a mother. You did not show up for me. Your silence was a deafening nightmare that I had to sleep through every night and hope that it would not jinx my pregnancy. Watching and feeling my child grow in my belly gave me the strength and the will to keep believing you had a justifiable reason for not being there for and with me. I held on to that growing being, because it really was all that I had, all I lived for. As fate would have it, I lost that baby too. This time it was even more difficult for me because I started to believe what my in-laws were saying, that there truly was something wrong with me. I still think you feared the same because for some unknown reason you came to me. I still remember that because I had grown accustomed to being shut out from the world, I had not on that day been wearing my scarf, or glasses, or the heavy make-up that had made me the joke of the community. They used to talk about how I dollied myself beyond recognition, but none of them stopped to think that maybe I was covering marks of pain with the layers of foundation and face powder. I do not think Nkondlo knew you were coming that day, because he would have instructed me to cover the bruises and scars that walled my body. I did not need to cry when you walked in. Every moment of my days was full of tears. Even though I did not see you drop a tear, I swear I thought I saw through my bloodshot eyes a sadness and anger in your eyes. I vividly remember you running straight to the corner of the room where I sat broken, in black clothes, mourning more than just the loss of another child, but everything that reminded me of how lonely and miserable my life had become. I expected you to embrace me, to hold and comfort me. I thought you would wipe the tears off my eyes and tell me you were taking me back home with you. I was very wrong. You were not angry at what had evidently been done to me. I can still feel the anger in your hands as you grabbed me by my hands and forced me up. You slapped me and told me that I needed to pull myself together and stop being an embarrassment to the Mdlongwa family. You went on about how I needed to remember that I was a wife and that while I was wallowing in self-inflicted misery, my husband was not being fed, or clothed in the dignity with which a married man was entitled to. Your coming to see me was an extension of my father-in-law's fury and demands for me to do what Nkondlo paid cows for. To stop being an irresponsible, good-for-nothing wife who could not give her husband children. The "waste of cows" they used to call me! You were not there because you wanted to make sure your only daughter was okay after her second miscarriage. You were there because someone had to remind me that I was the problem and needed fixing. I was honestly disgusted and crushed by the very realisation, that for as long as Nkondlo's cows were in my stepfather's kraal, I had no voice and my mother was there to remind me of it.

You have always been a very instinctive woman. You would know things without getting an explanation of them, but for some reason you failed to connect my battered body to the cycle of miscarriages. As if my puffed-up eyes and missing teeth did not scream an all too familiar story. Cold whispers deemed me to have barren lands, without ever questioning who kept poisoning my well. I can tell you that I do not believe you thought me barren when you walked into fragments of me. You knew at that moment I had lost my children to the kicks and punches of a man you consistently instructed me to submit to. No wonder you were not moved when the third and fourth children were lost the same way. At that point you must have thought because your daughter was not barren, as you had made her believe she was, it was not your responsibility to explain to Nkondlo's family why I still was not giving him children. You practically turned a blind eye on my cries for rescue because your cows were safe, even though it meant your daughter was not. There is nothing more painful than a consistent feeling of rejection, of insignificance and exiled isolation. You inflicted that on me. To this day I still bleed!

"You are your husband's and submitting yourself to his law is your only calling" you would say, even when it meant that a woman lost herself in the process. I can just about see you shaking your head in amusement at how trivial my reasons for resenting you are. I guess because my father had been a better man to you, I was hoping you would understand why I think I deserve better. My stepfather must really have changed you, and that is something I cannot reverse. Accepting this forms the basis for my choice to step away from your shadow, and to stop expecting you to be a mother to me. Because, that is a role whose execution you have failed to honour.

As I write this letter to renounce my relation to you, I also want to tell you that I have decided to end it. At least you will not have to be ashamed or embarrassed by my choice to end the pain this way, since I have renounced myself as your daughter. While I am grateful to have lived, I regret that I was born to you, and that a greater part of my life was marked by a pain and distress your protection and love could have eased. It would have been nice to have a mother that actually did what mothers do – protect, encourage, comfort, celebrate and inspire. You did not give me that, or even try, and that is what kills me the most.

Goodbye mother, or must I say, Hlelekile.

The daughter you failed,

Zilingo

The place of a woman

"Excuse me Owethu, Dr. Ndlelenhle is on the phone for you. He says it is an urgent issue, so he insists I get you on the call. Yes, he confirms knowledge that you have a press conference in the next ten minutes but as you know, he is the type of man you do not want to cross, so I told him I am putting you through. Can I?"

As I reached over for the phone, I could not help but run a mental scan of possible reasons why my predecessor would call me a few minutes before I took the podium for my first press appearance as the President Elect of the country's opposition political party. Instinctively, I concluded he wanted to give me last minute advice to ease my nerves as I stepped into his big shoes. That is the only plausible justification I could place my finger on that would make a man who consistently taught me that punctuality is synonymous with good leadership delay my press conference. Five minutes later and I am a total wreck!

My nickname in the political arena is "Margaret Thatcher", the former British Prime Minister who was nicknamed Iron Lady for her uncompromising politics and leadership style. I have served in different positions at the Drivers of Change (DOC) political party for at least ten years and most recently received the shock of my life when all ten provinces nominated me for consideration into the party presidency at our annual convention. My shock did come from a place of doubt of my capabilities to lead DOC to even greater heights, but it just felt almost impossible that a unanimous decision to entrust a woman with the leadership of our strongly traditional political party was made across all the provinces. That move in itself was history made and I was the subject of this revolutionary moment in our politics.

The weeks leading to the convention pretty much confirmed my fears, that my nomination was not supported by the larger population of misogynistic members of the party who did not hide their hope that I would lose the election because I am a woman, and to them, lacking in understanding of the density of the position of Party President. The same people who for the past two years had not expressed discontent at my competence as the Deputy Party President suddenly expressed that they did not have confidence in my ability to grasp the demands of a presidential position. For them, a woman needed to know her place, and aspiring beyond the appointed position of Deputy President was an insult to the sympathisers who gave her that subordinate position to start with. Two weeks into the campaigns, I almost threw in the towel. I was overwhelmed and felt at some point that maybe they were correct in calling me a "place holder!" That maybe I should be grateful for the very fact that I was sitting as the first female Deputy President of the political party and stop dreaming beyond what my biological disposition allowed me to be in a patriarchal society where women are incapable as and when men dictate.

At the beginning of the third week of the campaigns, Dr. Ndlelenhle extended an invitation for me to meet the representatives of the provincial executive committees whom he emphasised fully endorsed me as their preferred candidate for party presidency. I did not stop to question why it did not seem to bother him or the committee members that a greater population our party supporters were against me, I was just elated! Knowing that I had the vote of confidence of the authoritative members of the party, the ones whose votes would put finality to my election reenergised me to run a campaign that built confidence in my leadership. For every box I ticked as incapable in the eyes of the chauvinistic party members, I worked hard to tick a box of competence in the view of the provincial committees. I had realised at that moment that I could not change the fact that I am a woman, a young woman, but I had the power to tell the story of my role and contribution to building our party over the ten years I had served it as a member and as a holder of multiple positions. I centred the greater part of my campaign around mobilising individuals and constituencies that had benefitted from leadership. It came in handy that all my charity, social service and capacity building programs had been spread across the ten provinces. Women and girls came forward with testimonies of how the seed funding for projects that my fundraising committee made accessible to women at different levels of the society empowered them to find the financial independence to earn the respect of their communities. Young men took it upon themselves to tell communities about how I had championed the cause for men who were victims of gender-based violence because I did not just stand for the respect of women, but for men too. They told stories of my inclusive policies and ideas.

My speeches did not articulate ambitious promises that would increase my chances of winning the election without guarantee of fulfilment of the promises, but they hinged on helping people understand how they contributed to everything I had done for the different provinces. I proposed to sustain a campaign that challenged people to recognise and embrace the power they had to make leaders do their job in a way that progressed communities. In an ideal society where people buy into leaders that bring results, you would expect a campaign of that nature to challenge more than the bare minimum in behaviour change of those that hated me for being a woman and young. You would think that showing them they were better off with leaders like you would make them rise above their pettiness but it did not unfortunately work out that way for me. It was quite the contrast actually. I was accused of trying to buy people's allegiance and favour, which I could not secure without referencing my so-called "good deeds" which by the way were merely a product of the space, opportunities and resources that came with my position as Deputy President. It was said I never did anything out of an honest desire to serve my people, but just as a tool to get me into the Presidency. Ten years of unwavering commitment to my political party poured down the drain to suit a narrative that delegitimised my potential as a woman. The worst of that experience was that it came from both men and women. I was angry, but not defeated, because at the back of my mind, Dr. Ndlelenhle's assurance that I would be elected into office remained unshaken. If I could not convince the masses to accept me, then my best bet for winning the election was the loyalty of the committees and the promise of the incumbent President. I needed to get in, and then challenge mindset change from within, right? Well, I was wrong!

On Friday the 13th of November 2020, I was unanimously voted the President of the DOC. I had thoroughly prepared myself for the triumphant moment. I knew to the last full stop, the speech I would deliver to the press as a public notice of my election. I was prepared to talk about how my nomination and election was by default a confirmation that history had been made where the representation of women was concerned. For the first time in the history of ruling political parties in Africa, a woman had been given the space to take up the highest position in the country. It felt to me like my political party, despite the train of allegations of electoral fraud, kidnaps and assault, corruption and nepotism and the negativity that people who opposed it within and out of the country claimed that it characterised with, had taken the world by surprise. We had made history by championing gender equality through practical empowerment of women into positions of influence. This was the narrative I was refining before I received the call from Dr. Ndlelenhle. This is the narrative the phone call shattered!

As I placed the phone back on my desk, I could still hear the cracky voice of my predecessor as he trailed on about how apologetic he felt for the miscommunication. That is what he called it. A glitch in the way the intentions of the party had been articulated to me when I was nominated for the Party Presidency. The man congratulated me for my victory and told me he was proud of the woman I had become – resolute and unwavering in my support of the party. He instructed me to check my email for the speech the party had prepared for me to present at the presser. I do not think he had even listened to my protests and explanation of how I wanted to present a speech that came from my heart because that would be the premise of my leadership, heartfelt! He told me I had so much to learn and part of that was understanding the voice I needed to take to the public was the voice and interests of the party. That meant I did not get to choose. It had been decided for me, by MEN, what I would say.

"You thought the party leadership would disrespect the majority of its followers to make a decision that is out of its character by voting for you on the basis of a call for gender equality. Our choice to nominate and vote for you was a calculated move and I am shocked that you still have not grasped our ways. With an election coming up in two years, we were at risk of losing it to that devious opposition party. Intel had it that they planned to field a female presidential candidate. The world would have gone wild supporting it and we would not want that would we? You Owethu were perfectly positioned to fulfil our grand plan. We placed you at the front because that is how we will get the votes and financial investment to reclaim our popularity in this country. You are the party's biggest project to date, and you need to be proud, you are enabling us to stay in power longer than our old tactics would allow us. That is the place of a woman in this party, to enable the agenda that has been set by us men, because we have a deeper understanding of politics that you do. Presidency is not sustained by heartfelt leadership but sacrifices that may mean you step on other people to get things done. It is not personal but merely the politics of the day. Now get out there, smile and read the speech I sent you."

These words replayed in my mind as I tried to pull myself together for a press conference, I was no longer sure I wanted to take part in. I had less than five minutes to stand before the entire nation and lie that I was happy and humbled to have created the path for other women in politics. There was no path. As had been the case for years, a woman had been manipulated, I had been used. I could feel my entire world weighing on my small shoulders. My entire political career had been a facade. Every position I had held was a token for my gender. It had never been about what I contributed or what I had the potential to channel into the success of the party. I was a woman first and that is the picture everyone saw first. Even my nickname "Margaret Thatcher" was a sarcastic reference to the strength and boldness that would always be pruned by those who held the true political power. I was a puppet. A pawn in the chessboard of national politics. That is the place for women. That is the woman who took to the podium, smiled and told the world that I was proud to serve my party, and my country. That I was committed to creating a world where women and girls could dream because those around would ensure their dreams were realised. That was the woman who stood in front of the television cameras and praised DOC for remaining the party of choice, where dreams and aspirations had nothing to do with gender but the handwork and commitment of individuals who believed in making a difference. That is the woman I settled to be, a disposable tool in the greater scheme of things. I was disgusted, but what choice did I have?

Naivety told me that maybe in the two years before the party replaced me with Ndabezitha, I could prove myself and have them change their mind. This was a huge gamble because he was the jewel who was supposedly the true and preferred candidate that would run for Presidency in the country's next election. By that time, the female candidate fronted would have gained the party the kind of support and popularity that a last-minute switch of candidates on grounds of my "ready-made" scandalous behaviour would not compromise. It did not matter that I had a better curriculum vitae and track record than his three years in the party. He was a man, and the party was ready to walk him through the ropes. In ten years, I had failed to challenge the deeply entrenched misogyny, surely two years would not give me a different result. I knew this, but I just was not ready to accept it, at least without putting up a fight. I needed to. This should never be the place of a woman…where a man wants her to be. The place of a woman should always be right where she wants and believes herself to be.

Nyasha Melissa Chiyanike

Nyasha is a 19-year-old medical student at the University of Zimbabwe. She comes from the town of Rusape in Zimbabwe. Nyasha's writing journey began in 2016 and she has been blogging motivational stories ever since. She has also won several local writing competitions.

Screwed from birth

Slowly the unpolished wooden coffin descended into the dusty pit and it dragged with it all her hopes, dreams and everything she had ever believed in. A scream of anguish built up in her dry throat but it just would not escape the seal of her quivering lips. Emotions burnt inside her chest, banging on the walls, begging to be let out but somehow she kept shoving them back in. Tears kissed the tips of her eyes but that is only as far as they could go. She was broken, but showing it to the world was not an option. No one cares. *You are on your own now,* the voices in her head kept reiterating.

Without giving her even a second to breathe; life was hitting her hard with the momentum of a million blows. In a flash, mama was gone leaving her with an old man she had learnt to call father over the years. All she wanted at this point was another minute just to say goodbye and maybe for one last hug. Unfortunately the odds were not in her favour; there was no going back. A rare malignancy had robbed Kiki of her most precious gift. The doctors had said her mother was going to be ok but this is where ok had taken them. She wished cancer was a person because only then could she grab a knife and stab it a million times for all the pain it had caused.

The unkempt puny girl felt herself gradually drifting from reality to a place in her head where her mother was still alive and speaking. The sound of her mother's voice still echoed in her ears like a heavenly melody; one she would never want to stop listening to. Her mind crawled through all those stories her mother had told her. She had been named Christian after her father, but since many claimed her name was rather masculine she became popularly known as

Kiki which corresponded well with her affectionate personality. She found herself once again replaying the story of her life. Her mother had always narrated their painful experiences in a shockingly beautiful manner;

"Just a month after my high school sweetheart had left the country to study Medicine abroad, I realised that I was carrying his child. We had always played it safe but clearly safe had not been safe enough. He had said he would come back for me as soon as he got his degree. We were going to start a family together and live in a mansion facing the East so that we could watch the sun rise each morning. Now he was miles away and I was pregnant.

My parents did not take the news too well. They felt I was too much of an embarrassment to them. So, I was frogmarched out of my own home by my father while my mother stood right by his side without showing the slightest sign of compassion. I even sought a haven at my lover's home, but his mother proved to be a bigger devil. I mean she was a woman, she was supposed to know better, but no; she threw me out like a dog. She spat on me and called me a gold digger. I was sixteen, pregnant, alone and confused.

Thoughts of suicide visited me each night, but I knew what was growing within me was sacred and deserved a chance to live. As soon as I had you; I instantly fell in love with you. I knew straight away that you were the best thing that had ever happened to me. You looked just like your father and you still do. I named you after him but you had to take my surname. I lost all forms of contact with the love of my life but in your eyes I would still see him. We had to put up with street life until I met

Nathan; the man who took us in and raised you like his own. We owe our lives to him."

She had never liked the last line of this story and yet it was the one her mother had emphasized the most. The idea of owing their lives to a random man, simply because he had helped them out, seemed rather far-fetched and unethical. He had done it out of a good heart; supposedly. So, why did it have to feel like a life-long debt?

A rough, dry, scratchy voice hauled her from her mental world right back to the graveyard, "At least we still have each other," said Nathan, the last person she wanted to hear from. Dang it, she was back to her day-time nightmare. She forged a smile for a second and quickly looked away. Rubbing her chapped hands over her cloudy, squint eyes to try and remove the dust that was making her gaze hazy; she approximated a plain face.

Nathan was a rather weird looking fella. He had a tiny face with everything clumped up at its centre. He wore a pair of huge brown spectacles that covered nearly half of his face and to his lips always stood erect a smoking pipe. A few grey hairs littered his balding, mottled scalp. Regardless of the weather; he was always muffled inside a heavy brown coat that matched his glasses. Occasionally, he would add on a brown bucket hat to his monotonous signature look. Having to call him "dad" was the worst part for Kiki. This man was old enough to be her great grandfather. Quite surprisingly, he still had the strength of a beast.

Kiki knew very well that her mother never really loved this man, but she had been in it for survival. There was something about the old man that she never liked, but she could not quite put her finger on it. For all the years she had lived in the same house as Nathan, they had never had a proper conversation outside their random, short and awkward greetings. He barely spoke, but she occasionally heard him screaming at her mother late at night. Once she had been woken from her sleep by her mother's screams and she had noticed a black eye the following morning. She had noticed several other strange bruises on her mother on different occasions. "Mind your own business young lady," her mother would always say whenever she tried to bring up the issue. Love hurts, she would always think, and there was no doubt she had no happiness in this place. Only one thing was certain at this point, Kiki was in for a rough ride.

The days that followed did not fall far from Kiki's expectations. Fewer words were used in the house and gestures emerged as the first language. Occasionally, she noticed Nathan staring mostly at her thoracic and gluteus areas and this made her gut uneasy. She was tempted to reprimand him but fell short of the courage to do so. Each time, Nathan would gradually lick his cracked lips and wink. *Disgusting!* Kiki would think to herself.

"You must miss her so much. Your mother," Nathan finally reached out to Kiki after several weeks of awkward tension in the house.

"Yeah," she tried to keep it as short and as cold as possible, but he was not about to let it go so quickly.

"I miss her too.....so much. I miss her in ways you can never understand. I have certain needs that your mom used to take care of, and now that she isn't around anymore, everything has become complicated. Anyways you are a kid; you wouldn't get it."

Before she could fully comprehend what he was getting at, he was already right in her face, grabbing her neck with spontaneous agitation. "Shhhhhhhh," he hissed through his brown teeth, letting out a pungent smell of rotten onion. There was no doubt he had no form of relationship with a toothbrush. He grasped her mouth to suppress her muffled cries. Her eyes watered instantly partly because of his horrible breath and mainly due to trepidation. "Don't make this any harder for me," he added, as she tried to set herself free. "You owe me so much. I have fed you, clothed you, sent you to school and put a roof over your head for years now and for what? It's time for you to pay back! There's barely any free meal under the sun. Right now you basically have two options; give me what I want or it's back to the streets for you." Slowly she found herself giving in and at the hands of the man she had called a father, she lost her chastity.

She felt as if truckloads of maize were being repeatedly dumped on top of her. Each and every inch of her weak body ached. Like a frog in severe drought, she gasped for air as he thrust himself upon her. She could feel blood flowing between her legs from an epicentre of excruciating pain. He forced her to beg for more and sent her into a dark hole of self-blame and regret from which she could not rescue herself. She could not help but think that had she done things differently maybe she would not have been in this situation. She felt so dirty. Like a foreigner in her own body, she could not help but yearn for the ability to escape this filthy prison that housed her soul. When his work was done, he shot a thick blob of saliva straight into her face, and like a piece of trash left her swimming in her blood. "You better clean your mess up," he said with absolute disgust as he triumphantly made his grand exit.

Each extra second that Kiki had to spend in the same house with her rapist fuelled her anger but the anger was not the only thing that was growing. Nathan's lust rose exponentially at twice the rate. Where she was supposed to see a father; Kiki saw a monster. Where he was supposed to see a daughter; Nathan saw a wife. There was a seemingly irreversible conflict of interests.

What started off as a single rape turned into two, two into three, three into four, until the couches, the walls, the beds and the blankets had lost count. For Kiki each time felt like the first. There was no getting used to this. She found herself drowning in shame. She hated everyone and everything; cancer for taking her mom, her mother for leaving her, Nathan for abusing her, the world for not noticing that she needed help, her Creator for not taking her and herself for not being able to save her piteous self from this hell she was living in.

The movie of her trauma was constantly on repeat in her head. Echoes of her groans and cries haunted her day and night. She feared all men and avoided any sort of contact with them. Even her male teachers to her seemed like a great threat. Focussing on her books became a mammoth task and each day she would fail to reach her potential. The feeling of safety became unknown to her. School to her had become a torturous waste of time. Eventually, she stopped going to school at all and sadly, no one came looking for her.

For days Kiki took all her rage and shoved it under her bed but each night it would creep up and engulf her soul. She bottled her emotions until she was drained and hopeless. She had overshot her threshold. Enough was enough. Taking with her a few stolen coins and the only other dress she owned, she snuck out at night and set on a journey from her small home town to her country's capital. The train was by far the only mode of transport she could afford. Comfort was the least of her worries. Her sole goal was to escape the hell that had become of her home. She had to endure her turtle's journey to freedom.

Her entire life she had heard stories of the great capital; Sunshine City where milk and honey flowed. She had read about it in books but it had always been her dream to be a part of this wonder. Finally, she could start a new life away from the enemy that had broken her. This was it, she was free. She flexed her muscles of imagination and for the first time in a long time almost smiled.

Her fantasy was cut short when she arrived in Harare during the course of a hailstorm. Sunshine City was not so sunshiny after all. She was in a foreign place with no relative or friend, no cell phone, no food and her visibility was greatly reduced to a few inches. She managed to drag herself a few metres from the train station to an alley where she huddled herself together and spent the night. Her tummy rumbled in hunger providing a very unique kind of lullaby. "Tomorrow will be better," she tried to convince herself but deep inside she knew the worst was still to come.

Life in the city was unbelievable. The streets were littered by never receding numbers of people who mostly seemed focussed on their own lives – too busy to notice a skinny little girl who helplessly stood around begging for food. Bins became her diners. Boxes became her bedding. Rats and cockroaches became her fellows. Clearly her escape plan had been poorly orchestrated, but this is where life had taken her; she had to face it.

There was no luck for Kiki on the streets. She could go for days without placing anything in her mouth. She constantly felt nauseated and would vomit each morning. On her empty stomach it was always a greenish sour fluid that came out. Her body must have been reacting to the new environment and unusual feeding schemes. Her belly was bloated and painful. She knew very well that she needed medical attention but there was no way she was going to get it.

Slowly she could feel herself deteriorating. She got thinner and thinner by the day and her protruding stomach did not get any less painful. With time she began facing difficulties breathing and her limbs ached. She was frail. Her face and hands were slightly puffy. Eventually, she started haemorrhaging. It seemed each day brought with it an extra pinch of difficulty to her already crumbling, pathetic life. She put on a great fight up until she finally gave up on life. She was tired of living on a battlefield. The sixteen year old lay on a pavement waiting for her hour.

Her entire life flashed before her eyes. It had been nothing but a series of Friday the thirteens. She was determined to figure out where she had gone wrong but everything seemed to take her back to the drawing board. There was no doubt she had been screwed from birth. Had she been born in a different place, at a different time, to different parents then maybe she would not have grown to be the trash that she found herself to be. A part of her hoped that the afterlife was real, because maybe then she would have another shot at happiness, and maybe she would once again meet her mother and tell her all about how life had slapped her in the face countless times.

Gradually, she felt herself creeping into her grave but fate kept on pulling her back and telling her it wasn't time yet. As she approached her place of rest, she felt a gentle hand resting on her shoulder. A handsome young man gave her a compassionate look and with the voice of an angel began to speak, "I saw you from afar and couldn't help but notice your situation. Please allow me to help you." The most soothing smile followed up on his voice which was so rich, so deep and yet so surprisingly smooth. His words echoed in her ears causing a slight rush of adrenaline and an instant tachycardia. This must have been her guardian angel. She wanted to give him the approval but unfortunately before she could do so, she passed out.

Gingerly, she tried to open her eyes. A smell she had never liked pierced her nostrils; it was the hospital smell. Slowly she began to fully visualise her surroundings. A huge needle was embedded deep into her left hand. There were a lot of tubes and instruments all of which she did not understand. She realised she was surrounded by people dressed in white. Was she in heaven? "You are in safe hands ma'am," a young man in a white coat with a funny looking pendulum around his neck said as he fluffed her pillow. "You are at Redemption Private Hospital, do not be scared." She got the reassurance that she was safe but a whirlwind of unanswered questions still ravaged her mind.

Fully aware of her state of confusion, the young doctor took her through the events of the previous day to ensure she was fully calm. As soon as they got to the same page, a more senior doctor stepped in.

"We have good news and bad news," he spoke softly to her.

"Start with the bad news," she replied.

"It turns out you were two months pregnant. We tried all we could but we failed to save the child. You lost a lot of blood and succumbed to acute kidney failure. Any attempt to conceive ever again may be very fatal to your own life. I am very sorry ma'am."

A nurse handed her a box of tissues. Clearly they did not know who she really was. She had given up on crying a long time ago. There was no doubt she was hurt. She only looked up for strength and for seconds stared at the ceiling.

After a period of awkward silence, Kiki finally asked what the good news was.

"Well ma'am the good news is you are alive. Had you arrived a minute later, things would have ended up differently. We also obtained your name from the small book that you had in your pocket and tried to search for your relatives with very little success. One of our staff members, Doctor Christian however claims your surname is familiar and he would like to speak to you. Maybe he can help. He will be in here any second from now."

"I have no fam…." She could not finish her sentence as the doors suddenly opened up and in came a male version of her in a white coat. It was like looking into a mirror just that this image was an upgrade. This was no rocket science. Shocked and excited with a degree of hesitation that sought approval she exclaimed, "BABA!"

Regret for dessert

"School ends at 4 O'clock! Where have you been?"

Hesitantly, my lips set apart to let out yet another lie, but this time they were too late. A drastic clap landed on my left cheek, knocking my soul out for a second. A billion stars danced in my eyes as I staggered backwards and landed on the naked brick wall that stood behind me. I clasped my throbbing cheek in an attempt to contain the pain, and with resentment I stared at my mother in silence.

I had been given countless warnings concerning my 'little cabin boy' as she liked to call him. Like any other normal teenager, my feelings were all over the place and I had allowed my first love to take precedence over everything else in my life. The looks, the brains, the charm and the humour; he had it all. I was head over heels for Kundai and nothing was about to change that.

Initially, I had thought Kundai was a prince of austerity, but time had revealed to me that he was simply poor. I still enjoyed his company; our walks in the park, movies and popcorn in his cabin and our visits to the local stadium. I was willing to snuggle myself into his impoverished life for eternity, but my mother on the other hand was not going to stand and watch me throw away my life like that. She had bigger, better plans for me. I had always tried to keep my relationship with Kundai a secret, but the moment she found out, all hell broke loose. My mother hated the idea of me messing around with an empty pocketed boy whose future was clearly bleak.

"I swear the next time I get the slightest feeling that you went to see that poor rat again, someone will curse the day they were born." The seriousness in my mother's voice as she presented her threat left me with no doubt that she was willing to go to any lengths to keep me away from the love of my life.

"What will people say?" that had always been the anthem in my family. It had always been about the outlook to the public. Prestige was what mattered most, and thus it came first while everything else followed. As long as people thought highly of us, we were good to go.

I was tired of living this museum life. I was tired of our petty acts of perfection. I was tired of making sure my skirt always covered my knees and my clothes were never too tight. I was tired of kneeling, bowing and living the 'yes sir' kind of life. I was tired of acting like the most decent girl on earth. All I wanted was for once in my life to stop living under the impression of this picture perfect existence. Like other children, I wanted to make my own mistakes and learn from them. Unfortunately, I never had the privilege to use my freewill. My parents had written my story for me already.

As if she intended to apologise, my mother looked to me and as usual reminded me that all she did was out of love. I never understood her idea of love, but she was still my mother; so, I had to put up with her. "Now go clean yourself up, we have special guests coming for dinner," she went on to say.

Bearing with me the burden of knowing my mother was never going to allow me to be with the love of my life, I dragged my sorry self to my room. I sat motionlessly in the foam filled bath tub as I drifted in the vortex of my own problems. Soon enough I plastered myself with layers of make up under which I masked all the hate I felt towards my own mother.

Scented candles and the special cutlery we only used on Christmas day were elegantly lined up at the dinner table.

From apples to zucchinis; the extensive assortment of foods that lay on trays and in glass bowls shocked me. Whoever this special guest was must have meant a lot to my parents.

That night's dinner broke the record as the worst. The special guests turned out to be a self-absorbed, middle aged businessman and his chauffeur. The moderately ugly, well-groomed man, Dominic, kept rambling on about his achievements, which no doubt failed to impress me. Meanwhile, my mother's eyes shone with impish glee and I could tell from my father's smile that he too was enjoying the show.

The slap I had received earlier on had served a unique purpose as a starter to this plodding dinner. Just when I thought my life could not possibly get any worse; they served my hopes as the main course. I had always looked up to my father as a figure of respect, so the fact that he had to bring forth the message shattered me at a whole different level.

"You know we love you right?" Those words were never a misleading indication that whatever followed was disastrous. "After thorough analysis, your mother and I have decided that Dominic is the perfect man for you. We understand that this is a bit of short notice, but you have to get married soon." Just like that; my parents were marrying me off to an older man whom I had just met. I was only in high school and to make matters worse, I found nothing about Dominic appealing.

The first thought would have been to disagree, but the last time someone had spoken against my father they had ended up in the hospital. Disappointment, anger, denial, fear, hate and confusion; all those feelings consumed me. I was too young for this type of thing. I kept telling myself that I still needed to continue with school, but the fact that I was not intellectually gifted watered down my argument. Whilst

I was constantly repeating my 'O' Levels, my little brother had skipped grades and was already in law school. I had always been made to feel that paying school fees for me was an unnecessary burden on the whole family. I could not deny the fact that my presence in the family had not added any solid value. It was probably wise to dispose of me this early.

I knew very well that resisting my parents' decision was never going to work. Regardless of that, I still needed a second opinion. I needed someone to strengthen me, to tell me that I had a shot at winning this battle. I needed to speak to someone I trusted. I found myself calling my best friend, Ayanda and venting out to her. I knew she had no power over anything, but I still hoped she would tell me that this whole marriage idea was bogus.

"Your parents are right. You should get married now, at least you are guaranteed a good life. Kundai will take you nowhere," those were not the words I had hoped to hear. Sadly she was right. Dominic was my only shot at a good life. Kundai was just as hopeless as my academic future.

The thought of letting go of Kundai sent chills all over my body. I was not ready to face him and tell him the truth. I knew this kind of thing would break him. We had made so many promises to each other; how we were going to hold on to each other for life, how we would name our first child Jayden or Jane; how we were going to fight poverty no matter what...we had endless dreams and hopes for our future together and now I had to let go of it all before it had even begun.

Without a simple goodbye I stopped answering Kundai's calls. I ignored his texts and avoided him at all costs. Quietly, I dropped Kundai from my life and convinced myself I had closed that chapter for good.

Marriage was not something I had anticipated, but now that I was in it, I had to dance according to the tune. Sooner than I expected, I found myself enjoying Dominic's company. I sat in cars I had only seen on television and ate food I never thought existed. No one had ever told me that being rich could be this much fun. I became a reference point for the latest hairstyles. My nails were constantly on fleek. Each day I was spending money twice my parents combined monthly salaries. Older women envied me, age mates called me a role model, while younger girls wished they could be like me.

It turned out marriage was not as bad as I had expected. My husband put in sizeable effort in being the ideal partner. He was always home early, helped out around the house, cracked the funniest jokes and brought gifts each day. Before I knew it, the thoughts of Kundai were long gone and I was enjoying my paradise. My new elite way of life dictated an irresistible urge to flaunt it on social media. I became the hottest influencer on Instagram. My life felt like a movie that everyone binged on.

Out of the blue, the show began to gradually deteriorate. Dominic started bringing fewer gifts and his conversations became shorter and shorter. Coming home late became his trend until eventually he would not even show up at times. His phone began getting more attention than I did. Business trips lengthened and became more frequent. Too many red flags were popping up and I would have been a fool to ignore them. The spirit of Sherlock Holmes was awakened within me, and I decided to embark on a stealth investigatory mission.

Each time he entered the password into his phone, I watched him with an eagle's eye. I might not have been bright in school, but when it came to sneaky games I surely deserved distinctions. I did not need days to figure out what the password was. Whatever he was hiding in that phone; I was going to get to the bottom of it.

I waited for the perfect moment to strike. As Dominic took his morning shower before work, I threw my fears aside and reached for the phone. At that moment, I unlocked not only his phone but a whole new dimension of his life that I wished I had not discovered. "Wife", that was the first contact name that struck my eye. The idiot within me tried to convince me that 'Wife' was actually someone's first name. *People give their children weird names all the time*, I tried to calm myself as I gathered enough strength to open the messages from this person. My eyes rushed to a text message with an image of a little girl attached and the caption read, "Our little girl excited before her first day at school. If only you were here. We miss you daddy." The text was accompanied by pink heart emojis; the same ones I had always used on Kundai.

It all began to make sense now. This was why he had said he did not want kids. He had said he was not ready for such a big responsibility and that he still wanted to enjoy uninterrupted quality time with me. Shallow minded me had bought each and every lie of his. I was all about giving him fun, and now the joke was on me.

I wanted to throw the phone against the wall and hit it with a hammer till it turned into powder, but that was not going to solve anything at this point. Another part of me wanted to grab a sledgehammer and make pulp out of him instead, but again that was not an option. "I'm guessing you are done now," Dominic softly said as he approached me from behind and he grabbed his phone from my trembling hands.

It was one thing to realise your husband has been playing you the whole time and it was another when he rubbed it in your face. Dominic immediately made a call and judging from his flirtatious tone, it was to this "wife" of his. As if I was not there, he spoke to her with so much love and respect he had never shown me. Right there in my presence, he mocked my pride and emotions. I had done absolutely nothing to deserve any deception, but there he was juggling my feelings like a professional clown.

It seemed wise to immediately leave this toxic relationship; but was I being too emotional and irrational? Would I be able to handle the embarrassment of going back home when everyone knew I was now married to a big fish in the business world? What about my dignity and pride? I was not ready to give up the fancy life!

My mother had warned me that marriage was no everyday honeymoon. She had warned me about the possibility of cheating. She had said that all men were like that, that cheating was normal in marriage, and that it was my role as a woman to stay strong. She had predicted that like all other women, I was going to face numerous hurdles, but the one I faced had never crossed my imagination.

Now that he knew I was fully aware of the lie we had been living, Dominic became so comfortable with trashing my pride and hurting my feelings. He no longer bothered to keep any secrets from me. He would openly tell me he was going home to his real family, his real wife and not some gold digging school dropout. Whether or not I had food on the table quickly fell off from his list of worries. He knew I was stuck and like his sock puppet, he pushed and shoved me around.

In what was supposed to be my house, I quickly became a maid; just one who had no salary at the end of the month. I was basically turned into an all-purpose gadget; a washing machine, dish washer, cook and everything else he desired at any point. I soon realised that although I was a slave, I still had hope for change. The whole time my mother cheered me from the side line. "That is marriage for you," she reminded me each day. As for her, the hand-outs they continuously got from Dominic were enough for her to convince me to endure any form of abuse. I tried so hard to be the perfect wife. I sought validation from him, but nothing ever came my way.

I was prepared to put up with his drama but when violence joined the party, the cards were reshuffled. I became his punching bag, an outlet for work stress and all family problems. He would argue with his wife; the real wife, and then pour out his frustrations on me. "Men can be like that," my mother was still shouting from the terraces, but this time I was not going to sit around and be killed. I knew I had to leave before it was too late, but again going home was not an option. A part of me blamed my parents for everything I had experienced. I was carrying so much bitterness within me and all I needed was an escape.

There were not many remarkable things about me, but my firmness was definitely something to be grasped. I threw in the towel and confidently bid Dominic farewell. From a pure heart I wished him well, I just wanted to live my own life as far away from him as possible. He on the other hand was poised that I was going to desperately run back to him in no time. Whatever he had to say was not going to stop me. I packed what was mine and headed back to the town where I had grown up.

I had no idea where exactly I was going but as long as it was away from an abusive husband, I was ok with it. Surprisingly, my feet directed me to the last place I expected myself to go. I found myself once again standing at the door to Kundai's cabin. I stood there for minutes and reflected on the pain I had already inflicted on him. I was probably the last person he would have wanted to see.

A part of me hoped that Kundai had not moved on; that maybe I still had a shot with him. But then again, I would still understand even if he would not even look at me. I did not deserve forgiveness and so my expectations of getting it were low. I however needed him now more than ever. I was broken and there was no better candidate in the world to restore my smile than him. I had to humble myself and go back to the true love of my life.

Hesitantly, I pushed my hand to the wooden door which was being torn down by termites and knocked softly. I stared at the ground and even the confident ants mocked my pride. I felt ashamed for being back, having left the way I did. I could hear soft footsteps approaching the door and as they got closer and closer my breath became exceedingly harder to control. I felt my nerves tingling beneath my skin and my limbs burnt. I could not wait to see him but at the same time I was afraid. I could not begin to imagine his reaction to the sight of me.

The door swung open and I made eye contact with the figure that stood before me. My bag immediately fell from my hands and it felt as if my joints were liquefying. "Natasha!" my best friend exclaimed as she nervously smiled at me. She was just as shocked as I was. My eyes raced down from her face and could not get past her bulging belly. My logic told me she was around seven months pregnant. "Babe who is it?" Kundai's voice echoed from inside the cabin. I had only been gone for less than a year.

Without further ado, I grabbed my bag and walked away from this hub of disappointment and heartbreak. Tears raced down my cheeks and spilled over to my sweaty neck. Endless questions bombarded my mind. Had she always planned this? For how long had they been in love? Had they been fooling me the whole time?

I was done for. I had nothing left; no husband, no boyfriend, no best friend; just a family that had sent me off once and that I was not sure wanted me back. I remembered the words of my former school teacher, "Life changes fast. Life changes in an instant. When you sit down to enjoy your dinner, remember life as you know it can end as quickly as the food on your plate."

The main course was over and I chewed on my regret for dessert.

Cut off

Dear diary

I'm so confused, scared and hurt. They did something to her. I cannot keep it out of my head. I need to understand what happened in that hut. I need to know why it happened. I have a lot of questions that keep taunting me each day. It has been a couple of years now but I cannot seem to get past this. I know I am next in line and that scares me even more.

Hastily, I slammed the little pink book shut and slid it under my pillow. "I'm coming ma!" I shouted back as I blinked a million times to push back the tears that were already pooling in my eyes. At this point in my life I had become a seasoned stoic, so immaculate in her act of being fine when a lot of pain was being harboured deep within. My heart was in a cage of thorns and with each beat, bled a little more. I was smiling in everyone's face but drowning in my own tears behind their backs. Only the pages between the hard covers of my tattered diary and the faint black ink had the full view of the battle I was fighting.

I remembered vividly the heated argument my parents had engaged in on the night before we left home for the holidays those few years back. For reasons I did not know, Mama seemed to be against the idea of going to the village. "She is dirty, we have to go and get this done," Baba kept yelling. He placed so much emphasis on the fact that "she" was now old enough. I had no idea who "she" was or what "dirt" he was making a fuss about. As far as I was concerned, we were a God fearing family; as clean as they came. In all earnest, I grabbed my older sister, Efuru's hand and together we prayed for Mama to ease up. We both wanted the same thing, a unique get-away opportunity away from the usual noise of our city lives.

Premature judgement made us mark not only the following day but the vacation at large as the best of our lives. Our fervent prayers had been answered and we embarked on our greatly anticipated road trip. Excitement overflowed and energy levels climaxed. We talked, sang, giggled and marvelled at the transition of the landscape as mile by mile we distanced from the city. The rock and roll tracks from the tiny radio created a thrilling atmosphere of adventure as the brand-new Mercedes Baba had recently acquired bolted along the highway in sync with the music. The journey before us was great; there was no time to waste.

Gradually, our enthusiasm declined as we delved deeper and deeper through uninhabited woods. Eventually, a lethargic spirit settled. I hugged Efuru's arm and rested my head on her shoulder; we were inseparable. Despite our remarkable age gap, Efuru had always been my best friend. We slept, woke up and slept again but still the journey went on. After what seemed like a lifetime of travelling, we finally made it to our destination. Despite the fact that it was already late into the night; a delegation of men and women awaited our arrival – the prize for being the rich relatives.

The next day by far surpassed our expectations. A celebratory vibe drifted through the village. I could tell from the huge cooking drums and clay pots that were already resting on the fire that this was no ordinary day. Like chocolate left in the sun; my heart melted as I watched our large, beautiful family of diverse individuals go about their duties. There was Gogo with her edentulous smile that effortlessly warmed up the atmosphere. Grandpa on the other hand cracked a series of dry jokes and surprisingly maintained a straight face while the rest of us collapsed in laughter. A number of women busied themselves with the cooking while some men were already flooding their bellies with malt beer. Countless cousins whose similar names confused me raced up and down the compound. Everyone was so eager to get to know us. This was heaven on earth. The only regret I had was not having visited this place earlier.

"Today is Efuru's big day," a tiny girl whispered in my ear with great excitement. I had no idea what she was talking about, and neither did Efuru herself. Whatever it was seemed to amuse everyone else except for one; Mama. The whole time she wandered around the huts and would steal glances at my sister and I. She was probably still mad because of this trip she never wanted. "She'll get over it," we assured each other.

Slowly, I noticed an assembly of elder women from the village including Gogo gathering at a hut that was right at the edge of the compound. Something about this little hut was peculiar; it was isolated, old and had dense bushes surrounding almost its entirety. One of them began to walk towards us at a brisk pace, only to stop a few feet away. She called out to my sister who left me standing beneath a mango tree. Efuru ran towards the lady who seemed a bit uneasy and impatient. I watched as the two walked away. The lady put her hand around Efuru's neck and over her shoulder in a manner that reflected pure love. My sister likewise hung her arm around this lady's waist.

As soon as they got to the hut, the congregation of women cascaded in and the door was shut behind them. Never in my life had I appreciated being left out. I wanted to know what they were up to. I also wanted to be in that room. Quite surprisingly I still managed to keep myself in one place. I sat on a rock beneath the tree and tapped my foot in impatience. I could not wait for Efuru to come back so she could narrate everything to me. I took in deep breaths and shifted my attention to the beautiful view of the village.

When I least expected it; a sharp scream pierced my ears and headed straight for my heart, eliciting a reflex that catapulted me from where I sat into a mad sprint towards the hut. I knew this voice; it was my sister's! I wanted to scream back, to shout to her, to tell her I was coming to her rescue, but I channelled all my energy towards my feet. The tingling sensation on my face as I converged with the wind was the least of my worries. Thrice I toppled over but I still picked myself up and moved on without looking back. I threw my trunk right into the door of the hut and it swung open. Four strong hands immediately clutched my limbs to halt my run, but my eyes raced on. Before I knew it, I was witnessing a live horror movie.

Like flies on rotten fish, the women were gathered around my sister. Efuru lay helplessly on the table as one lady clutched her mouth to prevent any further screaming. Two others held down her hands whilst others pinned down her trunk and positioned her legs apart. As if she was some kind of surgeon, Gogo stood at the far end of this table and with shocking composure she gradually drove a blunt knife into Efuru's flesh. Mama had always said no one was ever supposed to touch down there, but here we were. An old woman was cutting off my sister's sacred flesh. Goosebumps erupted over my entire body as I looked at the blood stained, rusty knife penetrating Efuru's vagina. As if I was the one on the table, my synaesthesia kicked in.

"Stop!" I cried out, but was immediately thrown out like trash and the door was slammed into my face. Mama rushed after me and I fell into her arms. "It is circumcision Imara. It has to be done. Your sister is now clean. She is now a woman," she said softly as she held me tightly and wiped away my tears. I was shocked by her audacity to tell me to calm down. I wanted her to storm into that hut and save her daughter, but here she was trying to stop me from doing what she herself had failed to do. I tried to fight her off, but my strength was no match for hers. This was all too unfair. What did she mean my sister was now a woman? Had she been a man before?

I was dragged to another hut which was not very far from where they were mutilating my sister. Mama locked me in and claimed it was for everyone's good. It killed me to know I could not save my sister from her pain. I cried out in rage; begged the ancestors, the universe or whatever was in control to come to Efuru's rescue. I prayed for a miracle; one that would turn back the hands of time to the moment when we had prayed for this trip so we would reverse it all.

From the tiny window in that dingy room, I kept my teary eyes glued on the door to "the hut". The door was never opened and no movement occurred for what felt like an eternity. Eventually, one by one the ladies left the hut, but the one I actually wanted to see never did. For hours I sat at the window, but Efuru never walked out of there.

"Daughter of Heaven", that is what her name meant; Efuru. Her life had been nothing short of her name. A true angel, she had always been. Everything of hers was centred on love. Never in her life had she acted with any intent to impose pain on anyone. Efuru would never kill a bug. Her respect for all life was out of this world. I tried so hard to fathom the reason for causing her so much pain but I could not find any. My sister was to me a figure of perfection, and it killed me to know she was suffering without my support.

Like a prisoner; I was fed from the window. They said my sister needed time to recover and that I was a loose cannon, capable of disrupting the process. They kept telling me to calm down. They said she was going to be ok and each day I sat at that window with the hope of seeing Efuru walking out. She never did.

I watched all the movements to and from the hut. They would never allow me to join them. All I wanted was to see my sister, to look her in the eye and tell her that all was going to be well but no; they kept us apart. I held on strongly to the little hope I had, that all would be well.

Days passed and our imprisonment streak continued until one morning I noticed Gogo stagger to the hut with her walking stick and the fruit basket she normally carried there. Seconds later, she quickly walked out and called another aunt who hesitantly entered the hut. I nervously watched as the lady walked out shaking her head. I could feel it in my bones that something had gone terribly wrong. More and more people were called to the hut. Soon the murmurings became audible enough; Efuru was no more.

I felt the air in my lungs race out together with every last bit of strength I had within me and I could not hold it back. Grief immediately swallowed me up and it brought with it a lot of regrets. Maybe I should have stopped her from going to the hut. I should have fought harder for her. I should have been a better sister. I felt so stupid for having prayed for this trip to occur. I had failed my sister; my own blood.

I wanted answers. I needed to fully understand what had happened to my sister and why it had happened. "Efuru was too weak. She could not handle circumcision," that is all they had to say for what they had done to her. They said they did not want anything conspicuous, and so her burial was rushed. She did not even get a proper funeral service. A pact was made to never again discuss the conditions of her death. Just like that, they left my sister to rot in the village black soil together with mice and cow dung.

As if nothing had happened, we returned home and continued with our lives. To everyone else who asked, Efuru had been involved in an accident at the village and she had failed to make it out alive. I was charged never to discuss the death of my sister with anyone to any further detail. My parents were making efforts to live as if all was well, but I was never at peace. The fact that I had failed to protect my sister haunted me daily. My little diary was the only escape I had.

I read every religious book and every science textbook I had within my reach, but never at any point did I come across anything about female circumcision. I knew very well that my sister never deserved to die the way she did. It pained me even more to know that I had done nothing about it. What had happened in the hut still made no sense.

On this day like any other, I once again concealed my tears and ran to the living room where my mother had called me. As I approached her I felt something within me change. This feeling was foreign and irresistible. I had been raised in a typical African family where standing up to adults was taboo, but suddenly the urge to confront my parents bubbled up within me. I still needed closure for the loss of my sister. I was tired of hiding the pain and living in fear.

With a level of confidence, I never thought I would be able to pull, I walked straight up to Mama and firmly asked, "Why did you kill Efuru?"

My father who sat right next to her threw away his newspaper and with ultimate agitation sprang towards me. Had his hand landed on me, I was probably going to join my sister, but my mother quickly jumped to block him. "Let her speak," she said gently. He retreated to his seat with his blood-shot eyes scanning each inch of my diminutive figure with utmost disgust. He tried to hide it, but clearly he too was not at rest. He trembled with rage; he needed to vent and at this point I was the closest outlet.

"Why did you kill my sister?" I asked again, this time with a frail, breaking voice as tears threatened to choke me.

"Your sister was too weak. She could not handle circumcision," this was still the answer they offered. Efuru had never been given the liberty to choose her fate, and yet they still had the nerve to blame it on her. I needed something better than this monotonous half-baked excuse. An admission of their guilt and the assurance of my own safety was all I sought.

Mama looked me in the eye, and just as she saw my pain, I could almost see through her soul. I could tell that she too was fighting her own demons. She drew me to her bosom and caressed me with her motherly love. "I'm so sorry my baby," she kept saying as she burst into tears. All the pain I had retained over the years also gushed out. The dam wall of my emotions had ruptured and crying set me free from the shackles that had been binding me.

Mama's apology was still not enough. "Sorry" was not going to bring Efuru back. Neither was it going to protect me and all the other girls who were at risk of going through the same hell.

I knew very well that nothing I could do would bring Efuru back, but I had to fight for others beginning with myself. I was afraid – afraid of being harmed, afraid of opposing the same culture that had moulded me, afraid of being the dirty child. Through all that fear, the words still came out, "I will not allow you to take away my womanhood!"

I felt a firmer, masculine hand clutch my shoulder. I expected it to lift me and throw me to the wall; to slap, punch and possibly finish me off, but instead it drew me in for a hug. I knew then, that my parents were both on my side, and for the first time in years I did not feel alone.

Tinatswe Mhaka

Tinatswe is a feminist storyteller and lawyer from Zimbabwe working in law and gender equality through lobbying, advocacy, documentation and grassroots outreach.

Bloody cloth

Maybe one of these days the soldiers might come and shoot her husband in the head, oh what a joyous day it would be.

Mwenje smiled at the thought. The pain of stretching her face made her wince. She moved the warm cloth from her bruised lip, to the cut that sliced her brow in half and blurred her sight. The sting was worth it. The thought of a world where Zivai did not exist. No one would even notice if they took him, and that would be the best part. He would die alone and ignored. Everyone was too busy, either mourning their own or staying inside trying to stay safe. Not that that had stopped the military. Her mind wandered from her husband briefly as she thought of the soldiers, and all the tragedy they had brought with them in the last two weeks. On the excruciatingly horrifying days, violently disfigured corpses were found lying on the streets. On the better ones, there were soldiers demanding identification cards. It was not safe out there, it had not been for days. Between the prices going up and lack of basic goods, people had been pushed to protest. In return the ruling party had sent its soldiers to their neighbourhoods. They knocked down their doors, raping women, beating, kidnapping and killing anyone who resisted. It was political carnage. The slight burn in her skin brought her back to reality. It was the salt she poured in the water. It did not work, but it made her feel good, in a way that made her think she was in control of her healing at least.

Mwenje needed to replace the water in her buckets, there was too much blood on the cloth. Her blood. He had almost killed her. Not that this was the first time. If she was being honest with herself this had not been her worst night yet, and she was certain it could get worse. Much worse. How had she got here? Mwenje limped to and from the bathroom with the buckets of bloody water, rearranging the mess Zivai's episode had caused. She had the mind to keep it exactly how she left it, but previous incidents had taught her that only made things worse. As she picked up the scattered pots and their discarded contents, she immediately decided she would make another batch of food. It was late into the night, and all this cooking was way out of their budget, but there was a level of satisfaction she needed to maintain in the house to avoid things like what had happened earlier that night. It had not always been this way. It had not always been so bad and so frequent. Had it been four years ago, Zivai would have been home with her. She would have her feet on the kitchen stool, while he made them dinner. They would have cracked jokes and tasted the stew together, teasing each other about the possibility of a love-making bout later. She had never questioned how and why she fell in love with him. He took care of her, always. Physically, financially and even mentally. He had a solution to every single problem she ever had back when they met, and consistently for at least two years into their marriage. She had married him because she was sure she would never have anything to worry about ever again.

When Mwenje met Zivai, she had just moved from the rural areas to find domestic work in the city centre. Someone needed to make money to feed her mother at the very least. Zivai lived down the road from the street where Mwenje had been taken in as the house girl. He had been so loving. So romantic and nothing like she had ever experienced. He took her into town, bought her flowers and held her hand during their long night walks through the neighbourhood. He was better than any man she thought she would marry. Or than any that had ever had interest in her.

He lived in a two roomed house in the township. She had been so taken by him. She hadn't hesitated to marry him a short year after they met, it could only have been a better life ahead.

"Ah that was fast! Okay. Just be careful. These men have ways of blinding you with things," Madam Cecelia had said harshly the day she told her she would be leaving the job and getting married. Her crassness had startled Mwenje. She suspected she was jealous, but how could she be? She owned this house. She had a house girl, ate meat every day and had more than one channel on her television. Madam Cecelia was colourful, bold and slender. She ran her own business, cooking food for parties for rich city people. Madam did not have a husband or man of any kind, and Mwenje did not know why. That had never been one of the very rare stories she told when they were working on her orders in the kitchen.

"I don't like men very much. All they do is take take take!!" She had said one afternoon while reading a newspaper. And that was the closest she had ever come to talking about one.

Mwenje had moved out of Madam's house immediately after her marriage announcement, then embarked on her new life with Zivai. Something in her felt so fulfilled. It had not been till a few years ago that things had changed. She was not quite sure what had happened to Zivai, or what had changed in her that he hated so much. Three years ago, the factory where he worked had closed and left him jobless. He had started shaking her by then. Then the shaking graduated to shoving, pushing and breaking glass. He did not like to be asked about looking for work. A year after that, he had spent his retrenchment package on alcohol, and maybe sex with other women, she suspected. The day she asked him was the first time he had ever slapped her. She had briefly wondered if she deserved it. Nothing was ever clear after that. He had been apologetic at first. Shocked at himself, as she was, and making up for it ever so inadequately. He had eventually evolved though. Unapologetic and unhinged in his expression of dissatisfaction. They barely spoke now. She did what he said, and he lived his life how he pleased. She could barely put together the memories of their marriage prior to that. Her memory failed her. And here she was tonight, two years later, looking at the reflection of a broken woman.

"I don't know why you don't just pack your bags and go back to the rurals. He is poor now. Ha! Go home." The house girl from across the street had said to her one day as she swept their yard.

"Maybe you will only learn to mind your business when you have a husband of your own. Silly!" Mwenje had shouted back.

"You have one and what has he done for you? Look at your face. You are the silly one!" She had given her a look of pity, shaken her head and retreated into her yard.

Witch. Mwenje had thought.

Pack her bags and go? Where? She had mused. Her mother had been dead a year and she did not know who lived at the homestead now. She had not even attended the funeral because Zivai had insisted he had no money and forbade her from asking anyone else, claiming they would make it to the memorial, which they never did. Between brushing off the neighbours and keeping herself from her distant aunts and old friends, Mwenje did not have anywhere to go. For so long, she had not realized that leaving was an option. Those remarks had not been the only ones and every time she went outside, someone had something to say. So, she just stayed at home.

Of late, the idea of running away seemed more and more worth it, no matter where she would end up. Mwenje looked around the kitchen area that made up half of their home and felt gratified that half of the work was done. She could focus on preparing Zivai another pot. As she cut the onions, her eyes teared up, she was too sore to stand up to rinse it in water. She fixed her eyes on the knife and shivered. It did not seem fair she had to use this knife to give him sustenance, to prepare his food, take care of his needs and make his life better. He had used it to make hers worse. Much worse. She knew it so well and could have described its features perfectly, because on one night she found it gently pointing between her eyes after she had come home late from a queue for bread. She knew it was sharp because he had once pulled it straight out of her hand when she had not answered him about his unironed clothes. She might have known the knife more than her own husband at this point. A time had come and gone where she longed to mend things and take them back to how they used to be. But it was no longer just her in the picture.

As she threw finely shredded vegetables into the pot of hot oil, a bout of nausea rose in her stomach. She ran to the bathroom to throw up, before briefly kneeling over the toilet seat. She wrapped her arms around her chest and over her waist, giving herself a moment to gather. She would not be able to keep this a secret much longer. She was pregnant, it was starting to show, and it was getting impossible to hide. Zivai did not know. He could not. She could not stay. She would never be able to leave if she did. It was strangely fortunate for her that he detested being in her presence, and her appearance often went over his head. The last he had looked at her was five months ago. He had come home too drunk to walk, slurring and insisted she removed her clothes. She had obliged. A part of her accepted that she belonged to him. He had taken her in and given her a home. Even if she had left who would want her now? Something had shifted when she learned of her baby. If she had to imagine the worst, Zivai would beat her until she lost it. They could not afford cooking oil, what more a child?

She had run away once. No bags and no preparation wandering aimlessly in the streets, blood running down her head, and ended up at Madam Cecelia's door. She had opened the door, looking not the least bit surprised that Mwenje sat in front of her. She had given her a bath, fresh clothing before Madam had said, "I used to be you. And until you are ready to leave his house forever, do not ever come back to mine. I cannot see this again."

"I–" Mwenje had started to speak above her cries.

"I used to be you. I hope I will see you again, before it's too late." She had interrupted before standing up and leaving Mwenje in the kitchen she used to clean. That was the last time she had seen her. It had been a year and a half since then. The thought of Madam caused a sense of urgency through her veins. She would leave now.

I used to be you.

The words played over and over in her head. What was her story? It did not matter. She would go there and hope for the best. Even if she did not take her in, she would not come back here. She would find some money and go back to her homestead. God would make a way. Maybe not the same one that had watched her suffer under the hand of Zivai, or the same one who had watched her soak bloody cloths in water for   years now. But maybe the same God who had put Madam Cecelia where she was. Mwenje rushed to the bedroom and hastily shoved some clothes in a plastic bag. She would be quick and run in between the houses until she got to Madam's house. It was the longer way, but it was safer. Mwenje carried her plastic through the kitchen and headed for the door. It had been the closest she felt to freedom. She no longer remembered who she was before coming to the city, but she was a few moments away from starting over. As she reached for the door, it suddenly opened. Mwenje froze. Everything leading up to this moment proved to her that there was no god in her life. She stood face to face with Zivai. He was drunk than when he had left earlier. His dark eyes narrowed, shifting from her plastic bag to her morbid face. After a few of Zivai's drunken encounters, she had long anticipated that one day she might not wake up from his hand. She had longed for that day sometimes. And as she walked backward retreating into the house, she felt like that day had come.

"I married you because I thought you were clever!"

Zivai laughed obnoxiously as he clenched the neck of the green bottle tightly in his hand. He walked into the house and shut the door behind him, chugging the last of his beer. He had been so handsome when they met. She could barely look at him now. Zivai was twice her size and his appearance was just as intimidating as his actions. He was tall, with a heavy build and a protruding stomach despite the fact that she had only lost weight in the recent years. His beard was long and rugged, long in some parts, patchy in other ways that always left him looking unkempt and broody.

"So where were you going?" Zivai asked calmly.

"Nowhere, I–"

"Liar!" he screamed, throwing the empty beer bottle across the kitchen. The breaking of pieces of glass echoed in Mwenje's head as they cracked against the wall, and then against each other on the floor. She preferred to focus on everything else except for Zivai when he beat her. It went by quicker that way. Zivai charged for her, then placed his hand around her neck and slammed her against the wall. The pain was too intense to ignore. She had not recovered from his tantrum only just a few hours ago. She could not take this. Neither could her child. She wrapped her hands around her stomach instinctively, then began to scream. His hold tightened around her neck and she struggled to breathe.

"I'm pregnant Zivai please!" She let out. He released his hold and her body crumbled to the floor. Mwenje looked up, and before she could meet her husband's eyes, the sharp pain of his backhand cut across her face, over her brow in the same place he had beaten open her flesh.

"Who is the father?" he demanded.

Mwenje's ears began to ring. Between her blurry sight in one eye and her tears in another, she could barely make out the room. She could see Zivai's dark figure move closer to her.

"Tell me now!"

He raised her from the floor by the neck again and tossed her across the kitchen. More breaking! Mwenje's body fell straight into the corner of the cupboard which ruthlessly tore her buttock. As she reached for the small table that sat in the corner of the kitchen, hoping to bring herself to her feet, it broke and scattered the pots, plates, knives, and all that had sat on it.

"It's yours." She cried out as she fell back to the ground.

"I haven't touched you!" Zivai screamed.

"Why would I? How can I? Look at you. I give you this life and this is what you do? Whore!"

"A child in this economy, who will pay for it?"

"Tell me where you were going before I really hurt you Mwenje. I come home and my wife is carrying a secret child and running away to God knows where. What do you take me for?"

Next, Mwenje felt the hostility of the worn out sole of Zivai's boot, as he launched it into the stomach she had protected with her arms. His kick inflicted a sharp pain which ran through her stomach, sending electric waves of agony through her back, and all the way back up to her neck.

"Tell me!!!" He yelled. "I will kill you both."

"Madam Cecelia!" She let out as she placed her hands on the floor to lift her body. She felt dizzy and broken. The warmth of urine running down her thighs caused her to curl, tightly clenching her knees as close to her stomach as possible.

"HA!" Zivai stood still and let out a drawn-out chuckle of genuine pleasure.

"You leave the man who loves you in the hopes of finding help from a dead woman. Schupet!"

Mwenje could no longer speak. She elevated her neck and looked up to her husband's face. She could barely see him. The misery on her face was momentarily replaced by shock as Zivai laughed even harder. The confusion caused by his merriment made her doubt the predicament she found herself in. For a second, she wondered if she was in a lucid nightmare.

"Oh, you didn't know? They killed her and her little house girl. Left them dead on the veranda. You should be thanking me. That could have been you! Serves her right for thinking she was better than us all."

If Mwenje had not been on the floor already, she would have fallen on it. Whimpers escaped her mouth as she wondered if Madam had suffered. She pondered over whether they had violated her. Dragged her and forced themselves on her, before leaving her to die. Mwenje had no one now. Not that she had had anyone before, but the hope of it had been enough to push her through the door.

"Clean this up!"

Zivai had kicked the pots on the floor before staggering to the bedroom. Mwenje lay still on the floor. The pain in her stomach had surprisingly subsided. The rest of her body throbbed, and although she lay in a pool of cutlery and vegetables, she was sure her baby was okay. *It might not have turned out that way*, she thought. Silence surrounded the house. Zivai had fallen unconscious the minute his head hit the bed, and Mwenje had no more whimpers to let out. She thought about the way he had kicked her and wondered if that would be that last time in the next five months of this pregnancy? Did he believe it was his child? Had he gone to bed knowing she could not leave? Would he finish her off in the morning? She wiped her mostly functioning eye and began peeling herself from the floor.

Ashamed, Mwenje thought of the moment she stood before the door ready for freedom. But there was no freedom outside. There was rape, and there was death. There was no freedom in here either. On her knees, she gathered all the kitchenware into a pile. She stared at the appliances, stained with blood, tears and dirt. Her eyes landed on the knife again. Mwenje reached for it and gripped the handle firmly. She ached at the thought of all the ways she might end her life and put an end to it all. Her child might be safer if it never came at all, she thought. She stood up and dragged herself towards the bathroom. She would sit in there until she had contemplated her fate. She walked into the bedroom where a glimpse of herself in the mirror had stopped her in her tracks. She had started using it more often lately. It was because every time she looked at herself, she did not recognize her own reflection. She caught the sight of her bloody forehead and swollen eye. It would not be a life worth living, she thought. She should have left earlier. She should have listened to Madam the very first time. The thought of a dead Madam Cecelia caused Mwenje's stomach to turn.

I used to be you.

The words rang in her head. She would never know what she meant. Only that she was willing to save her. She would have been willing to save her baby too. The sound of Zivai's snore startled her out of her musing. Her eyes fell on his face, and back to her reflection in the mirror. Her left hand fell to her stomach and she rubbed it softly.

I will kill you both.

More words rang in her head. She believed him. Mwenje felt a bout of nausea rise to her chest. She thought she might be sick again and almost turned to the bathroom. She turned to the bed instead. She towered directly above his head. Without a second thought, she stretched her arm out and pointed the edge of the blade where Zivai's beard ended, to aim. She firmly clenched the knife with both hands, lifted it slightly, then stabbed hard with all her might, before dragging the blade across to slit his throat. She was not shocked by her precision; it was the way she had always been taught to do on a goat. Blood splattered everywhere from the fresh perforation. It was in her eyes blinding her, covering her eyes, gushing against her shirt. She did not let out a sound. Zivai's body seized slightly, then Mwenje took a step back and fixed her eyes on his face. His jaw dropped slowly, and aggressive gasps escaped his mouth. His eyes opened widely, immediately meeting hers. She held her stare and did not move. She could not tell if the wideness of his pupil meant he was shocked, or if that was his soul detaching itself from his defeated body as his senses retired. He shifted his body as if to stand, then landed on the floor. It made sense. A man like him had to resist death, even though he hated life.

Seconds later, Mwenje stood above the motionless body of her dead husband. He had fallen facedown, and the knife had torn through his neck and now peeped through the base of his skull. The pool of blood trailed from his throat, through the cracks of their polished cement floors, and under his now powerless hand, right to the edge of Mwenje's feet.

She would need a cloth.

Saving Trymore

Nothing disgusted me more than the pleasure of a man.

This man in particular. I sprang to my feet, picked up my clothes and rushed out of the room. I hated the moments after. They were the worst. They were especially different now because I chose to be there. What other choice did I have? We had to eat. Trymore had to eat. The first few days after our new arrangement, I would leave the room in a rush out of fear. Fear that the General might decide he wanted a second serving, and I could only stomach one at a time. That the other soldiers might envy his pleasure and take me for themselves, force themselves on me like they had done the others, and like the General had on me. Now I rushed simply because I looked forward to running down the mountain and taking my mind away from what life had become. I looked forward to stepping on the sharp rocks that stabbed my bare feet, and the pain of the thorns as they scratched my skin. I looked forward to pain that resembled what I felt on the inside.

The day Idai changed everything, we had stayed behind while our mothers went to the field to collect the last of the remaining crop. We survived through planting maize on the little land Mai Trymore had, taking it to the mill and selling mealie meal in surrounding villages. We usually all went. It was quicker that way, but the rains had become heavier and Trymore was too small for the harsh floods that flowed through the trenches, and far too big to be carried on any of our backs. We had heard from the neighbours who had cell phones and relatives in the city, that there would be heavy rains coming. They were calling it Cyclone Idai. Ironic that in Shona "Idai" meant they want or must want, and yet the last thing we needed was having our lives disrupted. We were living hand to mouth already, and winter was fast approaching. Trymore and I had stayed in the kitchen hut; he had played with his wire car in the corner while I prepared dinner. The wind had grown stronger, the roof shook more than usual and one by one neighbours had knocked, telling us to leave. Some were headed to the main road, others up the mountain. They had worn discomfort and pity on their faces when I had mentioned we would wait for our mothers who had gone to the field. It was when the wind had shaken the hinges off the door, leaving the wooden structure to blow away into the harsh storm, that we had decided to head up to the mountains. It had only been when Trymore sat on my back and we wrestled against the water that flowed down the man-made path, holding onto the few trees that had not been washed away, that I realized we might not survive. We had found a cave halfway to the peak and we had stayed for what felt like an eternity. The rains were too violent and the winds far too strong. The hunger had consumed me at first, but it became a distant ache in the wake of a realisation that my mother, Amai, was somewhere out there and probably dead.

Idai had stopped eventually. And that is when I had met the General.

"Girly, I'm sure even you know nothing is free."

He had said, as his eyes travelled from my feet and fixated on my breasts. I wondered briefly what he saw because they had barely grown out; puberty was taking its time with me. I knew I was beautiful, but I had the body of a teenage boy and the other kids in the village always made fun of me about it. I felt my skin crawl. He was tall, heavily built, with an above-average pot belly that hung over his green cargo pants. His gun hung on his back, with the sling pressing on the belly fat. He was dark as charcoal; his gums were bright pink, and his teeth surprisingly stain free. His patchy beard covered half his face, and he had what looked like breadcrumbs on his moustache. His eyes were dark and cold as he stared me down. That had been the moment resentment was born in me. Desperation had led us here, because over the past few months, the soldiers had tormented our way of life, how could these be the people I trusted to save us? Ever since the presidential elections, they were everywhere. Asking for proof of identification at every corner, burning houses and beating people. They said it was because among us were supporters of the opposition party and traitors to the country would not be tolerated. Relentless in their violence, the soldiers had killed our sense of community before the cyclone finished us off.

"Please *mukwasha*," I pleaded, voice barely audible.

"You know what to do young lady. A nice pretty ripe girl like yourself."

A few tears began to fall down my face. I had long fancied boys, but I had never seen a man's genitals. I felt a knot in my stomach.

"You and your brother can rush back to find your family in the floods then."

He turned without a second look and slammed the wooden door behind it. I turned to Trymore. His eyes were bloodshot, and his mouth was white as rice. He sat at my feet, his small body too weak to stand. Was I all he had? Was this our life now? Why had we fought so hard to survive only to die miserable? Should I have let him starve to death out of mercy? What kind of life would he live? I thought of how it would soon be him being solicited by the soldiers; I had heard the stories. They went after the little boys too. When they were off herding cattle, or in the fields. We did not have cattle anymore though. Or fields. They would never get to Trymore and I would make sure of it. I had to save him. I was all he had. He was seven years old and had lived in the hut next to ours all his life. We did not have much, so we had shared a rural homestead with him and his mother. Mai Trymore had had two children earlier in her life and they had both died of complications during childbirth. After the second child passed, it had not been long before her in-laws accused her of witchcraft and her husband had left. We lived in the neighbouring homestead and when my father had passed away, his family had ostracised my mother too. That is when Mai Trymore had taken us in. It was almost as if fate had brought our mothers together. And now it had brought us together.

I carried him to the rocks nearby, lay him on the ground, and covered him with the blanket.

"There will be food soon. Sleep."

I had walked to the eroding door and knocked, hands trembling. The soldier had opened the door and immediately smiled.

"You have smartly reconsidered. *Wakangwara.* Come in." He said it as if there was no wrong in exchanging food for sex. As if we had a choice. As if there was a single scenario, I could have said no. As if he would not help himself to me eventually no matter what I said.

The room smelled like cigarette smoke and period blood. It was stuffy and the slight scent of urine hung in the air. There were six single beds, all squashed in a line, going from one wall of the metal cabin to another. At the top of the beds were two small windows, with rusted bars protecting the opening. I wondered for a second why the soldiers went out of their way to make us miserable when it was clear the government was not taking very good care of them. My eyes had immediately locked with a girl. A young girl. I knew her. She had been in my class about four years ago when I had last attended. My nostalgia had quickly turned into raging fear when there were four other girls from the village sitting beside her. No one else looked at me. Their eyes were fixed on the floor, faces taken by grief. I recognized them all. One from my village, Ndima and two from the neighbouring one, I could not remember if it was Shinja or Mutambara. My fear subsided because there was one of him and six of us. Maybe I would not have to sleep with this very ugly man. He laughed and chuckled as he spoke to us, only asking us to nod if we understood. We were only to come to the cabin at night where we could have a place to sleep, on the floor, and their leftovers from time to time. In exchange, we had to open our legs and shut our mouths. I wondered why he was the only one here. Where were the others? Would they choose us? Would they exchange us? Tears rolled down my face and I wished I had been one of the many dead bodies I had seen since the cyclone. He said I was not to worry, and a few of the other girls could confirm they were just fine, but we were free to be homeless if we wanted. We were to address everyone as General and that was all we needed to know. During the day, we were to go down the mountain, away from their cabin. The trips down the mountain gave me hope to find ways to start a new life.

"Some of you are pretty, maybe you can find a husband during the day. You will be used up soon, and we won't need you."

"Leave now. Be back tonight."

He said dismissively, but with certainty that we would return.

I had bolted to my feet with the other five girls when he grabbed my arm. I thought I might vomit, but I did not have enough food in my stomach. My insides tied, my body went still, and my sight blurred from tears that now seemed to be running out. They sat at the bottom of my eyelid as I stared down at the cuts and bruises that covered almost every inch of my feet. They had looked exactly how I felt on the inside at that moment.

"Not you girly."

He slammed the door shut behind the last girl, and immediately unbuckled his belt. He removed his gun and placed it on one of the dirty beds.

"Your brother needs food too, so you have to do extra." He chuckled again. It was clear that he felt good about himself. Almost like he had been with us as we fled home and hid in the mountains. Like he could smell my desperation. There was no urgency in his demeanour either. He took a few seconds to look at me, smugly.

I could barely hear him. He seemed miles away. He pulled me by the shoulder and threw my face into the filthy mattress. The smell of period blood and urine entered my nostrils again, harsher this time. My hand brushed against the gun as my body bounced slightly from being thrown on the bed so aggressively. I locked my eyes on the gun and did not break contact. My eyes had travelled to the faded wooden part that hung right behind his neck when he wore the sling. It was dented and the wood looked like it might cause a few splinters. I looked past a metal part, onto some wood again, and towards the barrel of the gun. He should have used it to kill me instead. I stared at the trigger, wondering what it might feel like to kill a man. This man in particular. All of them actually. What it might be like to take the weapons they oppress us with and drive them to their maker. God would make them answer, I thought. Would he? If God could do something why was I here? Why had the cyclone happened?

Why did I have to live without Amai? I analysed the semi-circle trigger. It had started to fade where the forefinger was meant to be placed. I briefly glanced at my forefinger and back at the trigger. My finger seemed much too small to pull it. I was too small. Too small to fight, and too small to end all this. I whimpered faintly from the pain, my body still and lifeless. The General patted my buttocks and spoke. He still seemed far away, so I did not hear him.

As the ringing in my ear subsided, I heard the zip on his cargo trousers closing. He reached for his gun and I was jolted back into my own body. Without the gun there, I stared into space. I knew at that moment it was only the beginning. I decided the gun would be my point of focus. And it was. It was my focus point later that night after my eyes adjusted to the dark when it hung from the wall at the bottom of the bed. It was my focus point on the nights that he left it on the floor or when it sat against the wall. When it was out of my sight, I would look at someone else's. At night the rooms were dark, filled only with grunts of the soldiers, muffled sobs and odours of long and tiresome days. When the Generals were done, we would move to the floor, one blanket each, and when they left in the morning, we would share their leftover food among ourselves. I had always made sure to leave Trymore outside by the same tree. The Generals agreed. Even at the age of seven, he got more respect than us who were twice his age. They liked him. He feared them. Not because of what they did to us. He did not know. He was afraid because he too had seen the violence before the cyclone. He did not understand it. But he understood how it made him feel.

"When will I be old enough to get in before bedtime?" Trymore asked every night when I left him at the Chirinda Big Tree.

"When you are this tall." I would reply as I signalled my hand to a height he would not reach for another five years.

It was not long before we no longer needed somewhere to sleep. The days that followed our 'arrangement' with the Generals were filled with scavenging for materials that had been swept away by the floods so we could build our own home. The other girls stayed together because they preferred to stay up the mountain closer to rocky shelters and caves. They had given up on any prospects of normal life after this. I could not blame them. I knew before Idai their families had many cows and fields that stretched longer than most people in our village. When they had funerals and all-night prayers everyone wanted to be there because they knew there would be goat meat. There would be jam and fresh bread baked in their wall somehow. Survival was not life to them. I understood why they could not even bear to try. We were different. And I had Trymore now. I was sure if we found shelter close to the bottom, we would find a small piece of land dry enough to plant on. We would grow new crops and start a life of our own. I was strangely optimistic. I had accepted my plight every night and hoped to turn it into something else when the sun came up. Maybe the relentless spirits of our mothers were reincarnating in me. Or maybe I had spent too much time looking at gun triggers, and the hopelessness had started to bore me. Either way, I was brave and extremely so, because the day we finished building our wood and plastic den was the first time I spoke to the General since the day I begged him to let us in.

"General, if Trymore and I could please have money rather than a place to sleep we would appreciate it greatly."

The cuts and bruises on my feet had started to heal. I kept my head low and eyes fixed on the ground while I waited for the General to answer me. He did not need to help us. I did not quite understand sex, but I had come to observe that it was given and taken always in exchange for something. Food. Shelter. Money. Love apparently. So, it sounded simple to me that if I still needed a livelihood but no longer needed somewhere to sleep, the General might be willing to give me something else. He had shaken his head with laughter and made remarks about Trymore being a brave boy for being in the presence of soldiers, and how a little determination would take him a long way. He agreed to give me a dollar for every visit I made up the mountain, and I was to never get more than five dollars in one week. I used the money for food. Food at first and then seed for the crop after. It would take months, but I was accustomed to dividing little things and making more of them than there seemed to be, we would sleep in our own blankets, in our own space and Trymore would be safe.

The sound of running water catches my attention, and I slow my run into a brisk walk. It is relatively safe in Ndima now that everyone is either dead, fled or now living in the neighbouring Chimanimani regions. I avoid the stream. Ungodly sights flow down it now. Carcasses of the cattle the villagers lost remains of broken furniture, cobs and cobs of maize that had been stored away by families for the winter.

On one night while taking my evening bath, I had felt a hand graze me, looked down and seen a dark mass that looked like a body flowing down. It was small. Not much bigger than what a small boy might look like. I had not wanted to confirm. I grabbed my dress from the hanging branch and ran back to our den as fast as I could. I had no idea for sure if it was a body, but I had seen enough. As I thought back to that moment, I wondered if my mother's body had also trailed the path of the stream with passers-by avoiding its touch and wincing at the mere sight of it. I wondered at what moment she had accepted defeat and known she would not be coming home. Whether she had embraced the end with a brave heart because she had never been anything less than courageous. I had not grieved for her. I could not find it within me. If she had a grave, she would be turning in it. Reeling and ashamed of what her daughter had become. Maybe that is why I could not grieve for her. I had previously grieved, all the time, for my dead friends and my missing neighbours, for the innocence of my body and the death of my spirit. For Trymore's interrupted childhood and the loss of his mother. But never for my own.

Mwanangu

"Sorry...what?" Pregnant? She must not have heard right.

"Five and a half months to be exact. Honestly I'm not sure how you did not feel it."

Mukundi snorted in disbelief, then let out a chuckle hugged by what sounded like a little cry. It couldn't be. He was mistaken. She was a lot of things. Misguided, tragedy stricken and possibly chronically depressed, but pregnant certainly was not one of those things.

"Your tests could be wrong of course?" The sound of her own voice brought true light to her ridiculousness. She knew she had not been careful in her sexual encounters. "Careful" was not a word she had been able to identify with for a long time now. Something about living in perpetual misery hindered her from making good decisions. Being disappointed in herself was actually quite a familiar feeling. She completely contradicted the values she claimed to have every other week, and after a while she had come to realize she did not have the luxury to uphold those values. She had two options. One was to be guided by those values and end up just like Tete, counting coins to buy a small pack of mealie meal for the night. The second was to forget everything she thought she knew and do whatever got her furthest, no matter what anyone would say.

"I'm happy to refer you for an ultrasound if you like." The doctor interrupted her train of thought. He was dark skinned with a heavy beard, and a pair of very thick lenses sat on either side of his nose. His teeth looked especially well taken care of, and a matching white lab coat draped perfectly from his broad shoulders. His left hand held a blue Eversharp pen and fiddled just a few centimetres from the little transparent cup that held her urine. She wanted to keep staring at them just so she would not continue the conversation. She wanted to focus on the hairs that stood out on his fingers and his neatly cut nails where the pen sat.

"Sorry?" Why did she keep asking what he said when she could hear him?

"It's okay. I understand, this can be shocking. However, if you did not know you were pregnant, we need to check on the health of the foetus."

Her heart sank, almost as if she was hearing the news of her pregnancy for the very first time. As if this man had not been trying to tell her for what now felt like eternity. Bloody hell! What was she supposed to do with a foetus? A child. A child she was having not only out of wedlock but in someone else's. How many children did that man have? She could not think clearly, and the room could not feel any smaller.

"I know it's hard, young girl like you. Next time I suggest coming with the father."

She felt sick. Mukundi as a mother was one thing, but Mukundi as a teenage gold digger who fell pregnant to become a second wife was a nightmare she was not prepared to face.

“Adult things have adult consequences *mwanangu*,” Tete hissed at her one night after she had come home with takeaway for them both. They rarely ate fast food and it was so beyond their reach, they never craved it. She vividly remembered how annoyed she had been with her aunt's remark. She had not even slept with Zeke yet. He was still Mr. Ziki at the time. A simple “thank you” from Tete would have sufficed.

"*Ewoi*!" Mukundi had jibed back to Tete before retreating to her little room.

"Ma'am!" the doctor brought her back to consciousness. She could not take much more of this.

"Okay." she managed to reply. The doctor took out a pad and rambled on about which doctors were best on her budget and that it would not be long until the baby came. She could not afford to write exams; did she look like she could afford a child? He talked a lot. Were they supposed to do that? It was causing tightening in her chest, and she put her hand over it. Her forefinger caressed the chain that sat on her neck. It had belonged to her mother. She gripped it tightly as tears welled up and sat on the edge of her eyelids. She desperately wanted her to be here. She would not have been happy, but she would be here. She almost wished Tete was here too, so she would not have to repeat this news. She had felt for a very long time now that life could not get any worse. But, the humiliation of explaining to Tete, the only family she had, that she had made a child with her married boyfriend who she slept with for tuition fees, made her wish she was in the ground. The thought of her parents made her shiver a little. She had not heard much else of what the doctor had said. What a sick twist of faith, that she had gathered the little money she had to visit a doctor because she thought she had a sexually transmitted disease, only to find out it was much worse.

The sun blinded her as she stepped out of the doctor's surgery and walked toward the bus rank. The day was so overwhelmingly beautiful, it was ironic. One thing Mukundi knew was to never underestimate the insignificance of what felt like the most earth shattering events in her life. It did not really matter what kept her up at night, or for how long it did so, because life carried on for everybody else, and she had to make hers work. It had taken her a long time to understand this, but eventually she had to. She knew other eighteen-year olds did not need to learn that lesson. They were busy swapping their fruit lip gloss, kissing boys in class, and probably never thought about school fees or saving for candles to do schoolwork at night. Their biggest worry was making it to the Zengeza Market on time to buy second-hand tops that left their belly buttons out.

She felt God had his favourites, and he had to be a man. Was it why only women seemed to suffer?

She braced herself for the hour and a half ride home in the omnibus. She got in, got comfortable and leaned her head against the cold window. Tete liked to eat early, so Mukundi would get home just in time for dinner. She would not tell Tete tonight. She would sit her down tomorrow morning after she had had some time to think.

Almost six months. The words rang in her head. Had she gotten pregnant the very first time she had sex? Was that even possible?

Tete was the oldest of all her aunts. The first born in Baba Mukundi's family of three. They had grown up at the rural homestead in Gokomere, a few hours' drive out of Harare. Her father had moved to the city and after a few years he had started a booming car sale business. He did not have any degree or qualifications, but he was witty and sly, and that made him everyone's favourite person in the room. They had always known he would be the rich one of the three.

It had not been long after his car sale started when he bought himself a house then built one for his two siblings in Beatrice two hours from the city. Babamukuru, his brother, worked with him, while Tete enjoyed the benefits of having raised her two brothers. By the time Mukundi's parents met, fell in love and got married, her father's business was doing better than ever. She did not quite remember feeling extremely wealthy, but she had never wanted for anything. She had gone to a good school and learned to speak what they called white people English. Between her white schools and carefree parents, she had grown to be everything Tete resented in a woman. Defiant and ungovernable! Questioning everything and constantly on the lookout for better options. Mukundi had never learnt to seek the approval of people around her, especially not her distant relatives. She was free.

"I work so you don't ever have to do anything you don't want to, mwanangu." Her father would always slur during his Friday night bottle of whiskey, before he launched into stories of his childhood and having escaped a limited life. He had never explained in detail what he had done to gain all this success. He only had half of his secondary school education when he had left Mberengwa, and between that departure and the purchase of his second or third car sale, the story had a gap that he had never filled. As fate would have it, a few days after Mukundi's parents had passed, three police officers had let themselves into the yard, arrested Babamukuru for fraud and subsequently informed them that they would be hearing from the banks. And indeed, they did. Her parents had been involved in a fatal car accident after driving into a tree, dodging a herd of cows on the highway. The area they had crashed in was remote and by the time they had been found and help had been called, it was too late, and they had both died on their way to the hospital.

Mukundi had played those few days in her head over and over again, shaken by the swiftness of injustice, the quickness with which life could take away whatever it wanted, but also by the pain of the truth. Which was that her father had lied for decades. He had falsely registered properties and applied for loans with multiple institutions across the country. The car sale business had never taken off. In fact, it made sense because when she looked back it always seemed to be the same cars parked outside. Baba Mukundi had greased hands, cheated and lied for years to live the dream, only to leave her with nothing. They had taken it all. The house, the cars, the jewellery. Only Tete's house had survived the purge, and after Babamukuru was locked away, they only had each other.

The sound of tyres screeching jolted her from her nap. Reckless driving was the way of Zimbabwe's public transport. She looked up to realise the vehicle she sat on was already approaching her stop. She had dozed off much longer than she thought. It had felt only like a few minutes. She hopped out of the omnibus and started on her short walk home. The keys in her hands became slippery as her palms began to sweat. She fixed her eyes on her once most fashionable sneakers as they grazed the dusty gravel. They were too small for her now. Small, old and tattered. But she had not got rid of any of her old clothes. She wore them as much as she could. Not that she had a choice. Her wardrobe comprised of old clothes only. Hers. Her mother's. Some of her father's. But all old. Over the years between ordinary wear and tear, cheap soap and her growing curves, her clothing options had dwindled. It did not matter though. She had gone from being a 12-year-old that needed the latest fashion, to being a 17-year-old who was grateful that her five-year-old sneakers had not ruptured in the sides after being taken to a street side cobbler about three times now.

As she approached their humble little yard, Mukundi could not help but feel that this was the last time she would feel like herself again. She had not been sure of who she was for years now. But at least she had belonged to herself. Tete would never trust her again. Zeke would own her. Her very own fifty-year-old prison guard. This child would always have to come first. Come first at what? She briefly asked herself? This world had no prize. Not theirs anyway. The smell of fried vegetables entered her nostrils as she opened the door. Why was that suddenly so nauseating?

"Tete?" She called as she walked towards the kitchen.

"Kitchen!" Her aunt yelled back.

Tete Alice stood over the stove, putting her back into stirring the sadza. She had become like a mother to her. One she felt constantly at odds with, but somehow completely protected by. She did not allow boys, friends that wore short skirts, lipstick, and everything else that was outside of what the bible and tradition dictated. Her mother had long taught her the opposite. She had often done things like try cigarettes, stroll around without a bra and swear in front of Tete, out of spite. They did not particularly dislike each other, her mother and Tete. They were just too different. Much like Tete and herself. They needed each other though. Rather Mukundi needed her. She had saved her before. Maybe she could save her again.

"I'm pregnant. I'm sorry." Mukundi's words shocked her as they escaped her mouth. She had planned to wait, but there was no point. She had made her bed and now she would lay in it. She did not doubt that her aunt loved her, and she could find comfort in knowing that she might not need to take care of a baby on her own. That she could cry, and her whimpers would fall on the ears of a woman who knew her heart. But life was not so simple with Tete. The comfort would not come for nothing. Tete would send her away. That had long been the family position.

"Mwanangu, do you want to kill me as I stand?" Tete's head hung from her neck and Mukundi's eyes fell on her dirty shoes.

"You want us to die? Tell me where one finds the time for men when we are so busy trying to make it through the day? Did I not tell you that you are not an adult, child? It's a shame your mother gave you a rebellious spirit and did not show you how to use it."

Mukundi said nothing. Tete needed time to process the bombshell. As did she. Tete's words did not hurt her. They were a very small fragment of the doom that was about to become her life.

"You want to kill me as I stand!" Tete screamed. "If you want us to die rather, we just die of hunger."

Tete reached for the pots on the stove and threw the contents in the sink, then the pots right after. The sound of metal on metal rang loudly and the aroma of simmering sadza spread across the kitchen, even more than when Mukundi had first walked in. She watched Tete and thought she might lose consciousness with disbelief. Tete was dramatic in many ways but she had never thrown away food before. Especially not at a time like this. They had recently started buying mealie meal, cooking oil and on the good days, soya chunks in small portions enough for one serving. It seemed that many people in the neighbourhood had started doing that. The portions were called *tsaona*, which meant tragedy. It was a *tsaona* where it was one serving of cooking oil, a handful of dried *kapenta*, one tomato.

Mukundi raised her head to face the disappointed gaze of her surviving guardian. She propelled herself from the door she had leaned against, then sat herself at the white and red plastic wooden table that took up the small space of the kitchen. The burden of the last few months had been far too heavy anyway. Tete had not asked yet, and it truly could have killed her. But Mukundi had to tell her everything.

"Tete, Zeke is the father." She did not break her stare. Tete knew exactly who Zeke was. How could she forget the man who had stood as the best man at her own brother's wedding?

"*Ani?*"

"Mr. Ziki."

Tete stumbled and reached for a chair. She buried her face in her hands and shook her head vigorously. She regretted calling him by his nickname to her. Mukundi reached for the chain around her neck for courage and launched into the most respectfully detailed account of the events that had led to her sitting on the kitchen table that night. Mr. Ziki had always been there for her. He was a rural raised businessman who had been friends with Mukundi's father for years. He had been there to plan the funeral ceremony and memorial, and to help out after Mukundi's father's assets had been seized. He had in a few instances over the years acted as a father figure, bringing her a t-shirt or two, driving her to school when he saw her waiting for an omnibus down the road. She had started running into Mr. Ziki more frequently over the years, almost daily, it was as if he knew her timetable. He had a big house and a farm in their neighbourhood, so he always had a reason to be there. He had changed the way she saw life.

During their long drives, Zeke would give her scenarios and ask her what the right thing to do was. It was her favourite part of the drive because it was the only time he did not talk about himself. It did not matter that whatever she said was wrong to him and he would explain what the better thing was. He told her about his friendship with her father and struggling in Harare before they became successful. How without crossing their own boundaries and breaking rules they never would have had the town life they grew up only dreaming about. Mukundi knew that rule breaking is how her father had made all his money, why all their assets had been seized and why she sat in Zeke's passenger seat three times a week talking about fake scenarios.

"Use the little you have to get all you can. I have only lived on that principle and look at the car I drive. Conquer baby girl!" Zeke had said with an annoying sort of vigour.

He was tall, muscular and light in complexion, with a belly that slightly protruded. He looked like his age mates in her eyes. She had not been able to shake off that 'baby girl'. It had started one day, and it never stopped. He had told her she was beautiful and anyone who said otherwise was jealous. He complimented her legs and noticed her new hairstyles. It felt peculiar but flattering. She had not received any intentional and precise attention after her father's death. Not from boys, or by anyone lately. Her father had always done it so well, and she yearned for that intimacy. She had eventually opened up to Zeke about how Tete could afford to send her to the district school, but she would only write exams the following year because Tete could not afford both the school fees and fees at the same time. He had looked at her from behind his steering wheel and smiled.

"I'm sure I can do something for you." He had said, without a second thought, as he placed his hand on her thigh, rubbing it lightly then going back to driving. She could not describe in words what she felt about him, and "baby girl", and the incessant flirting. She just knew she did not like how it made her feel. But then she had looked at his car, like he always reminded her to. She looked at his watch and his shoes, the same as her father used to have. The things he spoke about buying for his children. She wanted that too. And she would never get it sitting on unsubstantiated hopes of a better future in a dying Zimbabwe. She imagined it was like one of the many scenarios they spoke about and decided almost instantly she would do whatever it took to get hers. And six weeks later, she had found herself in the Holiday Inn, naked, numb and past reckoning. Her life thereafter had consisted of more life lessons from Zeke in the car and skipping Friday afternoon lessons to meet him at the hotel. She would arrive at the hotel room and Zeke would let her order whatever she wanted off the menu while he made loud business calls before he took out a bottle of whiskey and joined her in the eating. The last seven months had gone by so fast her mind could not think back to intricate details. Her memory had become so terrible. She did not mind though. She did not like the things she had to do for Zeke, so she did not mind forgetting.

By the time Mukundi finished narrating her escapades, Tete had gone through all the emotions ranging from shock, disgust to agony.

"Pack your bags. We leave in the morning!" Tete meant it.

The morning had come fast. Patriarchy was efficient. Her parents had not been buried this fast. Distant relatives had tried to delay it as long as possible in an effort to loot as much as they could from what was left behind. Tete had allowed it, saying that elders and heads of the family could not be questioned. "What heads? Whose? You make no sense." Mukundi had yelled before storming off. Even the moving of all her belongings to go to Tete's had been swift, and she was starting to think things were only urgent when they were headed towards her suffering. It was 07.38 when Tete and Mukundi found themselves standing at the giant gate of the secluded suburban utopia. This was where Zeke lived. He would be so upset with her for not telling him first.

It was not like she had a phone. She did not need to anyway. He could not avoid this. Neither of them could.

"Mr. Ziki just left for work. I will get Mrs. Ziki!" The security guard said as he disappeared back into the yard. The pace of her heart quickened. Mukundi wondered if he knew they brought trouble. It was not long before a forearm in a pink robe peeked out the gate. It was her. She opened the gate slightly and then turned back to yell something. She was talking to someone in the yard.

"Sorry I'll be with you just now!" She yelled towards them, turning her head briefly. She was beautiful. Mukundi had not seen her in years, but she remembered her. And now here she was, pregnant with her husband's child. Mukundi glanced at Tete briefly and wondered what she was thinking. As she looked back toward the gate, she saw Zeke's wife walking downhill to approach them. Her skin was glowing and her head tie sat perfectly on her head. Her breasts were perky, and she had a plumpness about her that roused her hunch for a disastrous episode. As she stood just in front of her, Mukundi realized she was not plump at all. She was slender, and her body was little. When she turned her gaze and smiled to greet Tete first, her side view became perfectly visible.

She too was pregnant.

Nkosilesisa Ncube

Nkosilesisa, better known as Nkosi is a trained journalist, screenwriter and aspiring television producer whose interests lie in storytelling through whatever medium. To date she has written full length and short form films and has also written for television. She also interned at the national weekly newspaper "Sunday News" for a year and had a short stint as editor for an online entertainment magazine "Urban Culxure". She is currently with the Multichoice Talent Factory where she is working towards improving her skills in film. In her spare time, Nkosi runs a personal blog www.wordsbynkocy.com. Her other skills include public speaking and concept development.

Lost

There is a song I hate that they sing at every funeral. I am yet to attend a funeral where they do not sing that horrid song. There is always that aunt who cries too much, that relative who won't let the guests eat, and that song. It was terrible at my grandmother's funeral, it was terrible at Mini's mother's funeral, it was terrible when my childhood friend Tariro died, it was terrible at my father's funeral and it is not any less terrible now. The song is called "Asakhile" and it somehow rationalises death because we are not of this world anyway. I hate it. Not as much as I hate being here to bury Ntando, but it's pretty close. His mother sits in the front, very poised. That is a gift she has always had, the ability to stay level-headed even when nobody expects her to. On her right is Ntando's sister. I can never bring myself to remember her name. All I remember is that she is in her third marriage with her fourth baby daddy, but that should not matter right now. On Ntando's mother's left is a woman I don't know.

"Is that the girlfriend," Mini says as she slips into the seat next to mine. She expects me to know, there wouldn't be any way of knowing but she, like me, knows Ntando's type and this girl, next to Ntando's mother, pretty and slightly underage is definitely the girlfriend.

"I guess," I whisper. Mini takes another look at her for a couple of seconds then says "meh". In most universes, "meh" wouldn't mean anything, but Mini has been speaking in mono syllables for as long as I have known her. I know what meh means.

Mini takes out a packet of gum, tosses one into her mouth and starts chewing. She sees the look of judgement on my face but pretends not to, so we sit in silence until we hear a pair of heels walk in. Everybody turns around except us of course because we know who the heels belong to. Sometimes I think Fadzi takes the fashionably late thing too far, because she wants to be seen – not that you could miss her even if you tried.

"What's everybody staring at?" she asks as she takes her seat next to Mini. Mini rolls her eyes at her then Fadzi reaches for Mini's gum.

"Is that the girlfriend?" Fadzi asks. She is staring at the girl. Mini nods and Fadzi studies the poor girl for a little longer.

"See this is what I never got about you and Ntando's thing. Rest his soul, but he had such a type and then there was you – made zero sense." You can always count on Fadzi to tell you what she thinks, no hold backs, no "mehs", just the truth. I am still trying to find something to retort to Fadzi when the priest gets up. The priest was Ntando's mother's choice of course. Ntando had his issues with God. I wonder if he resolved them before he died. The priest says something about us opening Ntando's favourite scripture. Wrong! Ntando believed in God – a God, a creator, a higher power, but that God was never necessarily the Christian God. Ntando would sooner quote you a hundred verses from Tupac than a verse from the Bible, but what we have here is what his mother needs.

I suppose this is what we all need when we lose somebody we care about. We need to believe that they are in a better place – that they earned their stripes. Then we start to convince ourselves that they were better people than they actually were because the thought of people we love being consumed in hell fire or wandering as lost souls in the afterlife is so unfathomable. It makes sense. Ntando's mother stands up – gracious as ever and talks about her son. No doubt she loved him, she did a terrible job of raising him, but she loved him still.

She says something about him being sent from God and Fadzi scoffs. It's not loud enough to upset the front row, but a few of the people in front of us turn back and stare. Fadzi stares them down.

"I don't even know what we are doing here," she mutters as she stares at her watch. Mini tries to shush her, but it doesn't work. Fadzi turns to me, "Well, Azania. What are we doing here?"

***

I have this thing where whenever I am at a cemetery, I try to find a backstory for all the dead that are close to the grave I am either visiting or digging up – depending. Next to Ntando's is a Phillippa Mhlanga. Born 16 June 1989, Died 3 March 2020, Buried 8 March 2020. I imagine Phillippa dying young – an untimely death no doubt and a cruel disease that could have just skated past her the way it skated past everybody else, but I suppose life has a sense of humour. I wonder what people will think Ntando's back story is. Someone starts another of those horrible funeral songs and for the first time since he died, it hits me; Ntando is gone.

Perhaps I should have gone for the body viewing, but I could not bring myself to do it. The last thing I need is a memory of him in that casket, still, unmoving, constrained by the dimensions of that box. There is no way I could have looked at him like that. I want to remember Ntando as he lived, funny, no regard for authority, disarmingly handsome, charming – not this guy in a suit. Fadzi says they put him in a fucking suit! That's not the Ntando I know – that's not the Ntando anybody knows. Whoever we are burying here is some façade of him, what people wanted him to be. My Ntando is gone.

I stare at the casket lowering into the ground and Mini already knows what's going on. She grabs my hand. "Not here." I nod quietly but the deeper into the ground the casket goes, the harder it is to stay on my feet.

"Listen to me, this is not about you, you cannot do this here," Fadzi says. She is holding my other hand and I am almost certain if either of them lets go, I might drop to the ground.

"I can't breathe," I say quietly. Mini reaches for my bag and takes out my inhaler, shakes it and puffs it once in my mouth. "Can we go?" I ask.

Fadzi makes an exasperated face for two reasons. The first being I am ridiculous for even suggesting it and the second being that she has to literally hold me until the burial is over. I watch his mother, his sister and the girlfriend cry over the lowering casket – a privilege I no longer have. But haven't I earned the right to mourn Ntando? Didn't I care enough about him? Didn't I see him through his best and worst times? But again, like Fadzi said, this is not about me. I could throw soil into the grave like everybody else is doing but what would that help. Ntando is gone. He is gone and I cannot mourn him.

"When's the last time you saw him?" Fadzi says out of nothing on the drive home. That question catches me off guard. I stumble for something to say but Minnie comes to the rescue. She says something about none of that mattering. Fadzi retorts with a statement of how she's just glad this is the last time she sees me crying over Ntando. As someone who had front row tickets to the drama that was me and Ntando, I understand her relief. As my friend. I don't know why she would say something like that. They leave me at home and ask if I need them to stay. I say I need some time alone and I really do.

My mind keeps racing back to Fadzi's question. The last time I saw Ntando. Of course, that doesn't help anybody now. But wouldn't that be a beautiful story to tell? How after years of trying to figure out what we were to each other, we finally got it right. I remember Ntando coming to my house on the day that eventually became the day he died. The best thing about me and Ntando was always that neither of us ever had to say anything. We understood each other.

So, when he came to my house that day, he didn't have to tell me that he wanted to leave that girl. He didn't have to tell me how unhappy he had been since the last time we had spoken. I knew. The same way he knew that although I had spent a few months before that being furious with him, I loved him in spite of who he was.

We had spent the night talking about the many things we had done wrong in the past and how we would do them right. We talked, we laughed, we cried, we kissed, he teased…and now he is gone. I will never know why he finally chose that day to be the day he came back to me. I suppose he just felt like it was a good day for homecoming.

I remember him leaving, I remember wanting to tell him I loved him – that I had loved him since the day I first saw him all those many years ago. I remember not telling him that I loved him, because of course he knew, and I would always be able to say it the next time. I remember waiting for his text saying he got home safely. I remember getting angry when I didn't receive the text. I remember crying because once again, I had let this beautiful boy make a complete idiot of me. I especially remember crying by myself because I could not let my friends know that this boy had embarrassed me once again.

I have been trying not to remember how I felt when Mini came to my house the next day to tell me Ntando had been hit by a car on his way home. I remember saying "Ntando is dead" out loud and it all became so real. I remember thinking of the first time I met Ntando and the last time I saw him. I remember thinking how those two times were so similar. I remember the first time he called me beautiful, the first time I called him stupid...so many firsts.

Now all I can remember is how I regained and re-lost the greatest love of my life, all in one day.

Sins of the father

I always think about the first time I slit my wrists. My mother made a whole scene about how I tried to kill myself then she called our local pastor to exorcise me. They were crazy! I would never do that to myself. I think I was 13 years old at the time and had realised that this was my life. A slit wrist was nothing in the face of that. Besides, I would not let myself bleed out. If I wanted to die, I would probably just jump. It would take nothing more than the time that gravity would need to pull me to the ground. I would not let myself bleed to death; I was not that cruel to myself. My mother gave me the "do not kill yourself when you get there" speech when she dropped me off for my first day at the university. I would do my best to comply.

I am convinced something is wrong with me. Of course there is no sure way of telling; my mother would lose it. How could she possibly react to her only child saying she needed a psychiatric evaluation? I only go on what the internet has told me. According to WebMD, I have Depression, Agoraphobia and Anxiety Disorder. It was a terrible idea to bring me here.

But my mother insisted, dictating more than she suggested that I needed to get out of the house. It would be good for me to leave the house, she said. She also said that being around people my own age would keep me from being such a snob.

She does not get it. She thinks I deliberately stay away from people. I do not. You know those chills that people get when they think about death? I get them when I think about talking to people or getting up in the morning or getting my next meal. I get those same chills when I think about existing. Life gives me chills.

I am possibly one of the few people who are genuinely fighting mental illness in a sea of millennials who will do almost anything to be associated with mental illness. I do not dismiss that people go through some intense things. I would be the last person to disregard people's problems but throwing around big words like depression fetishizes the whole thing. There are whole threads on Twitter about depression being real, and it is, but we can't all have it, can we? Or maybe we can. Maybe this is how every other person feels, but I am just being a baby about it. Perhaps I should suck it up. Maybe I should stop thinking that something is wrong with me. Perhaps I should pray.

Born to a pastor, my father called me Sarah, ironically after a crazy woman in the Bible. Something had to have been wrong with her, for her to think for a second that God had time to joke with her. In what world would God take time off His work to make jokes with a barren old lady? Being a pastor's only child meant I was one of the few people who realised that at the end of the day, pastors were human, just like the rest of us, if not more so because of how much was expected of them. Before he was a pastor, before he became the standard of how some people came to model their lives; my father was a regular man and he made regular mistakes. A number of times, his mistakes landed my mother in hospital, and when I was six years old, his mistakes broke my arm. My father's faults were regular, nothing unlike any other man's faults; at least that was what my mother would say and then she would instruct me to never speak of it again. We kept this vow of silence even when my father died in his sleep at Mai Vivian's house. She was a member of our church, and her daughter Vivian would sometimes babysit me when my parents were away. I was only ten years old and my father's death made no sense to me. I asked my mother why my father was sleeping at Mai Vivian's house, and my mother slapped me then she reminded me of our vow of silence.

I always thought this vow of silence, this deliberate action to ignore the truth and at best overlook it, was the reason why I was like this. I was programmed to ignore a lot of things that eventually, all they did was build up and leave me like this. A poster child for unresolved issues! I gave up talking to my mother about any of it a long time ago; her answer was always the same. "Pray". "It will get better," she assures on days when she feels like humouring me. The upside of believing in religion was that you always have this unmovable faith that things will get better by themselves. The downside of religion was that you always have this unmovable faith that things will get better by themselves. I was not one of those things; I was a ticking time bomb!

Before I got here, it got so bad, I really wanted to die. I could not count on my fingers and toes the number of times I have wanted to die. However I have really wanted to die only twice. The first time I really wanted to die was when one of our neighbours said that I was my father's daughter. She meant well, because she said it in relation to what she knew about my father and what we let the rest of the world see. The neighbour went on about how alike my father and I were, and by the time she was done I could not stand it any longer. I would have gladly died than let someone compare me to that man – that hypocritical, cheating, wife-bashing, child-injuring, die-in-Mai-Vivian's-bed-ing man or any man remotely like him for any matter. It was disgusting of her to make that comparison. I was going to use painkillers but my mother's faith made her reject all forms of medicine. There were none in the house.

The second time I really wanted to die was when my mother told me she was bringing me here. I paid a psychiatrist out of my life's savings. She was nice enough. I told her I wanted to kill myself, she did not overreact. She told me not to do it but she did not state any plausible reason not to. She did state reasons, but nothing I had not thought about myself. She spoke about my mother and what that would do to her; I had thought about that. She spoke about the future that lay ahead of me, I had also thought about it. What I needed from her was a new, conceivable reason not to do it. She failed to deliver. I left her office that day determined to end it all, but the next day was a public holiday and it would be difficult for my mother to get a burial order on time. I would never put her through that.

I was fine, or my variation of being fine when I got here. Then it started all over again. I searched under my pillow for a bottle, I was sure there was at least one left over. I took a giant gulp. I hated the taste of alcohol. It tasted like regret and self-loathing, and I could relate to it. The smell was even worse, but on most days it pacified me. I know it might seem as though I was self-destructing and that I was not actively trying to get better, but I had tried. A few days ago, I went to the university clinic and I told the nurse I was sad. She looked at me like she wanted me to explain my sadness. There was nothing to explain. I had sadness. The way the girl behind me in line had a headache and the guy behind her had a toothache. No one needed to explain or justify these things. They were just there. She didn't get it. So I started on the alcohol. It worked, the highlight being that I was such a lightweight and it did not take much to knock me out. Just a bottle or two and I would be out for hours.

Lately, I find that thoughts about death have slowly come back to me. It is nothing to worry about. They are not the "I really want to die" thoughts; they are the mild "I want to die" kind. I have always been able to contain these. I take another gulp of this horrid drink and I remember why I hate it. Sometimes I wish it could just choke me before it settles in my stomach, but my relationship with alcohol is complex. I hate it but I need it, it keeps me sane. I turn on my laptop; I have not done that in ages. I check my learner's portal. I have so much outstanding work to do, but maybe this is what I need. If I slack enough, they will have no choice but to remove me from here and take me back home. My mother will throw a fit but at least I will be home, alone, with no students, and no sounds of girls squealing in laughter when some boy has lied to them. None of this! I ignore the pending notifications and see something I have never paid much attention to before. At the corner of the page, there is a small pop up. It says "talk to a student counsellor now".

I send a message. From the response I can tell that this is just a student who believes they have amassed enough wisdom to tell fellow students how to live their lives; also the type to cryptically post "Depression is real" on their Twitter timeline. I give this person the benefit of the doubt then I give up after three exchanges. There is no way someone who types in shorthand can help me. If they found typing the phrase "how are you?" so unfathomable that they typed "hwu" to me, how could they possibly understand that I think about dying more times than I do not, and how could they understand that sometimes I dream about my own funeral, and those are the few nights in which I do not get night sweats.

I gulp down the remainder of the contents of the bottle; it is taking more than one of few bottles to get me to sleep these days. Eventually it will stop working, then I will have to find another remedy. I don't know what I will try next. I drift to sleep with the taste of alcohol in my mouth. Can't it just choke me already? When I wake up, I see a missed call notification from one of my lecturers, Mr. Munda. What does he want from me? I have nothing against the man but he just reeks of desperation. I will never understand why he wants his students to like him so much. As I think of how I will avoid this man until the university decides to remove me, he calls again. I answer, he asks where I have been. I tell him I am sick, this is not a lie. He asks what is wrong. I want to say it but I know how he will react. I say I have migraines. He asks if I am better. I say I am. He says he wants to see me in his office. I ask if we can discuss whatever it is over the phone. I really do not want to leave my bed, much less my room. He says student-lecturer interactions are very important. I say I will go to his office the following day. He is satisfied, he hangs up. He makes no sense to me. Regardless of how many students pass, he will get paid anyway. What is the fuss? Munda is probably one of those delusional teachers who think they can fix their students. I am not his pet project. There is nothing about me that he can fix.

Munda talks to me about the importance of education and how I cannot do anything without at least a first degree. He asks if I perhaps want to switch degree programmes. *I WANT TO SWITCH LIVES!* Of course, I do not say that to him. I tell him I am happy with my current degree programme. He asks what my problem is. How much time does he have? He goes about it for a while. The Jesus complex on his man is disabling. He schedules weekly meetings and I comply then walk away.

He stops me in one of our meetings; he says my marks are still not enough to allow me to sit for the final exam. I really do not care. He says he and I can come to an agreement. I see the look on his face. This disgusting man! I try to get up but he grabs me by the arm and locks the door behind him.

Alone in my room, I had thought about Munda…so upright and so proper on the surface but beneath all that, he was rotten, just like my father. My hypocritical, cheating, wife-bashing, child-injuring, die-in-Mai-Vivian's-bed-ing father! You just couldn't shake their kind, they were everywhere. I felt a feeling of…resigned disgust. I had never felt this way before. Life was revolting. I remembered the first time I slit my wrists. Then, I walked towards my window. I tried to think of reasons to keep going, and as always I came up with nothing. My window was only two floors up, but I had to give it a go.

Precious

My mother has warned me more times than I can remember about the city and its people. She says they are dishonest, do not keep promises, and they have no moral compass. She tells me that she sent me to school to get my degree and nothing else. I do not need friends, much less, the kind that I could find at the university. She says the girls drink beer and like to dance while the boys smoke and like to have sex. She has said time and again that I am not like them. At first when she gave me these lectures, I never realised how odd it was for her to talk so much about the city; she had only been to the city the few times when she thought my father was seeing a city woman. She always came back a few hours later after my father had dismissed her.

It is odder for my mother to have such strong opinions about the university; she has never been there. However, she is determined that I, her eldest, should do all the things she could not do. My mother is that rare breed of woman who is willing to throw herself fully into something that she does not purely understand as long as she believes that it is good for me. She feels that way about me going to university. On her part, she only went as far as form 2, which she quit when she fell pregnant with me. She never held it against me because, as she put it, she was not clever enough to see school through anyway. But I am different, she constantly says. My father agrees. He too is a simple man, much older than my mother, but with the same mind set. He is a lowly factory worker, but he appreciates wholly what a good education can do.

They are excited for me to get my degree. It is a whole four years away, but they can already see how all of this will play out. I will get my degree and get a good job. A degree is so powerful that I will get a management post just soon after I start working. I will buy a car within the few years of working and then later a house in the city. They are sure to remind me that this house has to be big and of course it should not be in one of the high-density suburbs; my mother adds that these suburbs are where the vilest activities take place and I have more sense than that. I will buy a house in the low-density suburbs or as my father calls it "*emayadini*". He says his young boss stays in one of the big houses *emayadini* and he cannot wait for me to be like him. He says my younger siblings will come and live with me while he and my mother enjoy his retirement.

Growing up at Malalume, just after Dombodema, I have had very little contact with the rest of the world outside of what I have been told by my mother, who ever so strangely seems to know so much about life outside our little village. The village was so proud when I got accepted into the university; they had every reason to be. I am one of the few people to make it out of Malalume. Most of the people here are born here, grow up here, go to school here, drop out of school here, then go back to their homes to live out the rest of their lives. My father is one of the success stories. He went to the city, found a job there and still comes home every weekend to be with his family. Most of the men who got the opportunity my father did left Malalume and never turned back. They leave behind wives and children; this is why my mother is quick to go to the city whenever she has the slightest inkling that my father is starting to misbehave. She does not want to be a statistic.

Being here has been nothing like what my mother said it would be, it has been worse. The girls, much to my mother's word, are not wholesome. I saw a few of them smoking the other day and that could never be me. Some of them wear pants, I understand the need to wear pants when it is cold but to wear them in the middle of the summer and just walk around in them? Who raised these children? They talk very loudly about the most obscene things. One of them was talking about how she and her boyfriend "got together". She spoke so loudly, I had to turn and stare, and I thought she would stop when she saw me staring, but she simply smiled at me then turned back to her friends and kept talking as loudly as before.

However, beneath all of that – beneath the jeans, the alcohol, the smoking, the uncultured talk, there is something I admire about these girls. They are free. Free to be themselves, no matter how deviant that self is. You never know what they will do next, one minute they are bald, the next they have braids on and the day after they have weaves on. They can leave their rooms without make up then come back the next day with make up on and looking like a totally new person. It is an amazing thing to watch. These girls keep reinventing themselves day by day and if I cared for their overall behaviour, I would be inspired by their ability to continuously change like that.

I could never keep up with that. Not even if I tried. That is what Garikayi says he likes about me – that I do not try as hard as all these other girls. He says I am beautiful. He is the first boy to say it and make me believe it. Back home, herd boys would say it all the time, but I always thought it was because they did not know better. However, when Garikayi says it, it is different. It means something. He is someone who has lived in the city his entire life and has seen all types of women; these ever-changing university girls. He has seen beautiful women on TV and he even says he has spent time with some real-life models. How can I not be weak at the knees when someone who has seen that much still looks at me and sees something beautiful?

I will never forget the day I met Garikayi. He was such a gentleman. It was during our first week here and I was trying to get my registration done. I remember going up to the lady at the desk and handing her my documents. She said something to me in what I know now to have been Shona. What the lady at the desk and most people here do not seem to understand is this. I grew up in a very remote village where everyone speaks Kalanga. We do not have much communication with people outside our little bubble, except for the occasional WhatsApp message on days when the network is not too bad. I am proficient in English and Ndebele because I learnt these in school. I remember politely telling the lady that I did not understand her and just as she was about to accuse me of pretending not to know what she was talking about, Garikayi stepped in – my hero! He played translator between the lady and I.

Ever the gentleman, he walked me to my room, saying he would be glad to teach me his language, but only if I helped him better his knowledge of mine. He said his Ndebele was very basic, just bits and pieces of what he had picked up on his visits to South Africa. I remember telling him that if he wanted to learn my language, then he would have to learn Kalanga, and that not being Shona did not mean I was Ndebele. I remember him smiling at me and telling me "Even better" and that was when I knew I was sold.

My relationship with Garikayi does not seem to make sense to a lot of people other than ourselves and that does not matter. I love him and he loves me. I do not have a lot of friends but Garikayi is mostly friends with everyone. I believe that is what most girls are bitter about. Garikayi is popular, handsome and speaks the best English I have ever heard from anyone. These girls do not understand why with all these choices, Gary chose me. I used to ask myself that all the time too, but his reassurance has always been the same. "You are different Tjawa, you are not like the rest of them."

Another thing I eternally appreciate Gary for is how comfortable he is with my first name. For the most part when I tell people that I am Tjawanga Kulube, they have obvious questions. What language is it? What does it mean? Where do I come from? Where I come from is frowned upon here, I have come to learn. As soon as they know I grew up in a tiny village and this is my first experience with city life, I become the other. Some even go as far as making fun of me for being from the wrong side of the country. That's when it hits me, I will never be one of them. Gary says I have no business trying to be anything like them, I am better than that. I understand that, but I have decided to go by my mother's name Precious – it invites fewer follow up questions. Shakespeare said what's in a name? Everything! Once I started to go by Precious, people cared less where I came from or to which ethnic group I belonged to. Most importantly, Gary and Precious made more sense than Gary and Tjawanga. In spite of that, there are obvious things about me that still invite people to ask questions.

I walk into class on one occasion and sit by myself. I like being early. One girl walks in, she is so beautiful. She sits a few seats away from me. She says "hi" brightly, I answer back almost quietly. She says her name is Ntombi, I tell her my name – the name I have chosen now. I can see her struggle to make conversation with me. My mother warned me about girls like her. She has long fake nails and long fake hair and she looks like she has had a very easy life. I have nothing in common with her, what could she possibly understand about me? Almost as if hearing my thoughts, she gathers the few things that she has and moves to the front row. She is probably there to get the teacher's attention. My mother warned me about girls like that too. Almost immediately, Gary walks in and walks past her. I do not like the way she looks at him. Gary sits down next to me and she turns around and is now staring. I know that stare too well. I have been getting it ever since Gary and I started our relationship.

They stare in unashamed disbelief. They cannot understand how me: good, old, plain, simple me can ever get and keep Gary's attention for this long. Maybe I should change my look a little bit; it would give people less reason to stare. Maybe if I dressed more like these girls and had extensions like they do, maybe they would understand why Gary chose me. I will talk to him about it and see what he thinks; he might know how to help me.

***

It is amazing what a simple weave can do. I feel like a different person and everyone sees it too. People are nicer to me, they do not stare anymore, Gary and I finally make sense to all the people around us. This has got me thinking, I finally feel like an equal in this relationship, I am starting to have friends of my own and I realise now that what I feel for Gary is not just gratitude or indebtedness. I love Garikayi. He has been asking if we can take our relationship to the next level, but I have not been ready-up until now. My mother warned me about city boys and how all they want is sex, but Gary is no average city boy. He loved me before I looked like all these girls; he loved me before I changed my name to Precious for the sake of all these people. Gary loves me. The me that comes from Malalume, the me that had her first pizza a few weeks back, the me that has been teaching him Kalanga for weeks, that is the me that Gary loves and at the end of the day, that is what matters. I am ready.

No one ever really enjoys their first time. I have heard this so many times and I guess it must be true. It has put a strain on us. I must have done something wrong. I will try to talk to him about it, I will do better next time. He has been so closed off lately. I have only seen him in class over the last few days, but I do feel like he needs the space from me while I figure out what I should have done differently. I also hear that he has been spending a lot of time with that Ntombi girl. People like to lie, Gary would never. He does not even like her, or any of the girls like her. Gary likes me. I am wholesome; I do not drink or go to parties and only started wearing jeans a few weeks ago. Gary likes me, he loves me. On one of my days of endlessly waiting for Gary to forgive me for what I may have done wrong, Lisa Ndlovu comes to me. She says I need to talk to Gary so that he can undo what he did to her friend. She says Gary leaked naked pictures of her. The nerve! Girls like her probably have thousands of naked pictures circulating around and now that her actions are backfiring, she wants to blame Gary-my Gary. Lisa goes on about how I would not defend Gary if I really knew what he did. She is not instigating. She genuinely believes all of the things she is saying. Jealousy does that to people.

I go to Gary's room to tell him what Lisa said, and to find out why Ntombi thinks it is okay to spread such lies. I knock a number of times before he opens the door, his shirt is off. He is beautiful. He stands by the doorway, I try to enter, and he says he just sprayed insecticide, so it will choke me. I tell him I do not mind; I was raised on smoke. He does not laugh at my joke, but he keeps standing by the doorway.

I push forward, he pushes back, it is not violent, but it is a sure shove. That is when I see her. Londiwe Tshuma in his room, in his bed. She looks a lot like me – or at least a lot like what I used to look like. Her hair is neatly cut, like mine was. Her nails are trimmed, like mine were and I can almost bet that before she got into Gary's bed, she was wearing a simple t-shirt and skirt.

I realise for the first time that to Gary, I am not the exception, I am the rule. I really am not that unordinary. Gary has a pattern. His pattern is girls like me – girls who are new to all of this, girls who are always overlooked and will drop everything for the promise of even a little affection. It makes me sick. I feel my stomach go up and I throw up. I have never reacted so strongly to something before, but then again, I have never had to deal with anything this intense before. As I hold on to the wall while spilling my guts out, my hand lands on the calendar on my wall. I get up and empty out the bucket. My attention moves back to the calendar on the wall. I have not crossed it off in eight weeks. This cannot be happening.

A lot of people think that motherhood begins when you give birth or when you hold your baby. For me, it began when I knew a life was growing inside of me. A lot of people would think having a child this early is unthinkable, but I am more open minded when it comes to human life. The situation is not ideal, but it is not life threatening either. My mother was way younger when she had me, she will understand. I have told Gary and his initial reaction was unreasonable, he even went as far as suggesting that he was not responsible for any of this, until he eventually came to his senses and said he would take care of it. Maybe he will finally stop all these games that he has been playing with all these girls. I am willing to forgive him if he realises the commitment he has to me and to my child – our child. He will come around. I know he will. We just have to agree on how to tell our parents and how the payment of damages will go. That is the right way to do things. Granted, this is no ordinary situation, but this would be the best way to handle it.

Gary understands. He comes to me one night and says he knows what to do. He sits me down and explains how neither of us can keep a baby and he knows how to make it all go away. He brings a pill with him. He tells me to relax-he has done this before. I am not sure what feelings he hopes to inspire in me by saying that. He does his thing then he gets up to leave. I ask if he can stay, he says he cannot. I ask him why not, he says his friends will be suspicious if he does not join them for drinks. He says he will be back soon. He is gone for hours. In the hours that he is gone, his pill starts working. I feel my baby clinging to the walls of my womb as she slowly slides out. I say she because she is such a fighter. She wants to stay alive and I am rooting for her; what mother would not root for her own child? Eventually, she caves in; she is just a baby – a baby from a poor village girl and what chance does she stand against Science and Medicine. The battleground is not level, oh but what a fight she put up.

The last of her slides out of me and I am left sitting in a pool made out of my baby. She is warm. I put my palm on her; I swear if I listen carefully enough, I can hear her heart beating. She did not have to go through this. I look at the mess I have made. It's a funny thing – this body of mine. I take care of it. When it is hungry, I feed it. When it wants a bath, I bathe it. When it is cold, I give it a warm blanket. When it wants more than a warm blanket, I give it Gary – he keeps it warm. However, the one time I ask my body to keep this baby for me, just for 9 months, it suddenly can't comply.

It listens instead to Garikayi and his pill. Why not to me? Why not to my every instinct that wanted this child to live? It is a funny thing, this body of mine. This selfish, ungrateful body of mine!

Nadia Mutisi

Nadia Mutisi is a law student at the University of Zimbabwe. Raised by a writer, she grew up immersed in literature. She has won a number of awards for her public speaking and debate. A regular contributor to The Herald's Youth Interactions Column, Nadia is passionate about the growth of the arts in Zimbabwe's education sector. She participated in the SADC People's Summit public speaking contest hosted by the Southern African People's Solidarity Network and won an award as the best speaker. Nadia is also a social and economic justice ambassador, a role she uses to advocate for the marginalised in society.

Sinking roots

At nineteen, Rutendo attended her first funeral. Her cousin Mpiwa had died an untimely death and everyone including Rutendo was in shock. Mpiwa was the only one of her cousins she saw often and at most three times a year. Rutendo's father was an illegitimate child and had never felt welcomed by the rest of the family. No sooner than he had finished college at the University of Zimbabwe, graduating summa cum laude with a finance degree, he had retreated into his own space, worked very hard and built a successful company, Nexus Finance.

Rutendo had been shielded from the horrors of life by the high walls of their Borrowdale home and the family's large cash inflows that detoured them from life's hardships. The wealth of her family removed much of her heritage from her, leaving instead a strong aura of luxury, aristocracy and a tongue fluent in three other languages. Their Borrowdale home was well known for Sunday barbecues where the family hosted their affluent friends and engaged in conversation about the African Renaissance, Fela Kuti and the power of art. She was deeply divorced from the typical life of a Zimbabwean, had never been to *kumusha* and very rarely saw her relatives. She had never known death and had even considered at some point that death was a conspiracy theory that never really happened to anyone. She had not known then that death was real and that in the African context, it was the greatest unifier of people.

The mourners gathered in Mabelreign, at Mpiwa's home. The men sat outside on chairs. Silence blanketed the atmosphere. Mpiwa's father sat amongst the men, his eyes blank and emotionless. She had known how much Mpiwa was loved by her father and had expected to see tears streaming down his face. Rutendo knew why he would not dare cry. Rutendo, a ferocious debater always loved wrangling about feminism and made it a point to outline that feminism was not just for women, it was for men too. It was for men like Mpiwa's father who had been raised to shun any kinds of emotion, emotions were female attributes and it was taboo for a man to cry. Rutendo had shaken her head and been disappointed by the hordes of Zimbabwean men who defended patriarchy in ignorance. Her heart ached for the man who was disallowed by society to unmask his pain and she hoped that at night when the darkness swallowed him, he would at least cry.

Inside the house were women. They sat on blankets and cloths they had laid across the floor. The women had tied colourful head scarfs around their heads and wrapped around their waists, traditional African cloths they referred to as, 'mazambia.' Luckily, Rutendo had known enough about Zimbabwean funerals to be dressed accordingly. She was relieved she was not sticking out. The atmosphere inside was drenched in grief and unlike the men, the women wailed and sobbed. Some women, Rutendo suspected, only wailed out of solidarity and not compassion. The older women sat on the floor, their backs against the walls and their legs stretching out while the younger women who were doing chores in the kitchen occasionally tore the blanket of grief with loud laughter.

Rutendo circled the room where the older women were sitting. She shook each of the ladies' hands awkwardly muttering a phrase she often heard and knew was applicable but was foreign to her. 'Nematambudziko,' she whispered to each lady. As she moved around the room offering her condolences, she saw in every pair of eyes the shock that death brings that one never gets used to. She could smell the shadow of death as she moved around the house and stared sincerely into unfamiliar eyes. She could sense hope suspended above the opaque blanket of grief where no one could reach, and no words could beckon effectively.

One of the women broke into an old church hymn. She could remember it – they used to sing it at the Anglican Church before they had moved to the suburbs and became Pentecostals at the colossal church along Borrowdale road. Like a gauze applied on a fresh wound, the quiet melody of the women eased the flow of grief that coursed through the atmosphere. A stout masculine woman led the song, she closed her eyes as the song filled the room. Some of the women, caught up in an air of spirituality raised their hands in surrender and on their lugubrious faces, peace was painted. The bass of the men rose as the song proceeded, and soon the choir flooded the room with a comforting serenade. For a second, Rutendo had felt that angels must have been in their midst. This was the importance of religion – it was the bridge humanity used to cross difficult chasms. This was the beauty of being African, the people loved boldly.

Rutendo had watched her cousins and other girls she had never seen before manoeuvring the outdated foreign kitchen as if they had lived there in their past lives. She watched Nancy whom she had last seen three years back at a wedding deftly cutting the chicken into pieces. Puberty had caught up with Nancy, Rutendo observed. Amanda stood at the sink vigorously washing the plates that had been used for lunch, her face was still stern. Rutendo watched and quietly remembered the Adichie books that were the pillars of her arguments on feminism. Gender roles. She understood that no matter how much she fought it and no matter how many books she consumed and no matter that Adichie had been on the cover of New African Woman, her worth was always to be proven in her demeanour and in her skill in the home. Rutendo's own mother had often called her into the kitchen back at home to teach her how to cook a more complex meal. She had recently been taught to make chicken biryani and her mom had made a joke on tasting the biryani that she would demand a thousand cattle for Rutendo's dowry. They had laughed about it.

It did not matter that she had only A's for her O-levels but, it was important how she tilted her head to the side in mock humility as she spoke to the older family members. Her ability to remember every single person who greeted her along with their title even though she had last seen most of them when she was a baby counted for much. The words she had learned to nasally enunciate at Hellenic Academy were envied by every other person who met her but here they only evidenced the assumption that she was uppity, snobbish and good for everything else except being a woman. Rutendo knew from the books she would read under her covers late at night, the stories by Lola Shoneyin, Ayobami Adebayo and Tsitsi Dangarembga that being a woman was as heavy as being a woman. Women always had to carry something. If it was not babies, then it was expectations.

A number of women and men poured into the kitchen as they carried the groceries to the pantry. The small lady with the terrible voice that sounded as though her vocal chords were being grated, gave out orders – Mai Tendai was to cook the beef, Rutendo and the girls would cut the vegetables and the married ladies with the most experience would cook the sadza. The kitchen was soon frenetic as they rushed up and down. The marble kitchen surfaces only recently cleared were chaotic again, the just mopped floors now had fresh muddy shoe prints, vegetable pieces that had missed the dish littered the floor, the plates in the sink only kept piling as the women continued with their business, refusing to notice the clutter. They wanted to be overwhelmed by the mess after the bigger job was done. Like a network of bees, they cooked, and they cleaned. Their conversation buzzed in the air as they took turns to cook the sadza on the large fire that they had started outside. They spoke of Mpiwa's sudden death and then about their own children and the back-to-school promotions. Mai Farirai, ever so loud, big boned and easy to pick out, had made it a point to let the other women know how wise she was. She always bought uniforms downtown where they were half the price of those sold in the formal shops. The women had also gossiped about Maria who had left for the UK with an older man but had come back sick only two years after – it was AIDS, the ladies concluded. In Africa, any illness that made one grow thin was always suspected to be AIDS. Rutendo was amused at the harmonious working of the women – the way they each found their place and contributed. Rutendo being sucked into the network felt herself growing into the femininity expected of her – the industrious, sharp African woman. She could feel an unspoken unity between her and these women, most of whom she had never met. These women all wore the heavy title with grace or perhaps through conditioning had never felt the burden of womanhood.

The men sat outside, talking. Some drove around, picking up people and things sent for by the women. It was most intriguing when it was time to serve the food. The girls would move around with a dish and a jug and knelt for people to wash their hands. They would kneel too or crouch as they offered the plates of food. The girls were respectful, saying 'pamusoroi' before they began the distribution. These girls who moments earlier had spoken of sneaking out to go to the club later that night and had squealed as one of their own had told the juicy details about her rendezvous with her boyfriend suddenly became stately, principled young ladies before the older folk. Rutendo too was learning. Learning to engage in conversation with these people she had last met when she was a baby. She would laugh surreptitiously, hiding her discomfort. She greeted them all, saying *'Makadini,'* with the most lowly and humble voice she could muster. They often asked her to greet them with their title. It was this Rutendo found most difficult. She had never met some of these people and knew little about the family tree. Where Disney had taught her to say 'aunt, uncle or cousin,' she now had to apply the appropriate terms, *'tete, babamukuru, mwana.'* The older men and women would ask her if she remembered them. She would shake her head and they would begin explaining who they were and how they had last seen her when she was three. Her annoyance at seeking out everyone's role, relation and title quickly turned into a sense of unity and belonging. She was *mainini* Rutendo and not just Rutendo.

When the coffin arrived, the men instinctively rose to carry it. There had been no announcement made to gather them, no plan crafted to coordinate the event, it had all just happened in a telepathic way. Their heads bowed, their faces mournful, they had carried the coffin into the living room. It had seemed amazing to Rutendo, how the women all stood in the side-lines, weeping as the men carried the coffin in. How had they all known what needed to be done? Rutendo cried as she watched the event, the finality of Death revealing itself to her, the unity and love of the mourners overwhelming her.

She left Mabelreign that night. She would be back the next morning for the funeral. There would still be so much to do – she would be a woman again; cook and clean and offer food and be respectful. As she drove off in her cream mini cooper, sunken into the leather seats, her ankles tingling with pain from all the standing. She laughed inwardly at the juxtaposition of the youthfulness she felt on the inside and the woman she suddenly became in that flowing skirt, calling everyone by their title, squeezing into the wonderful network of those who made things happen. She had clung tightly to their conversations in Shona, and loved the flow and warmth of the Manyika dialect. She replayed the stories told by the women, smiled as she remembered Sinikiwe, one of the girls who had taken a liking to her and had invited her to a kitchen party the following week. As she drove off into the night, Harare's streets hardly illuminated and playing a track by Dido, she could smell grief on her clothes; photos and memories of Mpiwa would flash in her mind. She remembered the time they had gone to Lake Chivero together and Mpiwa had said they should hang out together more often. They had both agreed but it was one of those things you said yes to but never really wound up doing. Her own mortality faced her, and she felt sad at the impermanence of everything.

At six thirty in the morning she was already back at Mpiwa's home. She was surprised at the number of people that had slept over. People walked in and out of the bathrooms, all of them in a hurry to prepare for the burial. Dozens had laid blankets and cloths on the floors in the bedrooms and had made themselves comfortable for the night. Nearly every two minutes, someone would walk into the kitchen and request for either water or tea. Rutendo wondered who was paying for all the expenses and worried about Mpiwa's siblings who instead of resting had felt the burden to make everyone else comfortable in their home. Was this really the most effective way for one to mourn?

This time Rutendo was aware of her duties. She had headed for the kitchen where she was told to stir the mealie meal paste until it became thick and simmered. She called it porridge but everyone else called it '*bota.*' They had taken out what seemed like hundreds of plates to dish out the porridge and distributed it to each of the mourners. Mai Farirai seemed to know who should receive what kind of plate and who did not eat sugar or peanut butter. This time, Rutendo applied herself – she had reckoned she could make up for all the time she had lost with Mpiwa by at least doing something at her funeral. As they cooked the breakfast, Rutendo was asked by several other women who did not remember her and who had never seen her, whose child she was. She repeated, 'Richard and Dinah's firstborn.' They began to call her '*mwana wa*Richie' meaning child of Richard. Rutendo's parents had not come with her. Her father was somewhere in London, preparing for a conference and her mother, Dinah had only sent her condolences and believed she had already made up for her absence since the child she had carried for nine months and who bore twenty-three chromosomes that were hers had attended. Some of the women had asked her where mom was and Rutendo had felt too ashamed to say the truth. Her mother was not a busy woman, besides the functions at church which blew hot air into her and gave her the much-revered position she now had, she had nothing else to do except meet up with friends. 'Where is your mom? These days she doesn't like us, we used to be such good friends but now eh,' most of the women seemed to repeat this statement whenever she told them she was Dinah's daughter. She knew something had happened that had made her parents drift from the rest of the family. She had been told they had never been welcome but that too had never settled well with her. Could they never have been welcomed to the extent of becoming so estranged from these people?

Warren Hills cemetery is just outside Harare. The rich red earth, the tall yellow grass and the grey tombstones create a poetic landscape. The clear big blue sky runs uninterrupted over the cemetery almost as if to allow one to experience heaven by simply gazing at it. As Rutendo walked with the crowd heading to the grave where Mpiwa would rest, she scanned through the tombstones, finding interest in who the people lying under the earth were. Upon each tombstone was an inscription of a scripture. She had wondered whether atheists too when they died would have scriptures as epitaphs. She had been sad at the thought of the thousands of people beneath the earth who did belong to God but only ever realised that reality as death drew nearer.

The men carried the coffin and louder sobs could be heard as people battled with the epiphany that they would never see their beloved daughter again. They gathered around the grave listening to the preacher who spoke boldly about Christ. After the sermon was done, the coffin was lowered into the ground and the men took up sand in their shovels, covering the hole in the ground where Mpiwa now lay. Grief choked the group of family and friends, its black hands strangling each of them and sucking the hope out of those who had known Mpiwa.

Rutendo remembered her favourite play, 'The Death of a Salesman.' She remembered in sadness Willy Loman's pitiful funeral and how only his sons, wife and friend had attended. But here was a simple girl, whose lifeless body now lay in the mud and hundreds had gathered to mourn and grieve and celebrate the life of one whom they so knew. She thought of their Borrowdale home, fancy and large but disconnected from family, love and identity. Nancy had stretched her hand to Rutendo's and now they held hands, the girls, mourning one of their own. They had all known Mpiwa better than Rutendo had and for this, Rutendo felt a pang of guilt.

Death, a grotesque and very real figure had finally shown his face to Rutendo and she knew he was running stealthily behind each of them. She knew that in a moment, he would grab them from the earth with finality, sucking them into a vacuum. Rutendo imagined their kitchen, the hanging chandelier, the heavy granite counters, the modern appliances and the linoleum tiles. She imagined one of them at home lying cold in a coffin and the mansion being so desolate, save for the dignified members of the colossal church who would come to comfort them out of duty but not out of love.

Mainini Rutendo, that is who she wanted to be – a simple domino among other dominoes. If she fell, they would all fall with her. Walking back from Mpiwa's grave, she offered the other girls a ride in her car so they would not have to use the crowded bus that had carried the mourners to the burial ground. The girls had been so mesmerised by the interior of the mini cooper, they had sat comfortably requesting for different songs to be played, the memory of Mpiwa, like a pendulum crossing their minds. It was here that Rutendo wanted to grow. *Moyo muti unomera paunoda.* The heart is a tree, it grows where it wishes.

The Storyteller

He reminds me of a train; the way trains pass through different cities stretching across the country, travelling for miles on end and capturing life in all sorts of shapes. I find that he is exactly that, a train. His body is now weary from all the years of walking the earth. He bends as if to fold into the dust, the result of travelling for miles through life accumulating all kinds of burdens and aches. His stooped body can barely stand. His veins jut out through his skin, defying age and the white stubs on his head like rust tell a story of ages of service.

He is at that age they love to affiliate with wisdom, and he knows it too. Quite a beguiling man even from his early days. He weaves tales and stories that always leave them in stitches or mesmerised. He often narrates the stories of his life and knits them together as if making an entire book from the many pages collected over the years. His proud voice smoothens the creases and creates in their minds a utopia that is believable. But he is old now and the days of adventure and youth and fun are long behind him. Now he sits on a wooden stool outside his house, his hands jittery but his mind full of stories to keep him company. I often wonder if there are some stories locked within him that he has vowed to die with. I wonder too whether he has laced his tales with lies that have morphed to become truth over time. His jittery hands speak of life's slow triumph over him and yet his eyes remain awake in defiance, very bright like Blake's tiger. It is these bright eyes that have caused me to lie awake at night and that have made this Storyteller quite an enigma.

He has boomed aloud in dark rooms as the children are eagerly expecting electricity to come back. He has told stories of his heroism, the high compliments he received over the years and often he throws in some verbose words, a malicious way of strutting his intelligence. He boasts of Cuba, the notorious dog he owned from its infanthood. He brags about Cuba's agility, his sharp canines and his dogged devotion to his owner that led him to chase a white farmer, much to the white farmer's embarrassment after he had tried to beat up the Storyteller for his tactlessness and pomposity. The Storyteller is always very happy about how European he is, even though he is an African man without a doubt. He says even during the liberation struggle he never saw a difference between him and the murungu. He says he could speak the queen's language with flair and there was nothing he did not know about British history.

The Storyteller knows everything. At least I used to think so. His convivial manner often made him lead in community discussions. His attentiveness and curiosity drew him into conversation with the most unexpected minds. The fire in his eyes, those bright eyes enchanted him to be a reader and he gladly consumed books. It is this that makes him such a mystery to me, his foolproof nature – how could one appear to have mastered life so well, to be well aware of the storms and gusts of life but still be able to walk through unscathed?

Others have told me stories about the Storyteller. I must confess, I was really excited to begin picking the loose threads in his foolhardy portrayal. They say the Storyteller came from Malawi, that he reluctantly left his family and loved ones in search of a livelihood and that he has not gone back home to see them since. They say he came down here before any of these buildings were even constructed, that he slaved on the farms of the *murungus* and used his wit to win their favour. He did not even speak Shona, he only accumulated it as he made friends. Often at night, before he learned to build with his words, he would sing the wonderful melodies from back home, beside the lake.

The Storyteller is unusually optimistic, and it is this that makes him such an enigma. His laughter, like an engine failing to start, is as sure to come as he is telling a story as we are sure that the sun will rise tomorrow. Life doesn't seem to be a bumpy ride, at least for him who wears wrinkles so gracefully and has no scabs or scars to show for the years lived and years grieved.

I heard once, from the lady who owns the tuckshop at Gwinyiro here in Dangamvura, that the Storyteller had a mousy, petite lady for a wife. She said the wife was diligent, a strong woman though willowy – would take the Storyteller's absences without quarrel and made vetkoeks for the boy who at aged ten knocked at her house claiming the Storyteller as his father. Her name was Jane and she raised him. Never once did the Storyteller look her in the eye to offer an explanation. The audacity. Men have audacity and apparently the Storyteller had a large portion of it.

The lady at the tuckshop, Mai Mufundisi who has a nasty habit of airing everyone's dirty laundry said Jane took everything with her lips pursed and that maybe it was not a clot in her artery that caused the heart attack. She says sometimes anger is like a lump, haven't I ever felt it in my throat? It must have been the anger then that clogged Jane's arteries – the anger of sharing her man with the whole city, a ladies' man this Storyteller. I wanted to ask as she narrated the story, was he not consumed with guilt? Did her death never weigh him down?

The man from the mill filled in the gaps left in the gossip shared by Mai Mufundisi. He told of the ten-year-old boy and how he grew close to the Storyteller. The Storyteller with a natural charisma had swaggered in the streets turning heads and grabbing attention but when the boy came into their lives there was an added spring to his step. After Jane had died and been buried, the Storyteller mothered the boy with Jane's affection as if her spirit had clothed him as the last rose was thrown into her freshly dug grave. He quit much of the drinking, came home earlier to spend time with the boy, read him the newspaper each morning at their daily breakfast of oats and bananas and drove him to the high school right outside of town. It was in raising the boy that he perfected storytelling, he wrote him little stories that the boy was embarrassed about but cherished, nevertheless. Tall boy, lean and athletic with deep set brown eyes and a cheekiness that could be seen in his crooked smile – a not so perfect reflection of the Storyteller.

At school, the boy had a reputation for charm and wit, inherited from his father. Jane had taught him to sing, and his voice dressed the atmosphere in the cathedral every Friday with opulence. It was after he had serenaded the school with his hymns one Friday that he complained of a headache. The boy had called the Storyteller and informed him he was not feeling well but was adamant that he could walk into town and wait at the Storyteller's office. They allowed him to leave school early. As he walked into town, they assumed he must have got dizzy and confused, did not check both sides of the road, was hit by a truck and was cold within seconds. At eighteen the boy had died young and the Storyteller once again was separated from home. You know, sometimes home is a person. They say the Storyteller was never the same again although we do not really know that. The blaze in his eyes and life in his voice when the children gathered around him tells a different narrative. I search for his pain like a lost priceless relic each time I serve him porridge. He either wears it well or it is absent. It is this that causes me to lie awake at night and makes the Storyteller quite an enigma.

On the death of his son, he neither sang nor told stories, only packed some bags into his car and drove off to God knows where. Mai Sibanda for whom I do the laundry every Wednesday said she was nine when the Storyteller left, and they had gradually forgotten about him. The memory of that beautiful car, what was it called again? The memory of it faded and the kids could not recall a time when they would ride the expensive beauty. Renault R18, aha!

The R18 was back though, some years later. The Storyteller was back to his old charisma and joy – he had a new Mrs and Mai Sibanda said she was a really beautiful woman, even though she had short tight coils while the other women flaunted their wigs. She was nothing like Jane. This lady had a body that filled her dresses and walked as if to advertise her bums. She had dimples engraved into her cheeks, a wide smile and a contagious joy that Mai Sibanda suspected must have been the reason the Storyteller had chosen her. It seemed the Storyteller was back for good. He resumed telling stories. It also seemed as if the death of Madalitso had been something that had happened to someone else whom the Storyteller had only heard about in the papers.

The beautiful lady was soon pregnant with a set of twins and for the next five years, they say she was always pregnant. Perhaps he was making up for the loss of his son, nobody really knew. The Storyteller's belly was also protruding, but from good living; he had bought a truck and the money he was making from his small haulage company was enough for him to renovate his already pleasant home. He reminds me of a train; the way trains pass through different cities stretching across the country, travelling for miles on end and capturing life in all sorts of shapes. I find that he is exactly that, a train; his body is now weary from all the years of walking the earth, he bends as if to fold into the dust, the result of travelling for miles through life accumulating all kinds of burdens and aches – his stooped body can barely stand, his veins jut out through his skin defying age and the white stubs on his head like rust tell a story of ages of service.

The Storyteller is in his bedroom, I walk through the narrow passage whose walls are decorated with pictures from long ago of his family. My eyes run over the pictures, I take notice of the Storyteller's children. There is only one who is familiar, the one with the perfume that announces her. Choziswa. That's her name. A real Londoner now, rolls words on her tongue and says 'innit' quite a lot. That must be the Mrs. Yup. The dimples. She is a beautiful woman indeed. There are two kids who look the same age but nothing alike, probably the twins. A large portrait beckons me, the Storyteller is youthful and handsome in this one. His eyes are alive, and his smile is beaming. There are many other photos to look at, some in black and white and others in colour. There is no time to examine. I walk steadily, trying not to spill the water in the glass on the tray, "Sekuru," I call the Storyteller, a statement that means the same as, 'may I come in.' Today, he is in bed reading and before I can say good morning, he glances up and in a raspy voice, asks, "Do you know the name of the pilot who flew the plane that dropped the bomb on Nagasaki and Hiroshima?"

"Enola Gay?"

"Good memory but that was the name of the plane, not the pilot. The plane was named after the pilot's mother – the answer is Colonel Paul Tibbets!"

I put the tray beside his bed and tell him that I have brought some water. It is a daily routine for him to start off the day with some water. He claims it revitalises the body. For a ninety-year-old he is fit enough to sit upright on his bed. He gulps the water, I follow his motions with my eyes. He has been alone for so long and ever since I came here, it has just been him and I. Chozi sometimes visits but not frequently enough. His bright eyes meet my gaze, I take the glass and place it on the tray.

"Porridge is almost done cooking; I'll bring it just now."

I take the tray and head on to the kitchen, questions unanswered assaulting my mind. Where were the rest of the children? What happened to the Mrs? Who did the Storyteller have to call home? I create scenarios in my head, perhaps the twins had died in an accident or the Mrs had had an affair and left. Or maybe one of the boys was a political activist, you know, those ones do not live very long in Zimbabwe.

I pour the porridge into a bowl. It is thick and brown. I go through the passage again, a museum of nostalgia and love. This time a boy about my age catches my eye, a flute in his hands and bright eyes glimmering, the charm and wit is almost tangible, Madalitso perhaps. Sadness grips me as I remember his tragic story.

"Sekuru," I call and enter his room again placing the porridge on his bedside. He glances and this time I am the first to speak, overcoming my fear of asking the Storyteller for stories.

"You have such beautiful pictures hanging on the walls, and what a beautiful family you have," I begin, hoping that will suffice as a conversation starter. Like the Spirit descending upon Zechariah and sending him into prophecy upon the naming of John the Baptist, the Storyteller, his eyes taking on a new shine, tells of Tessy, his daughter. Tessy had been so fond of cameras. It was for her that he had bought a number of cameras which they often used to capture their best moments.

"She died young. It was AIDS," he says, his eyes dimming for a moment. I am sorry for the Storyteller and am ready to leave the room but from the tone of his voice and the flow of his story, I can tell he wants me to hear. The Storyteller tells of Tendai and Mufaro, the twins. Mufaro had left for America and had never returned since. The Storyteller confesses that sometimes he forgets Mufaro's face, it has been thirty years after all. He speaks to him occasionally but Mufaro doesn't care much for the Storyteller and the Storyteller cannot account for the reason. Tendai, he is in Harare, a preacher at a Pentecostal church, the Storyteller visits sometimes but they never visit. Then there was Vincent who had taken over the haulage business, had got married to a clever and quick wife who was left devastated when he had an accident on his way from Mozambique. The Mrs had been too heartbroken at the death of Tessy, had prayed endlessly and called for prayers from all the friends she regarded as saints when Tessy was in hospital fighting for her life. When Tessy died, she felt God had betrayed her and in less than six months, the Mrs had suffered a heart attack. Once again, love had left the Storyteller. He reminds me of Chozi, this one he reckons I know just enough about.

"I'm writing a book," he finishes as if to discount his pitiful story and crown it with something worth celebrating. I could understand why he should write a book; his life had been so unfortunate. It was either that or living to see ninety was the unfortunate part. He outlived almost everyone he loved. I felt sorry for him and motioned him to eat the porridge before it got cold. I guess he did not vow to die with some stories anyway, perhaps nobody ever asked.

"Thanks for letting me tell you a little story, no one ever seems interested in these ones," he adds.

He looks so vulnerable, frail and alone. I leave the room, pace through the museum which with my new knowledge has turned into a museum of grief and sorrow. I am bewildered at how one could not fall apart with such terrible stories locked within him. The Storyteller finishes eating, I see him limping through his museum, his heart must be stronger than his bones for him to pass through this museum daily. As I observe him in his quietness, a being who is so aware of the chiming of time in his life, who knows within him that the gates of eternity are probably one small sickness away, I marvel. I wonder if he aches within him, whether the arthritis hurts more than the memories.

There are children outside now, I can hear them screaming. It is a Wednesday, they normally come for a story, but they are very early today. "Rose," the Storyteller calls, "let them in, it's time for a story." I respond quickly, grabbing the keys from the shelf and rushing to the gate to let the kids in. Smiling wide, their shrill voices creating a pleasant cacophony they enter and race each other to the front of the door where they take off their shoes in haste.

"Sekuru! We are here!" The children scream.

"Sit down," he commands. "Which story would you like to hear?"

Some shout Cuba and some request for the story about the baboon that spoke to him. I am not sure if I believe that story about the baboon, but it is a favourite of mine.

He sits and begins to tell the story, starting it off with a song he has taught the children and that they all know by heart. His voice harmonises with the shrill chants of the children,

'*apunzisi bwelani dzuva likupita*
mitambo yakumwamba, ilikuenda'*

The song places heavy emphasis on the passing of days and I watch the Storyteller and the children heading towards their graves as Time refuses to be persuaded to slow down. I observe the white stubs of hair on the Storyteller's head, the lanky legs of Joshua whom I used to carry when he was still three, Ruva's glossy clear skin that will give way to pimples as long as Time has his way. The song ends and the Storyteller begins the story with strength and power in his voice creating a believable utopia.

I stand leaning on the kitchen door, the sink filled with dirty dishes, but my eyes focused on the Storyteller and his bright eyes that filter the many tales he has inside of him. He has lived very long and seen too many things; it is a wonder he still stands. Like a train, he knows his way and has accepted his route, smoothly he goes never questioning the terrain and accepting what life has to offer. Just as a train whistles along its way, the Storyteller sings and tells tales forgetting the heavy load inside of him.

Teachers, come the sun is going
The clouds in the sky are moving*

Of Sunsets and New Dawns

It was supposed to have arrived at two pm, but it is now six o'clock and the bus is nowhere in sight. It is custom for these buses to arrive much later than communicated for whatever reason. By now, Tsitsi should know better. Waiting for the yellow Pioneer bus at Roadport is Tsitsi's seasonal ritual, something she has in common with numerous other Zimbabweans who await groceries from South Africa. Tsitsi glances at her phone nervously. She is worried about having to walk alone at night to Copa Cabana with the bulky Shangani bag. She remembers the accumulating stories of children going missing and wonders if she, almost eighteen, still qualifies as a child.

Roadport is always busy as buses arrive and depart. Litter is strewn all over the place and the smell of urine constantly clings to the air. The structure of the building attests to the glory of Zimbabwe fresh out of the colonial era. But, the old-fashioned floors, the paint peeling off the doors and the mobs of vendors and money changers swarming the place and suffocating every traveller tell Zimbabwe's true story – plunder. Tsitsi is no longer bothered by the state of Roadport or of Harare. The jarring evidence of underdevelopment no longer catches her eye. It is now normal and as any normal thing it blends with everything else. She stands with her little purse slung around her neck and hidden inside her blouse. She constantly feels for the purse to check if it is still there.

The night slowly swallows the fading sun rays. Just as Tsitsi is about to call home, the Pioneer bus with a coat of dust on its sides, leaning slightly to the right and with hundreds of Shangani bags atop enters through the gate. Sighs of relief can be heard from across the station. Finally,

Tsitsi lets out as she breathes deep. Though determined to receive her package and head on home, she is sad as she approaches the bus. Sad at the monotony of events. Sad at the receipt of these goods once again at crowded Roadport from a detached conductor matted with dirt and sweat. She had for so long imagined her mother carrying large boxes filled with new shoes, clothes, Lay's chips, Romany Creams and that Ultramel custard she always saw on television. They would then open the boxes together at home and Gogo would hold up the new goods in the light and pray a long prayer of thanksgiving. Unfortunately, Tsitsi was here, at Roadport along Robert Mugabe road expecting a man to exit the big yellow bus and hand over the bag.

As she waits, she notices people waiting to board the luxurious Greyhound bus. They look clean and stylish in designer trainers and with their high-quality backpacks. There is a family standing there too; a mother and a father along with their two plump children. You can tell they are well off from the iPhones they hold loosely in their hands and the conversation she can overhear that is strictly in English. The dad is going through a checklist of all the important things they ought to have on their journey. She concludes that he is a present father. She finds that impressive.

Tsitsi feels inferior as she stares at the rich family. She remembers her own dysfunctional family. Her old Samsung phone that is falling apart begins to make her uncomfortable and she slips it into her front pocket. She has been praying for a new phone for her birthday, but she knows that like every year, she'll just get a basic vanilla cake from Mai Tafadzwa from church.

She spots a Shangani bag being carried out of the bus. The block letters printed on the bag make her certain that it is hers. She runs to receive it and thanks the conductor for taking care of it. Finally, she can begin her journey home. She sacrifices the little money she had saved up to take a taxi to Copacabana. From there she'll take a combi home.

The dark stout man looks at Tsitsi suggestively. His tongue lolls outside his mouth as if he ought to pant for him to breathe properly. "Taxi," he says flatly. Tsitsi passes him by. She sees a blue Honda Fit in a pretty neat state, walks toward it and asks the driver how much it is to go to Copacabana. He is a small man with an unusual beard and a bald head.

"Three dollars," he mutters. Tsitsi opens the car door assenting to the stated price. The driver takes the bag and places it in the back of his car. Tsitsi sits in the car waiting for the driver to take her to Copacabana.

Copacabana is always busy at eight pm. Harare really comes alive at night. Vendors sprawl their goods on the street and with shouts advertise their wares. The rank is full of combis going to different places and commuting people to different lives. The Shangani bag is slightly heavy. Tsitsi struggles as she tries to walk while carrying it. A couple of men who pass her by try to make conversation with her. One asks how many cows he must bring home for him to marry her. She snarls at the man and carries along, determined to get into a combi. Copacabana is like Roadport in a number of ways but Tsitsi dislikes Copacabana. It only reinforces her and Gogo's unfruitful imaginations. There were days she and Gogo would sit outside beside the fire and envision one day owning a car. She was here however, at Copacabana opposite Food World, her eyes searching for a combi heading to Warren Park.

She gets into the combi, settles on the front seat and sits the bag on her thighs. The combi is soon full. The journey home begins. As she stares blankly through the window, her thoughts occupy her. She is back at Roadport watching the perfect family as she is about to board the big Greyhound bus. She imagines what it would be like to arrive in Johannesburg and find her mother waiting for her at the bus station. She drifts to her birthday and creates images of the perfect cake, a two-tier vanilla cake covered in white and gold roses. She dresses herself in a royal blue jumpsuit and she has a crown on her head. Every year she dreams of a birthday celebration that remotely looks like the ones she sees on Instagram, but she is always disappointed. She remembers her obsession with Instagram back in 2015; how she would go to flea markets in search of secondhand items that looked like what the pretty rich girls with lots of followers wore. She would buy the clothes and head home to twist and bend and pout and devote herself to taking pictures that had to look effortless. She could not understand why her photos were never as exquisite. For a time, a melancholy settled over her until she deleted the app altogether. At seventeen it made sense why her photos in spite of the effort were always far below the standard. The walls with blotches of mildew never made for a good background and the blood red floors that screamed 'ghetto' did not give off an aura of affluence. She had made peace with it and began seeking comfort and inclusion at church instead, where she was now a member of the choir.

She will be eighteen soon, she remembers. She should be happy, but the thought is accompanied by gloom. The government will call her an adult. She only now comes to realise the reality she had for so long denied in hope: her childhood had really flown by without her ever living or spending time with her mother.

'Hope deferred makes the heart sick.'

She remembers the statement but cannot really place where she heard it from. Tomorrow she turns eighteen. The sun is setting on her childhood but unlike the usual beauty of sunsets; the pouring of the sun like honey onto the canvas of a darkening sky, a fitting swansong to a beautiful day, the sun has set but her dreams have not budded.

She sighs heavily at the thought of burying the still-born dreams that she will never experience. Her mother will never pick her up from school or pack her lunchbox. Her friends have stopped asking when her mother would visit. She too has stopped asking over the phone. To Tsitsi, turning eighteen cemented that her only family was Gogo with all her nagging and pestering. "My mom will come and take me!" Tsitsi would sometimes scream in anger. She would be eighteen tomorrow. Her screams had had no echoes that crossed the Limpopo. Mother had not come and was not coming.

She would be writing her final exams in a few months. Mother had told her to apply to the University of Pretoria and said she would pay. Mother often calls early in the morning to speak to Gogo. She complains about her boyfriend who she somehow cannot leave. Tsitsi overheard their conversation once and the words are emblazoned on her mind: 'I can't tell him I have a child, he must never know.'

She must not be going to learn in South Africa then. Her friends from school are talking about going to London or Canada. They often ask her where she is going to learn as if she has much of a choice. They forget that she is not like them, she is only there because of a scholarship. No one notices anymore. She talks like them now and they like her because she is smart. Nevertheless, her Harare and their Harare are worlds apart and she always tries to remember.

The combi passes Long Cheng Plaza, the Chinese mall. Tsitsi remembers how her friend from Church, Tawanda had been left homeless after the government had torn down their house. "It was built on a wetland," the government had argued. Long Cheng was still standing proudly though its foundations were sunk deep into a wetland. Tsitsi remembered the days back in primary school when mist hung over the wetland early in the morning and the *vapostori* in their white flowing garments huddled in groups and prayed – it almost looked like a supernatural affair.

She sees the stadium in the distance and recalls the miracle crusades held by charismatic prophets. She remembers Mai Jackson being caught up once in a stampede and coming back home limping. Gogo thinks the prophets are fake. She told Tsitsi she was sure they were fake after she asked Mai Jackson about her experience and Mai Jackson with wide eyes had said she saw an angel. Nonsense, Gogo prayed more than Mai Jackson and unlike Mai Jackson, she never gossiped. How could she have seen an angel? "They mess with their minds, Zimbabweans will go for anything just to forget their struggle," Gogo had said. Tsitsi believed though, in the prophets and the healings. She had always wanted to attend the crusades, but Gogo, strict with Anglicanism forbade it.

The combi is now in Warren Park. It is pitch black outside but Tsitsi knows where they are, the same way an ancient river knows its way. The traffic lights are not functioning, there must be no electricity. "*Hakuna* ZESA," the man beside her says disappointed. They have a gas stove now, so she is not worried.

She drops off at 'Pamasimbi.' The road traffic chaos started when combis became the main method of public transport. Any suitable place became a bus stop and the physical features around the chosen place would be used to name the place. 'Pamasimbi' refers to the green metal rods that line the road. Tsitsi drops off. This time, the conductor helps her balance the bag on her head much like how African women carry water home from the well. She walks in the darkness, fear gripping her chest. She sees through the fences of some houses. Women and children are sitting around fires cooking. She knows these are things her affluent friends never have to go through and feels sorry for these families that have accepted life as it is.

She identifies the silhouette of the *muzhanje* tree. She is home. It has always fascinated her how these big *mazhanje* are called the English *mazhanje* and the small wild ones are known as those that belong to them, the indigenous people. Gogo, a tall and rounded woman with unusually dark hair for an old lady and wise eyes scolds Tsitsi for coming back late. Tsitsi tries to justify herself but Gogo shrugs as if holding Tsitsi accountable for the unreliability of the bus. The dim candlelight is sufficient for them to see each other's faces. Gogo smiles as she stares at the bag wondering what might be in it this time around. With glee pasted on her face, she picks it up with much more ease than Tsitsi could muster. She places it on the mahogany table that was passed on to her at Mukoma Teddy's funeral. They unzip the bag. The zip purrs as it is opened. The anticipation of both Tsitsi and Gogo boils. Gogo takes out the goods one by one. As she does, Tsitsi's face grows longer and longer. The contents of the bag are all essentials save for a cheap bag for Gogo that she cannot stop rejoicing over and a new pair of sneakers for Tsitsi. Gogo then breaks into her ritual, a long prayer of thanksgiving, but this time Tsitsi is not mouthing Gogo's famous prayer lines or listening to the words of the prayer.

Her heart is troubled. *Did she forget that it's tomorrow?* Tsitsi ponders.

Gogo offers Tsitsi the food she had dished out and left on the kitchen counter. Tsitsi goes outside. She sits on the steps outside the kitchen, dips her hands into her sadza and rolls it into a ball. She stares at the fire next door, hears the gurgling of the sadza on the boil. She is annoyed that she stood all day to receive essentials only. Her eyes water as she wanders deeper in thought. Tomorrow she will be eighteen. What a way for the sun to set.

Sibonginkosi Christabel Netha

Sibonginkosi is a poet and a short story writer who was born in Chipinge, a small town bordering Zimbabwe and Mozambique. She has lived in Chipinge and Bulawayo (Zimbabwe) and Johannesburg (South Africa). Her writing is deeply inspired by her personal experiences of migration and struggles as a Zimbabwean girl child in the diaspora. In 2018 she was a finalist in the Africa Book Club short story competition for her short story, The Baby's mother, which is published in the collection. She participates actively in Bulawayo's vibrant art circles while also pursuing studies towards her first degree. She is passionate about social development and is a youth worker within the NGO sector.

The office

Tinashe

We are sitting in our "office", my workmates and I, which is basically three plastic chairs under a tree opposite the fish and chip store at the taxi rank. The chairs are the only comfort we provide for our customers and calling it an "office" is an inside joke between us and Tau, that guy who walks around selling low quality phone accessories all over town. He met us at the fabric shop one Monday morning and asked us who was watching our "office" if all three of us marastas were this far away from the taxi rank. We have called it the office ever since and each time Tau passes by he knocks on an imaginary door and says, "*Gogoyi tipindewo here* muOffice? Can I come into the office?" when we have customers who don't understand Shona and we all crack up laughing.

It is a gimmick that manages to get everyone laughing, which is something Tau is exceptionally good at. Sometimes I wonder if Tau really enjoys making people laugh or if he only does it for the sales. I find it difficult to believe that a grown man can enjoy looking like a moron for the sake of others. Either way, Tau's comedic gift serves him well when he is selling his wares. He is friendly with all the nationalities at the rank and he always manages to sell his wares without any difficulty, even though they are so low quality they hardly work beyond two days of use. The Nigerian guys who run the betting club love his Nigerian jokes, and the salon ladies think he is adorable. Even the South African taxi drivers call him their friend and he is usually exempt from any Xenophobic insults they hurl at us, as in, they usually add, "except you Tau" at the end because, of course, that should make it better.

George, Wilbert and I are sitting in our office when she shows up and asks if any of us can "crosh" dreadlocks, and I want to jump up for joy because of the three of us, I am the only one who can do that, so there won't be any question about whose customer she is. She is a young lady, as beautiful as Wilbert's girlfriend or maybe even prettier. She speaks to us in English without the South African accent and I can immediately tell that she is also from Zimbabwe. I am not sure which tribe though, so I continue speaking to her in English.

The customer, who looks as if she could be in her early twenties, sits in the chair that I was sitting on and removes the cap she had on to reveal a mass of shoulder-length black locks. She begins to explain how she would like me to not only renew them, but dye them as well. As we negotiate the price, I realise I am not really listening to what she is saying but just to the sound of her voice. Her accent, which I have decided must be the most beautiful sound on earth, reminds me of a girl I had a crush on back in High School. She was the only Ndebele girl at the school, and she spoke English with the ease and fluency that reeked of privilege. I agree to charge her a lesser price than I usually agree to, and she settles in so we can start the process.

She is silent for the first twenty minutes of the process and I realise she is unlike most of the women I know. I ask her a few questions about herself, what she does for a living, and where she is from, but she gives perfunctory answers without offering any more information. I want to dig deeper. To ask more personal questions but I realise I don't know how to do it without sounding like an interrogator, and the last thing I want to do is scare away a beautiful woman before she has even got to know me better. Instead, I decide to compliment the Africa-shaped ivory necklace that she is wearing and for some reason this serves as a good icebreaker. She begins to tell me that the necklace was a gift from her lover, Ronald. He is a poet and playwright based in Hillbrow whom she has been seeing for the past six months. She actually uses the word "lover" and explains that this is because they were not officially dating, because of the uncertainty of her job and it's travel requirements.

She says they are definitely in love and planning on getting married as soon as she finished her undergraduate degree and settled down, until he disappeared three weeks ago. I can almost feel my infatuation dissipating as she further exposes her naivete with her hero worship of a man who I am pretty sure has returned back home to Zimbabwe to a homestead with filled kids and a wife, after a decade-long adventure collecting disease in the city of gold. I let her go on and on about how his latest work was a stage play centred around Gukhurahundi, which is how she met him as she was doing research for her African Studies assignment, and could have probably been controversial enough to have him disappeared by those who do not want the truth to get out there. I decide to stop thinking too much about what she is saying and to just enjoy the sound of her voice as well as my view of her cleavage from where I am standing.

Victoria

I realise that the guy doing my hair has stopped listening to me and has only been grunting and shaking his head whenever he thinks it seems appropriate, but I do not stop talking about Ronald. This is the first time I have ever actually spoken about him to anyone because I wanted to wait until we had built something solid before telling people. Even my aunt, who introduced me to him, thinks he was only a contact and nothing more and so I cannot talk to her about his disappearance.

Ronald Mlambo would never run away, especially since he was in the middle of such an important body of work. He spent many hours locked away in the community centre basement, typing away scenes that he would later read to me so we could decide if they were the right fit or not. He was particular about how he wanted the play to come out and most scenes he would throw away as soon as he had read them aloud and decided they just were not good enough, much to my objection. On some days he was just visibly exhausted, both from the late nights he spent writing and the weight of knowing about the things that happened to people back then. To be honest, I was exhausted too, from the weight of that history. Learning about it and attempting to put together a body of work from it was not only a difficult task. It was traumatic and draining. On these days, we would go to Joubert park and sit on one of the benches and let the sunshine warm our bodies from the outside in. I would read one of his lighter poems from his first anthology, one he published when he was only 18 and only starting out as a poet and we would buy one ice cream cone between the two of us because he claimed to be too old for it.

"But wait, you two were not official lovers, right?" the guy doing my hair interjects when I got to this part, much to my annoyance.

"No, we were not, but we just clicked, you know. It's like he understood me and I him, because of the work we were doing. It was nice to have someone around who could relate to the trauma of having to listen to and retell those stories." I explain.

"Do you think he felt that way?"

"Yes! He often told me how special I was to him, how close I was to his heart and he would never be okay if he lost me."

"Did he ever write poetry about you?"

"No…not that I know of. Look, he was in the middle of an important body of work okay? He would hardly have time for love poems."

"Wait so he was a poet, but he never wrote anything about you? Not even a small, small haiku?"

Annoyed by his line of questioning, I change the topic to how much longer he is going to take doing my hair and he understands that as his sign to shut up. So, the last thirty minutes are silent, save for the few "sorrys" he mutters when he thinks he is pulling on my hair too much. On the inside, I fume at the arrogance of his questions. Who is he to question Ronald's love for me, to poke holes in my love story? Ronald loves me whether this guy believes it or not. In any case, he is just a hairdresser I will never see again in my life, so why should it bother me so much that he does not believe me? I need to focus.

The only man I have ever loved has vanished without a trace and only I seem to think this is a cause for concern. His flatmates said he had probably gone away for some writing inspiration, but I didn't believe them. He would never go away without telling me and he had only taken a small backpack that he took with him on day outings. If he had indeed planned on going away for a long time would he not have taken something bigger? Someone at the community centre said they thought he had perhaps gone to Zimbabwe for the weekend and something had happened which made him prolong the trip but even that doesn't make sense because he would have told me if that was the case. Perhaps we might have gone together even.

"Look lady, Ronald is unpredictable okay. These artists often are. There is no knowing when they will just up and leave for a new adventure or whatever. Now do you want to waste time talking about Donald or can we continue with your actual work," the manager of the centre snapped at me and I felt tears welling up to my eyes although I held myself from crying. I feel them welling up again now as I think about it but somehow, I miraculously do not cry.

I am a hot mess and I think Tinashe sees that as he hands me the mirror to look at myself after he is done. He seems worried when I hand it back with nothing more than a shrug. I whisper "thanks" and I hand him the 150rands we agreed on.

"Do you not like it?" he asks.

"No, it's fine, I'm just tired." I say before putting my cap into my handbag and standing up.

"Okay uhm take my number, and if you decide it needs fixing you can text me and I'll do it free of charge," he offers, taking out his cell phone.

I do not have my phone with me, so I take his cell phone and punch in my number instead before I wave goodbye and head home. I realise that all this talking about Ronald has made me even more exhausted than my schoolwork does, and I will probably spend the entire week crying alone in my room.

Tinashe

I spend the whole week feeling bad about how I treated Victoria. From the moment she left, I wanted to run after her and apologise for being an asshole, but I could not seem to move, and I spend the entire week kicking myself for being a prick and a coward. I eventually take the leap of faith on Friday, five days later, by sending her a message on WhatsApp.

"Hey. I am sorry I was an asshole the other day. I had no right to say that stuff about Ronald," I type out quickly and send before I chicken out. She does not reply until midnight and when she does, all she sends is a perfunctory "ok". I feel as though I need to do more to make up for it and so I offer to accompany her the next time she goes to look for him; which she agrees to. I still do not believe that anything has happened to him, but I hold myself from going down that road again as I do not want to upset her again.

We meet at the Bree taxi rank on Saturday morning and decide we will walk to his flat in Hillbrow because taking another taxi will be a waste of money. She is quiet on the way there and I cannot help but notice that there are dark circles under her eyes. Clearly this issue is affecting her more deeply than I thought. I bring up various topics on our walk, but she is not very interested and only offers one-word answers to my questions about school, work, her family and travels. She only seems to perk up when I ask about how she met Ronald.

"I met him at a book launch I attended with my aunt. I was her plus one and he was there as one of the performers. He performed a Ndebele poem in that imbongi style that Albert Nyathi does, and I remember thinking that he had such an amazing stage presence. Like he had the entire room under his spell and I just thought that was beautiful," she describes wistfully and for a moment the cloud that was hanging over her disappears, but only for those few seconds.

I realise then, that love is stranger and more powerful than we all think, because here is a beautiful woman, with a heart burdened by the agony of loss and probably other tragedies that I will never be privileged enough to know, beaming for a minute or two. I wish to lock her in that moment forever, despite my reservations about this Ronald character, I want to immortalise that memory of him forever just so that the dark cloud hanging over her would disappear.

We arrive at Ronald's flat and press the button on the intercom system. One of his flatmates answers and Victoria explains that we just wanted to look at his room so we could see if there were any clues about where he could be.

"I'm sorry I can't let you go through his things. I don't want to be held responsible if something goes missing in there, you know how Ron gets." The voice of a young man with a thick Xhosa accent speaks matter-of-factly through the intercom.

"Oh, come on dude! I promise we won't steal anything. We just need to see if maybe there are any notes or something that can tell us where he went," Victoria begs.

"That is an invasion of privacy, so no!" the guy refuses, again.

"He could be in danger! Do you not care at all?" she yells hysterically and the people walking into the building eye us suspiciously.

"You are not the police okay? Go away and wait for Ron to contact you himself," he says coolly before hanging up.

Victoria and I are silent for a few minutes after the "click" sound. I look at her tired eyes, unsure of what to say to make this situation better. She simply turns away and starts walking, leaving me standing there, still searching for something appropriate to say. I run to catch up with her and I stay silent as we cross busy streets and meander through thick crowds of shoppers and pedestrians. We continue walking silently until we reach Joubert Park.

She sighs heavily and sits on one of the benches overlooking a children's playground and a patch of lawn that was littered with clusters of women in burial society uniforms. I join her and stare at the people in front of me and wonder if they too are feeling as overwhelmed as I am. The children who are squealing in delight as they slide and swing are probably not, I figure.

"For the longest time, I have hated this place you know. I hate Johannesburg and its easy life and big city pace and everything about it. I promised myself that as soon as I could, I would pack up my life and go and live in Bulawayo. But Ronald…he made me want to stay. For the first time ever, I saw myself being happy here and I just do not know what to do without him," she blurts out, hot tears streaming down her cheeks.

I realise that there is a lot I could say to comfort her, but I hate it when people try to talk me out of my sadness, and so I shift closer to her on the bench, put my arms around her for a while and then offer to buy her ice-cream.

"Only if you promise to buy your own and not finish all of mine." She looks up at me, wiping away her tears.

"Trust me I'm not a saint, I only offered because I'm hot from all the walking you made me do," I tease, relieved to see her smile.

"Oh please! I did not make you do anything you didn't want to do!" she says rolling her eyes and we both laugh. We start to play a people watching game where we try to figure why each of the people in the park are there and their story. By the time we are ready to go, she has ice cream on her chin, and she is giggling loudly enough to disturb the burial society ladies who are involved in a very sombre discussion a few metres away from us. They keep giving us disapproving glances every time she laughs, and I cannot help but wonder what I would think if I was trying to figure out our story.

Would I figure that I am just an insensitive hairdresser who was privileged enough to spend a whole day with an angel? Would I be able to tell that I am trying very hard not to break her again, this broken angel? Or would I just conclude that it is a date, and we are in love. After all, people care to look at what is on the surface and on the surface only. Victoria has her arm hooked in mine and is laughing hysterically as I describe to her the most embarrassing moments of my life, the way Taurai from the taxi rank does every day. On the surface, I am making a beautiful woman laugh.

After I walk her back to her flat in Braamfontein, I walk back to Bree to catch a taxi to Maraisburg. I decide that this is the best day I have ever lived through since I moved to South Africa. I offer a genuine prayer of thanks to the heavens, something I have not done in a long time.

The Thing with Feathers

I hold it up to the light, my new golden pen. It has become my most prized possession of late. I lift it up to the window and watch the light shine through the glass diamond at the end of it. I smile when the light dances through the fake rock as I slowly tilt it, remembering the first time I saw it. Sabelo brought it for me from the city of gold on what had felt like the worst day of my life, until he arrived.

***

He walked into Haven with the swagger of a njiva and the stupid grin of a man who had seen the promised land we all dreamt of. The small children rushed to him before he had even walked more than five steps into the yard. He staggered back as squealing bundles, covered in chalk and ash and dust from playing in the ruins, all leapt at him from all angles. Even the children who were born after he left joined in the madness and excitement of welcoming back uBhud' Sabelo. Mbulelo, who had gone to pick him up at the Greyhound bus station in town, simply shook his head as he picked up the backpack that Sabelo dropped when the children jumped onto him. On his face was a small content smile that said he would happily pick after his younger brother, as long as he was home.

"Okay! Okay let me pass through please!" Mbulelo said, trying to make his way through the stampede that had somehow formed at the gate by this point. Almost everyone who lived in Haven, the small compound that once was a motel for travellers heading to and from Victoria Falls but was now just a mess of old derelict buildings that the owner let us live in, had come to welcome Sabelo back home. The only people who had not attended the informal welcome parade were those who were somehow incapacitated by their health and even they waved and cheered from their spots on the stoep where they sat, basking in the sun.

The overzealous children were followed by the women who made a great ordeal of breaking out into different chants at the same time. One half shouting praise to God and the other to Sabelo himself for not having forgotten about us, his family. It did not matter whether they were related to him by blood or not, all these women wept and fussed over him like mothers, aunts and sisters. That is just how things are in Haven. Everyone who lives here is connected to another, the way an actual biological would be. My "aunt", Sabelo's mother used to tell us this all the time when we were still children and I did not understand how a family could be so big with so many mothers and fathers and brothers. It did not make sense to me. Were families not supposed to have a clear structure? With a mother, a father and children? It simply did not make any sense to me until she told me about her own family back in Plumtree where she grew up. She told me that she too grew up in a big homestead, where her grandfather's children, her father and uncles all built their houses and lived close to their father. She told me about how all the children on the homestead, her siblings and the adults were all either her parents or grandparents.

"It takes a village to raise a child, Sili. And it is better to have that village be your family, don't you think?" Aunt NaMbulelo petted my head as she answered one of my million questions. It certainly had taken the whole village to raise us children, including Sabelo, and as the mothers and aunts offered him their welcome greetings, the men drew close to welcome him next. They surrounded him slowly, drew him into what must have been the biggest group hug ever, and cheered as they patted his back or shook his shoulders. They went quiet for a moment before a deep baritone rose from the middle of the group and began a guttural rhythmic chant. The voices of the men rose into the sky as they sang the praises of a great warrior who had crossed mighty rivers and evaded death as he sought his fortune to bring great pride to his family. The war cry for Sabelo went on for a minute or two before the men broke out of the huddle cheering and clapping once again, which made the children all excited once again, so they leapt onto Sabelo once more until they were sternly reprimanded by the aunts.

I was the last one to welcome him back home. I came out of the classroom where I had gone to hide myself from everyone's sight just as he was about to go and greet the gogo's who were too old to get up. I froze as he looked at me, unsure of what to think about this surprise. I wanted to take a step towards him, and I willed my face to smile but I seemed to have been paralysed and none of my body parts were working. Fortunately, my best friend smiled and started walking in my direction.

"Silindile." He whispered breathlessly when he got to me, almost as though he could not believe his eyes. His whispering of my name somehow freed me and suddenly, I could feel my limbs again. I threw my arms around his neck and released a breath I had not known I was holding for the past seven years. The relief alone of seeing him in the flesh and touching sent tears rushing to my eyes in the most unbecoming fashion. We held each other for a short while before we let go, and when I looked at his face, I was relieved to find that I was not the only one embarrassing themselves with tears. We looked at each other and laughed before linking arms and walking back towards the crowd while teasing each other about being cry-babies.

"We have so much catching up to do, meet up later?" he asked as he unlinked his arm from mine so that he could greet the grandparents who, if it were not for age or ailment, would have leapt on him just like everybody else. I watched his interaction with them for a while before I went off to help with dinner preparations. The aunts had decided that we would make a big deal out of it, so the kids had been tasked with chasing some of the roadrunners that roamed around the yard. Once they were captured, we would use the sharp knife Mbulelo had been sharpening to slaughter them before placing them in boiling water to remove the feathers. Sabelo's welcome home dinner was going to be spectacular and the entirety of Haven went into a frenzy over the preparations. We may have been caught unaware by his visit, but we were not going to let that stop us from going all out.

After the celebratory supper, everyone except me sat outside by the fire while listening to Sabelo's stories about the glamorous city of gold. They all seemed to have forgotten that before his arrival, we were in a crisis, not that I could blame them. Seeing him had also filled me with a bit of hope, just not enough to completely forget that we would all be homeless in a month. I threw myself onto the small bed I used to share with Aunty NaMbulelo before she passed and tried to sleep but the only thing that came were flashbacks of earlier in the day.

I was in the classroom when the men arrived and one of the children rushed in to inform me that two strange white men had come into Haven.

"They looked like they were going to Khulu Joseph's house." The child said. I figured then that this must have been something official because Mr. Joseph was the man that usually handled external affairs for Haven. He negotiated our rent on our behalf and all communications between the owners and inhabitants went through him. He had been a court interpreter in Harare before he found himself here, so he understood most of the processes.

By the time I was out of the classroom, most of the adults had also come out of their homes to watch as well. We all stopped what we were doing to gawk at what was not actually white men, but two-coloured men. One of them was very pale and the only thing identifying him as coloured was the mass of black curls that resembled wool on his head, while the other one had a slightly darker skin tone. They went into Mr. Joseph's house and for the few minutes they were in there everyone started speculating quietly about what it could have been that brought them here.

A few minutes later, they came out of the house and together with Mr. Joseph started walking towards us. They stood in the middle of the path between the houses and Mr. Joseph began speaking. In his official tone, he explained to us that the two men were Jesse and Calvin, the sons of Mr. Doug Rutherford, the owner of Haven. Apparently, Mr. Rutherford had passed on a few weeks ago and they were now the owners of the place. Jesse, the paler of the two brothers, lived in England but he had come back to take care of his father's estate. The brothers were going to sell the place, so we had to move.

At the mention of selling Haven, the entire place went into a frenzy. We were all stunned by the news. We had always known that Haven was not really ours but the thought that we could be forced to leave was not something we were ever prepared for.

"Where will we go? Haven is our home," one person cried out.

"You cannot just kick us out come on!" another said.

"Can we not come to some sort of arrangement?" I attempted to bargain, looking straight at Mr. Joseph.

"It is very unfortunate, but it seems the two gentlemen have made up their minds," he replied, and collective groans of disappointment rang out through the yard.

"Now we can discuss the issue amongst ourselves later, but the two men would like to say something before they leave." Mr. Joseph said to the crowd. At this point, Mr. Jesse stepped forward to speak.

"Good Day everyone! I am Jesse," he began in English then waited for Mr. Joseph to translate for him. "I understand you are all disappointed but unfortunately, this is the decision my family has come to. My father, the Mr. Rutherford who did business with you, was the only family member left here in Zimbabwe aside from my brother Calvin who will be returning with me to England. I must be back at work in three weeks therefore we have to sell all his property before then. The fact that there are squatters here is a problem we were not expecting, my father never mentioned this in his will."

"Squatters?" people shouted angrily. "How can you call us squatters? We pay rent!" they demanded.

"What my brother means to say is he did not expect people here," Calvin spoke in Ndebele, attempting to soothe the crowd. It did not work however, because people continued shouting and asking them to reconsider.

"You all have one week to vacate the premises. Good Day." Jesse spoke once again before he and his brother left. The people continued protesting and complaining long after they had walked out of the gate. I noticed Mr. Joseph walking back to his home and so I rushed to talk to him.

"What are we going to do Mr. Joseph?" I asked, hoping he had a solution.

"Start packing," he replied simply before walking off.

I was left there stunned. I could not believe that even Mr. Joseph did not have a solution. The man had worked in courts before. He knew the law inside and out so if he could not see a way out, the situation was truly hopeless. Haven had been my home ever since I could remember, I could not believe that we had to leave. And even if we did, where would we go? The rent we paid Mr. Rutherford was exponentially lower than the cheapest places in Bulawayo because of Haven's run-down state. In fact, most of the buildings here counted as ruins. But these ruins had been the perfect home for those of us who were down on their luck and just needed shelter and a place to call home. These ruins had been a hiding place for people who needed it, a haven.

I remembered Aunty NaMbulelo's story of how she got to Haven. She had lived in a green two roomed house in eNtumbane with her husband, a painter, and their two children, Sabelo and Mbulelo. When her husband passed, she lost their house to her in-laws because she refused to marry her husband's younger brother. She slept on the streets with her children for two nights before she met a kind street vendor who told her that she could find a cheap place to stay on the outskirts of town. This stranger directed her to Haven. Once she got here, she realised this was a community of people who had been down on their luck too before they found this place. Together they made a home out of an old derelict motel.

Sabelo had been home for a couple of days by the time we finally got to catch up. I had forgotten how alike we were when he was away, but at that moment, the old familiarity crept back in and we easily slipped into our old repertoire`. He teased me about everything, from how much shorter than him I was, to how my glasses could never sit straight on my face. I rolled my eyes each time and teased him right back about all his quirks. We knew each other so well the two of us, we had grown up together. Sabelo's mother had become my own mother when my own parents passed away in a car accident. She had become my primary caregiver even though she was only a distant cousin of my father's. As a mother, she had loved me like her own child and her sons had become my brothers. I often read or heard stories about how relatives treated orphans badly when in their care, but I could not help but thank my lucky stars that such stories were not my reality. Aunt NaMbulelo had made sure I never felt abandoned.

"Seeing you here reminds me a lot of her, you know." I said to Sabelo. He was sitting opposite me in the classroom, on the desk Mbulelo had built out of scrap wood so that I could have somewhere to prepare the lessons. He looked away momentarily before speaking.

"I could say the same about you. You are so much like her sometimes I forget that she was only your aunt," he said as he looked at me.

"Well I will take that as a compliment because she was an amazing woman." I said quietly. His comment made me very self-conscious.

"It is. I am sure she would have been proud of you Sili, the work you are doing here…what you do with the children…it is amazing! The people cannot stop going on about how important you are to Haven. You are more than just a schoolteacher and I am so proud of you." His tone had got very serious now. I turned away from him to look outside the window. The children were on break and some of them had begun a game of hopscotch. A piece of green chalk had been used to draw lines on the floor of what was once a building but had lost all its walls, doors and windows. I remembered that in a few days we would not have this place anymore.

"Except now we are about to lose Haven and I cannot do anything about it." My voice cracked as I spoke.

"It's all so unfair, Sabelo. I always dreamt of a day when we could have a proper school with a proper chalkboard and a playground. Every time I look outside and see the children playing in the ruins, I think of how they deserve so much better than this. Now even these ruins are about to be taken away from us." I sobbed.

Sabelo was quiet for a few moments before standing up. He walked to the window where I was standing and looked out of the window with me. After a few moments, he spoke.

"I remember when we were that young and we played in these very ruins. I never quite understood that these were ruins, I did not see them as something to be despised. The bricks lying around were just props for all the games I wanted to play and the old buildings that had missing walls and roofs were just opportunities for adventure. It is only now that I am an adult that I think these are ruins. My point is that even as a poor child playing in derelict buildings, I had enough to propel me to become what I am today. These children have enough Sili, you are doing the best you can," he assured me.

"I guess so, but in a few days, I will not be able to do anything for them. Who knows where we will be?" I said quietly.

"You have got to have hope, Silindile. Remember to have hope, just like mama used to say." Sabelo chided me with a smile.

"Yes! Yes, I guess it would be disrespectful to her to abandon hope." I laughed along with him. We stood at the window for a while longer, none of us saying anything. I knew that we were both thinking of her and how brave she would have been at a moment like this. After a while and a very deep sigh, Sabelo looked at me and pulled a small rectangular box out of his pocket.

"I got you a little gift," he said quietly as he handed it to me. "I am heading back to Jozi tomorrow so I probably will not see you again. I wanted to give you this now."

I opened the box and inside it lay a shiny golden pen with a glass diamond on the back of it. I gasped as I picked it out of its box.

"Sabelo this is beautiful! Thank you so much!" I breathed out. The pen was the most beautiful thing I had ever seen and probably the fanciest thing I would ever own. "I don't know what to say."

"Don't say anything, just write Sili. You are good at teaching, but I know you are even better at writing. I want to see a book you wrote on the shelves at a bookstore one day." He replied and once again, I realised how close we really were. My love for writing was not something I spoke about. It was more of a secret hobby. Sabelo was the only person who knew about it and most of the time he teased me about it. I looked at the pen in my hand thoughtfully as Sabelo quietly walked out of the classroom.

***

I look at the pen in my hand again and twirl it slowly this time, thinking about the first time I ever used it. When Sabelo left the classroom, I had marched to Mr. Joseph's house to ask for Mr. Cavin Rutherford's contact information.

I knew his brother had his mind set on selling, but I had hope that Mr. Calvin could be persuaded to see things our way. I wrote him a letter asking him to reconsider and in it I explained Auntie NaMbulelo's story of how she got to Haven and what Haven had come to mean to the people who lived there. I told him about the children I taught, how special they were and how they truly did not deserve the hand they were dealt. It was a longshot, a moon-shot but Mr. Calvin agreed to let us remain, despite his family's position on the matter. More importantly, he asked me to manage Haven because he would not be around to do so himself. This meant I was free to improve it as I saw.

It has been a year since the two young Mr. Rutherfords walked into Haven and the place has changed drastically. After Mr. Calvin let us remain, I asked the men to help fix up the ruins and they agreed. The old classroom has now been improved and it now consists of two rooms that house two different levels. The outside walls are now a bright yellow colour and there are drawings of Donald Duck, Mickey Mouse and other cartoons painted on. We also have a small playground with a swing-set and a slide.

I look outside the window again and I see the children playing, then I remember what Sabelo said to me the day he gave me the pen.

I look down at the notebook in front of me, and at the top I scrawl out the words "Have Hope" and underline them.

Ukuhlalukelwa

We buried Senzeni on a Friday, three days after we found her hanging on the pole of the clothesline at the boyskhaya. The same clothesline on which she and I hung our uniforms when we washed them on Saturday afternoons. The same clothesline which always had to be tightened after we hung a few things and the middle started to sag in such a way that the clothes would start touching the grass. Senzeni would, in an assertive tone which I guessed was one of the things she inherited from mother, yell for one of the boys laying around to fix the wire when it started to sag. She would remind them that we were also washing their uniforms if ever they started to protest and they would obey as though it was an order from mother herself. Senzeni also had mother's caramel coloured skin as well as her loud, commandeering nature while I had baba's dark skin and quiet, mouse-like demeanour. People said she was more likely to become a superstar because of her confident and outspoken nature coupled with the self-assured way in which she swayed her hips as she walked. They said my behaviour resembled an apology because I barely spoke above a whisper and I hunched my shoulders as I walked, as if trying to hide how tall I was. Mama said had she known how we would turn out, she would have named me Senzeni, and her Siphokazi because she was more of a pleasure to be around, and I was the one worth apologising for. I did not react when she said this, as I often did to other things. I simply carried on as though she had not said anything, wishing all the time that I had not happened at all.

Of all the times I had ever been angry at Senzeni, I had never been as angry as I was now. When little George, who was there when they found her, asked me questions about what happened to Sisi Senzeni, I simply shrugged and said, "I don't know." I didn't understand why the first emotion that coursed through my body was anger. Red-hot, seething, anger. I felt as if something had just been taken away from me, and not just my twin sister. When Auntie Buhle read the note she left behind for the family, I stood up and left. I couldn't stand to hear anything with her name in it. And she didn't think to leave me a personal note, as her sister and best friend since we were children!

I fumed all through the funeral gatherings, as well as at the final burial service on Saturday. It had just rained the previous night, so our shoes were soiled with the mud of the cemetery grounds and our stepmother Keisha kept sinking into the mud because of the stilettos she was wearing. When asked if she would not rather wear flip-flops like the others were doing, she refused on the grounds that flip-flops would ruin her "all-black" gothic inspired look, which, everybody had to admit was a very nice outfit – albeit a little too over the top for a funeral in Africa.

Everybody else wore their regular clothing, which, for the women was mostly a regular old political-party t-shirt from the previous year's elections. Even Baba's unpredictable little sister Aunty Buhle, dialled down her usually controversial outfits to a basic brown skirt that covered her knees and a cream blouse that seemed as if it had been borrowed out of gogo Chirizi's wardrope. Even her bleach-blonde dreadlocks that were usually adorned with cowry shells and bright beads were concealed under a basic brown doek. Gogo Chirizi insisted it was because Aunty Buhle was cultured enough to understand the need to respect the dead, unlike Mummy Keisha who was caught up with the frivolous ways of the West, but I highly suspected it was because Senzeni's death hit her harder than everyone else in the family.

I was often jealous of Senzeni's bond with Aunty Buhle, and on most days I imagined that one day I too would be able to converse with the ease and comfort that Senzeni had with her. It was as if Aunty Buhle was Senzeni's older sister and not our aunt. Each time Senzeni was home from boarding school and Aunty Buhle came back from one of her trips, they would cook and wash dishes together, which was odd because Senzeni hated chores of any kind, after that they would sit in the kitchen until the entire family went to sleep and long after; chatting in their posh private school English that I would mimic sometimes when I was alone in the bathroom. Senzeni once told me that the only person who knew all her secrets was Aunty Buhle and I had to swallow something that felt like a small rock before mumbling out a "nice."

Still, for the larger part of the year she was my sister and best friend. We did everything together, she, loudly and enthusiastically and me, cautiously and apologetically. Where she bulldozed through without any care for the consequences, I tittered hesitantly behind her, trying my best to make up for her recklessness. She needed me to remind her that there are consequences to things and I needed her to remind me that it is okay to take risks. We were quite the pair and I remember that every time I was not with her, I always felt a bit unbalanced. As though standing only on one leg, my world was never quite balanced without her around.

That is what it means to be twins, I think. She was my other half, a vital part of my existence and now I had to deal with the fact that she was no longer around. I don't know how people do it, I'll admit. I don't know how people move past things like loss and grief. All I know is running and I've been doing it ever since the day we laid Senzeni to rest. I ran from the cemetery and I did not stop until I had crossed the railway behind SOS Children's village and reached home and headed straight for the chicken coop. I stayed there until Aunty Buhle came to find me and scolded me for worrying Gogo and the family.

"You could have given her a heart attack! Honestly, Sipho. There are less dramatic ways to grieve you know." She said as she threw her arms around me and we both dissolved into tears and sobs.

Looking back, I realise that I have actually been running for the past ten years. I have been trying to escape the feeling of loss that Senzeni left me with and the feelings of guilt that I could not tell that something was wrong with her. I have spent the last few years trying to understand suicide and depression, and I am well aware that it does not always show and yet, I carry this burden with me. The fact that I was unable to protect my own twin paralyses me at times and it still gives me nightmares. I am faced with my own failure every time I look at myself in the mirror. The fact that my own twin sister felt she could not tell me that her teacher was making sexual advances at her is something I have never been quite able to get over and I do not think I ever will.

On the Monday after her funeral, the police came to school and arrested Mr. Mutupa, the tennis coach. All of the girls on the tennis team were sent to the headmaster's office and we did not see them the whole day. In the middle of the day, Daddy and mummy Keisha came to pick me up and told me that I would not be going to Northlea High School again. They said I would go and live with them in Cape Town and "it would help me heal" as Auntie Buhle put it. I am not sure if it worked or not, but I am grateful that they tried.

"Dear family,
By the time you read this, it will be too late. I am so sorry to do it like this but I have no other choice. I have no other way to handle this. It is all too heavy to carry and I simply do not want to go on living like this.

For the past two years that I have been on the tennis team, Mr. Mutupa has been forcing himself onto me. I did not know who to tell and I am sorry for that. He made threats to hurt me if I tell anyone and I am sure that he did so to other girls in the club as well. He corners me in the changing rooms or in the toilets every time we have to stay for extra practice and I am so afraid.

I am ending this because I don't know if I will ever be able to survive being the girl that was raped. I have thought about it and I want him brought to justice, but I do not think I am strong enough to watch it all unfold.

I am so sorry for being such a coward, I love you all.

Love, Zeni."

I sit on the sand as I re-read Senzeni's letter for what must be the millionth time. Aunty Buhle insisted they let me have it as soon as it was no longer needed as police evidence. I fold the aged piece of paper carefully and place it in the pocket of my windbreaker before looking up at the Atlantic ocean. I think of the word "ukuhlalukelwa", which Gogo said is the Ndebele word for depression. I think about how when I say it, it feels less clinical than its English translation and I like how it comes out of Gogo's mouth. Gentle, calming and soothing and less alarming than "depression." I find that when I think of it in my native language, I feel more balanced, much the way Senzeni made me feel.

"I wish you would have let me talk you out of it, Zeni. You know that was my job, talking you out of reckless ideas," I breathe out as the salty Cape Town wind hits my tear-stained cheeks.

This has become a ritual. Every year on her birthday, I come out to the ocean and sit on the rocks while rereading her last words to me. I like to think that the ocean would have been her favourite place, if she had ever lived to see it. The way the waves rage and hit the shores with a violent intensity reminds of Senzeni's nature. Reckless, wild and intense in everything she did, living with Senzeni was like living with a storm. A beautiful, loving, funny and bossy storm. I like to tell myself that if as a spirit, Senzeni got to choose any place to haunt she probably chose the ocean and so, I talk to her every time I come out here. It has become the only place that I can truly be at peace.

Mummy Keisha says we can never really control the events around us, especially the tragedies. But, if we try hard enough, we can let it turn us into better, stronger people. I think the idea of strength is only but an illusion that can only manage to keep up until the sun goes down. At night time, the same nightmare comes just in different forms. Sometimes it's Senzeni falling into a dark hole and me being unable to reach out to her and pull her out and other times it's Senzeni's voice calling me to come and help her, but I never see where she is and the more I think I am walking towards the voice the more it fades. The message in each one is clear, I failed to save my sister.

I often wonder how different things would have been if she had not taken her own life. Would Mr. Mutupa have been convicted if there was no dead girl with a grieving family involved in the case? Did Senzeni's sacrifice help those other victims and do they acknowledge this, wherever they are now? Did they go on to live good lives, knowing their rapist is firmly behind bars and most importantly, were they strong enough to live with the burden of being "the girl who was raped"? Would I have been able to do what my sister could not do? The truth is I probably would have told Senzeni and given her the opportunity to be strong for me.

"That is what sisters are for Zeni." I whisper to the wind before I turn and make my way home.

Chipo Moreblessing Mawarire

Chipo is a performing practitioner and blogger based in Bulawayo, Zimbabwe. She is the producer and contributing writer of Vagina Monologues Africa, a project inspired by Eve Ensler's Vagina Monologues.

Tombstone unveiling

Her one-man audience gave her the most perplexed look, one she had anticipated.

"Ma'am are you sure you handed me the correct message?" he said, trying with all his might to be courteous and not sound at wits end.

"Definitely, with the world going paperless I am careful how I use paper."

"I do not mean to pry, but in all my years' working here I have never been asked to write something so…"

"Honest?"

"I was going to say unusual," said Mucheno, instantly wishing he had not said that.

"If you must know, I am convinced you want to anyway. I believe that part of the bible that says the truth shall set you free. Possibly one of the few verses that make sense in that whole book anyways."

"I'm sorry, my job is not to ask why," he said, wishing the conversation could end sooner. "My job is to discuss fonts, style and design. I just wanted to be sure if it was the right one, I have had to redo jobs a couple of times before and so I try my best to avoid doing so again. I am really sorry ma'am can we please start over?"

"No worries, Mr. Mucheno, that is the correct inscription. I will be in touch," she said. Examining the invoice he had given her earlier.

"Alright. Sorry once again."

Natasha didn't reply. She just nodded and briskly left for her car. Eager to leave, being here only confirmed what life has embezzled away from her, and discussing such finer details made her feel suffocated and claustrophobic in an open space. She had to leave.

With the same energy, she opened the car door and let out a sigh once inside. She was not coping, she admitted to herself. Coming here was confirmation of what she had lost and how it made her angrier than sad. Moments of regret would sometimes hit her so hard she would stay up all night drowning herself in a pool of what ifs. On other days, she convinced herself she had done all she could. In hindsight, she was ready for the war she had just declared. Lulue was the one family member she had for most of her adult life and now that she was gone, none else mattered. Through her grief, she could finally say her truth and make things right by Lulue. She filled the void Lulue's departure had carved in her life by fighting all resemblance of injustice towards her kind. She could not be ignored anymore. She had a generational mandate to speak out and be the voice of a gender often left to the whims of violence and abuse of all forms. Suddenly, she was jolted out of her imaginary safe space by a car blaring its horn as if announcing an impending danger.

***

''When you die, I will buy you flowers every month till I die too.''

Ten-year-old Natasha had softly, but succinctly blurted out these words to Luyanda who was masterfully plaiting her hair one Saturday morning. She sat on the floor with her back resting on Luyanda's legs who was sitting on the bed while combing her hair. On that day, she was plaiting what they called *mabhanzi*, the most basic African threading. It was one of their special moments alone. Lulue had recently just learnt how plaiting natural African hair while moist was the best way to deal with the usually kinky coils. These plaiting moments grew more enjoyable with time, as the head adapted to the pull and strain which often leaves novices wincing in pain. Lulue always did Natasha's hair every Saturday at 11.30 am like clockwork. Lulue was consistent on time earning herself the moniker, 'the timekeeper'. On the contrary, the only thing Natasha did on time was her hair because 'her majesty', as she sometimes called Lulue, was responsible for it.

''Don't be crazy Tasha! Why are we even thinking about death?"

''I'm just assuring you that I will love you beyond the grave."

The smile on Luyanda's face she saw on the mirror reflection which stood in front of them assured her that she had struck a chord.

''With the way you are reckless I hate to break it to you that you will die before me lil sis."

Reckless and carefree as she might have been, Natasha was big on promises and expected other people to keep theirs too. "Keeping a promise says a lot about someone's character and how they value whatever relationship they have," she always said. To her disappointment though, she never met her match in that regard as people in their utmost mortal being are prone to fail at keeping promises. That broke her heart a couple of times until she accepted that to her it was a gift, a gift so unique maybe, just maybe, only she possessed it the world over. Lulue had taken her sister's promise as rumblings of a ten-year-old, forgetting the promise the minute it was uttered. In December 2003, Natasha bought flowers for Luyanda and it became a monthly ritual. She kept her promise.

***

From Mucheno's workshop, Natasha went to her parents' house. She called it her mother's house, rather because even while her father was still alive, it had always been her mother who wore the pants. It was the house she and her siblings had grown up in; Adam, Luyanda and herself. She had fond childhood memories of the place. The birthday parties, Christmases, playing hide and seek with Adam and their friends. It, however, also held her worst life experiences. Her very first heartbreak; discovering her father's unconscious body lying lifelessly on the bedroom floor when she was only eight and the charade that was Luyanda's lobola ceremony. The memory of her father's motionless body lying on the floor haunted her for days on end and the pain felt different every time. She had come home from school one Tuesday afternoon to find the house unlocked but there was no one in sight.

Assuming an elder was nearby, she went on to change into her clothes and have lunch. It was only after she made her way to her mother's bedroom to steal a new pencil, that her life was changed forever. The door was slightly open, but something was blocking it from the inside. Determined to get her pencil before she could get caught, she tried pushing and squeezing herself through the crack. When she finally pushed her small body through, she fell on her father's cold body. She laughed, asking him if it was so hot that he had to lie on the floor, but she got no response. She tried pulling him up and when she failed, she went and called Auntie Gina from next door to help her. She was befuddled when Auntie Gina called her nephew, Majaha, who took Natasha's hand and led her to their house so they could play. Aunt Gina was unusually hasty, sad and fast paced; making Natasha feel even more lost. After a while a police car arrived, her mother was wailing, neighbours were coming to their house one by one. That was the last time she saw her father; cold, motionless with froth on his mouth. Medically, a heart attack had taken his life, but traditionally it was an avenging spirit, something Natasha only overheard said in whispers during the numerous family meetings that ensued.

Natasha had loved her father immensely, so being told he has gone away and will be back did not help her situation. When he passed away, he was on his annual leave, time he fully dedicated to family. Natasha valued their story times and looked forward to them every afternoon. She did not mind missing out on her favourite cartoon to have her father read to her, tell her stories from his childhood most of which cracked her up as she would laugh uncontrollably until she teared up. As an adult, she would rekindle the memories in her head and bask in their glory and that always brightened her days. She often wondered how life would have been if he were still alive. How their lives would have turned out. No doubt they would have remained the best of friends. Adam probably would not have had that 'wild episode' which almost led to his arrest, save for the fact he was still a juvenile, and a few canes sufficed. Luyanda would not have…this thought always brought tears to her eyes. Luyanda's lobola ceremony.

She never understood why it was called "Luyanda's lobola ceremony". A 'make a dead man happy while killing Luyanda' ceremony is what it was to her. A goblin marriage! It perplexed her how everyone was trying to normalise this charade. The Gatsi monsters driving a convoy of cars, acting like they came in peace to initiate a conventional everyday lobola, yet they were there to uproot Luyanda's very being, to enslave her. Her paternal uncles coming all the way from their homes to officiate an obscenity. Her mother suddenly a 'yes sir, no sir' kind of a woman, something she had never expected to see in her lifetime. Luyanda was to 'go help her aunt Betty with her marriage' as they put it. Peter and his whole vicious family was disgruntled with Aunt Betty because after fifteen years of marriage, she had not given them sons as expected. So, seven daughters and two miscarriages later, it was decided that Luyanda had to carry the button stick from Aunt Betty and give Peter Gatsi at least one son. Peter and

Aunt Betty's marriage was not a conventional one either, she had been given away to appease an alleged avenging spirit which was tormenting her family, *kuripa ngozi*. The spirit was of one of the Gatsi brothers who is said to have been killed by Natasha's grandfather. Traditionally, to rectify that mishap and to avoid perennial spiritual attacks and a life of poverty across generations, the Moyo clan pledged Aunt Betty as a wife, but without bearing them a son to replace the deceased, the spirit was still seeking vengeance. Another Moyo girl had to fulfil that need, and so Luyanda was their next victim. Talk about some greedy spirit!!

So, Peter and his uncles had to officiate the marriage. Strangely enough, although Luyanda was the payment to appease the *ngozi*, the Gatsis were also meant to pay part of the lobola that is traditionally due to mothers. A cow, blanket and a complete outfit. This was superficially obligatory because mother and daughter are not of the same bloodline, so if she was not given her dues her wrath would bring bad omen on the families, yet another *ngozi* because of a *ngozi*!

Was her wrath of this injustice towards her daughter not stronger than not receiving her supposed dues from a blood thirst family? To succeed in their evil plan, Natasha's uncles had driven Adam into the terror of being killed by the *ngozi* if it was not appeased and so he could not fight on behalf of her sister. The terror-stricken Adam had to save himself, so he did not question them further and sheepishly followed all given instructions, something Natasha never forgave him for. Natasha's over imaginative mind tortured her.

Looking at Luyanda and Peter she trembled at the thought of her youthful and vibrant sister in the same bed with the frail and grey Peter. His sweaty and sticky old self taking away Luyanda's soul by every stroke. His rough ravenous hands all over Luyanda's zestful and tender body. How he would feel like a man thereafter, which is what they say younger women made them feel; manly and important. She felt her spirit slip out of her body at the thought of Luyanda not having sons, yes it meant Natasha being in the sweaty old man's bed, trying for a son. The more she thought of this, memories of Peter lecherously glaring at Luyanda from an early age became more vivid and she was sure she was not imagining it. The bastard had long wanted her and had found the perfect excuse to pounce.

Natasha had begged her mother to pay off the debt with money or livestock than with Luyanda. "A human being is not a commodity, certainly not an object to be exchanged as people see fit," she had rationalised. MaNdlovu unfortunately had no power in the proceedings, when patriarchy decides; a woman has no power whatsoever, especially one in the position of a daughter in law. With her husband dead, she was at the mercy of her in-laws. It was as if they long had scores to settle with her, but no matter how strong a woman is, the vile of chauvinism catches up with her and in MaNdlovu's case it was her daughter's forced marriage. Strong and hard-headed as MaNdlovu might have been, there are matters she had no say in and whenever she raised her head, she was reminded how she was an outsider. How as a mother the children were not hers, something Natasha's young mind could not comprehend. A human being for another; is what the tradition dictated. She tried explaining this to Natasha, but she was having none of it. She felt herself getting angry at her father for dying and leaving them vulnerable, with no one to stand up for them. These uncles also had daughters, but they were not about to sacrifice them when Adam Senior's daughters were available for such. Not having a father in such a scenario made them a herd of cattle without an owner, they were at everyone and anyone's mercy. When everyone else was giving reasons why it could not be their daughters, there was no one to speak for them, to defend them.

Luyanda had never been much of a fighter herself, they often joked about how Natasha had taken all the feistiness for the three of them. Being the first-born child, she was taught responsibility at a young age. Even with a nanny around, her mother made her liable for her siblings' wellbeing and mischiefs. With so much responsibility over her head, she had not had time to be a child, experiment and be irresponsible. Her father's passing away while she was thirteen and in form two had not helped her situation either, it meant more responsibility for her. She was about to go for afternoon study when the matron had told her to go to her dormitory and put her things in order because someone was on their way to take her home, no sufficient explanation given. Death was the last thing on her mind since to her knowledge everyone was in good health. Aunt Sethi, who came to take her home only told her the reason why when they were a few metres away from their home. Luyanda refused to believe the news until she saw her mother sitting on a form mattress in one corner of the lounge looking distraught with two of her friends from church sitting with her. She had never seen her mother so defeated, Luyanda wept for her loss and that of her mother too.

Her father's passing away made her an adult at thirteen. She felt the need to be there for her mother and not give her trouble and she wasn't about to add on it. So, when other teenagers were out and about, causing trouble at every turn, she was being a deputy and her mother's right-hand girl. She had the burden of being the level-headed child. While her peers were going away to study abroad or in other cities, she opted for the local university just so she could be near her mother. No matter how much MaNdlovu insisted she broadened her options, she was having none of it. And so, when her uncles invaded their home to uproot her, she was there. They used her love for her family against her. Created the worst-case scenarios consequences if she did not heed to their request. Used to carrying her mother's burdens, she did not show her or even complain. The thought of losing another family member scared her more than being the wife of an old man she had considered an uncle all her life. MaNdlovu tried talking to her but all she said was how she would do anything to save and serve her family. In an instant, a second-year electrical engineering student became a doormat for her whole family line. No one could get through to her to talk and act against it. It was clear in how she had lost the spark in her eyes that she was not well, yet she insisted she was ok with it. And so just like that, she gave up her life and went through with the charade.

This was too much for fifteen-year-old Natasha, but she stood her ground and fought for Luyanda, even if she refused to fight for herself. She said words she never thought could come out of her mouth, especially to her mother. She had more fight in her than the women in Lysistrata combined. But unlike them, withholding conjugal rights and benefits was not the answer. After the biggest mother daughter confrontation of her life, she took a deep breath and said;

"We cannot dump her into Peter's hands."

"Natasha, he is Uncle Peter!"

"He is not my uncle. This is not even part of our culture. We don't pay off our debts with humans."

"I understand your feelings my dear, but it is culture. Not believing it doesn't mean it will just go away. What do you think mysteriously killed your father and Aunt Anna? Do you want that for the family? To live in such uncertainty. We must put an end to this or else the spirit will kill everyone. Aunt Betty and Luyanda are saving the family. My heart is a wreck watching Luyanda go through this but if she doesn't, we will be disowned."

"Let them disown us then, why would we want to be part of such a vile family to begin with?"

"I wish it was that simple Tasha, a child has two parents for a reason, and I cannot bear the burden when something happens to you or your siblings and the family is needed. I could never bury you without them, there are family traditions and customs only they can perform. Instances where I'm considered an outsider."

"You have always been my example of a strong woman and I never pictured you giving in like this. Be weak all you want mum and give me all the excuses in the world, but I will not be a part of this."

"You know if I had it my way this would not be happening. You are hurting me with your words." She said reaching Natasha for an embrace, but she ducked.
"I'm beginning to think you are enjoying all this. You are the only one profiting from this anyway. Is it the cow or…?"

She was silenced by a slap on her left cheek which left a buzz in her ear, feeling dizzy and on the kitchen floor. She stared at her mother in disbelief. She had felt her mother's anger and frustrations in the slap. There was an insufferable silence as she regained her composure and MaNdlovu half regretting the slap, but the disrespect had gone overboard. Natasha picked herself up, regained her composure and said;

"You just lost a daughter."

She walked deliberately slowly, half testing the waters of her recent theatrics and half hoping her mother would embrace her and inexplicably make the pain go away, then banged the door after her exit.

MaNdlovu was astounded. She could only watch as her emotionally deranged daughter walked away, and it hurt. She felt like a wrecking ball had settled on her heart when the next school holiday Natasha refused to come home from boarding school but rather took odd jobs at the missionary school. When she passed her ordinary and advanced level exams, she never shared the news with her mother, leaving her to hear it from her sister Sethi tore her apart. Natasha got a scholarship to go to university and still did not come home, did not have the mother daughter talk about life ahead at university. She was devastated when Natasha came back for the first university holiday and stayed at her friend's house the whole two months, she had hoped things would be different. She has chosen strangers instead of her own family and swore never to set foot at her own mother's house. When her age mates had one graduation party after the other in their parents' backyards, yet no one knew where Natasha was, MaNdlovu faked illnesses just so she could not attend, and with every one of those invites was a reminder of how her daughter had turned her back on her and never looked back.

When she eventually came home, after Aunt Sethi had begged her, her visits were less than an hour long and she often refused to eat anything. She sometimes made up excuses to not even enter and rather talked to her mother by the gate through her car window. She never asked for Adam either, her sentiments were always that he had been the weakest link in the falling apart of the family. He was also rarely home most of those times as he was a black-market money changer. MaNdlovu's life was never the same after Luyanda was married off and Natasha left. It drew a wedge between her and her ever trusted first born daughter such that even when she visited, they were like two strangers on a bus with mutual courtesy. She was frail, shattered, and had lost interest in the art of living. She had weathered the storms, but had no drive left in her, like an aloe vera plant growing on a rock which stays alive but without the substances that define others of its kind.

***

Embarrassing an African parent is one of the gravest sins one can ever commit. Airing the family's dirty laundry in the presence of 'esteemed' guests was outright abominable. The preacher went on and on, but Natasha did not hear a single thing he said. Sitting in a valley of a rock and a hard place does not give one the liberty to be settled. A place where the 'wide and narrow' are not clearly defined, and one must decide it for herself. She might have disbanded herself from the family, so she cared less about the consequences, but she still loved her mother. She was also just a victim of the system. This made her rethink if this was the best way to seek justice. She reminded herself that she was doing this for Luyanda. For Aunt Betty. For all the other women who had been used as chess pieces all their lives. She was going to be their mouthpiece. If people disregarded the voice of the living, then maybe it was time to let the dead speak for themselves. Having reassured herself on her course of action she finally could hear the sermon.

"Luyanda lived up to her name, she was all about growth and spreading love, Luyanduthando. She surely spread love wherever she went, always with a smile on her face. Parents, names are prophecies we place upon our children so give them names that can manifest into good fruits. As we celebrate her life today may we also emulate her life? Live a life of love, growth and sacrificing ourselves for the people we love. Pursue peace, love, self-sacrifice, gratitude, selflessness and living a life of harmony. Amen!" The people ululated and clapped hands for him as he closed his sermon and Uncle Tobias took over from him. Natasha stared indifferently into the space and her mother was not impressed, she wanted her daughter to acknowledge the pastor, but this is the daughter she had lost over a decade ago, so nothing was about to change. She looked at her inquisitively, but Natasha was not moved. She just glared at her mother with the same disregard and went back to her thoughts.

"Thank you for the powerful sermon baba mfundisi. We feel comforted a lot." Uncle Tobias said, "Allow me to call up Luyanda's husband, our son in law Gatsi, to come and unveil the tombstone for us."

At this point, Natasha could not hide her disgust as the old frail Peter Gatsi made his way to the grave, how she wished that was literal. She looked at him with shots of hate before she looked down to calm herself down as her red-carpet moment was nigh. She finally had an audience. She had to utilise the moment well. Her thoughts were interrupted by Gatsi's old frail voice. "Thank you all for joining us today as we celebrate my wife's life. I feel lost without her. My life will never be the same without her, she was my anchor, my support system and had a way of holding things together like no other. I pray that the love we shared will carry me through this difficult time. Sweetheart, the children and I miss you. Until we meet again, rest in power my wife." He concluded. "Power indeed," murmured Natasha rolling her eyes to the stupefaction of those in her earshot.

"Please do join me as I unveil Lulue's tombstone," he said and went on to cut the ribbon that held the lace together. He carefully removed the lace that covered the stone to reveal a beautiful rose shaped midnight black stone decorated and inscribed in shadow blue. He went on to read out loud, "Here lies a goblin wife…" The murmurs and gasps of the crowd stopped him midway. Before he could gather what was taking place, Adam had come closer to read for himself. The rest of the Moyo and Gatsi clan followed suit. Everyone else was either whispering to each other, stone shocked or mumbling one thing or another. Natasha did not move, as she allowed the momentum to build up. Luyanda deserved a powerful final send off. The world owed her that much.

"What on earth…" whispered Adam into the mic before it startled him into throwing it to the ground. Everyone around the grave was talking, none of them listening to the other. While everyone lost themselves in the mayhem Natasha walked up to the grave, picked up the mic from where Adam had dropped it. She startled them all as she had not been on the scene just moments earlier. She was surprisingly calm and poised. One could swear she had rehearsed for this moment for ages, which she had. Her small thin voice was a force that compelled everyone to listen. Like a maid of honour at a wedding she stood with her head held up high, unshaken and ready to deliver her speech and all had to listen.

"Here lies a goblin wife. Sacrificed to make men happy," she said and took a dramatic pause as they took in what she had just said.

Everything and everyone fell silent. "Finally, I have your ears! Wish that had been sooner. Wish you had listened to Luyanda and Aunt Betty too. We would not be here today. We could probably be planning a family holiday or Christmas festivities. But because everyone was blind to the abuse which firstly befell Aunt Betty and later Lulue, we are here by Lulue's grave saying all kinds of lies and deceit, perpetuating the silencing of the voices of women and children. And maybe Aunt Betty would have married a decent man of her choice that I could properly call uncle, unlike Peter here." MaNdlovu gasped and in a bid to salvage the situation, Adam walked her to one of the minivans they had come in, he had to save her from the eyes of the people, yet he had not dared save Luyanda, thought Natasha. The crowd had her attention and her family was too astonished and not ready to cause anymore glares and murmurs by fighting her off. That is the danger of fighting an unexpected opponent with nothing to lose, it takes too long to find the appropriate response which is often too late and trivial. With the attention she had hoped for, she went on to read the inscription.

"Since I'm not afraid of the truth, unlike the majority here I will read the inscription again; Here lies a goblin wife. Sacrificed to make men happy. In loving memory of Luyanduthando Moyo. Born on 5 October 1983. Died on 26 May 2003. Buried 17 June 2019." People's gasps gave her the vigour to go on. "My sister died in 2003 at the age of twenty but only buried in June of 2019, with her spirit hovering around the atmosphere and her body occupying a space she knew nothing of. The day she was forced into a goblin marriage with Peter is when her slow death began. Every birth and addition to the evil Gatsi bloodline only made her grave even deeper. The day she left her mother's house to be a goblin wife is when she died. Her soul and true self left the earth and all that was left was the shell left to be called Mrs. Gatsi. My sister was murdered. By your silence when you saw things unravel. By the system which only prescribes women's place as child bearers and later calls them outsiders when matters concerning the same children are concerned. Given away to appease a spirit and bear sons for Peter and the whole Gatsi clan. Prey to her own dead father's brothers because he was not here to protect us. As if her dying every day in that marriage was not punishment enough, she died while giving birth to her sixth child, her second son, still paying off her family's debt, kuripa ngozi, as they said. Both she and the baby did not make it. Two innocent roses trying to blossom among thorns. Peter and my uncles killed Luyanda in a bid to appease a goblin. Peter is nothing but a goblin medium, and she, the price. A sacrifice to please a goblin. The system killed her in 2003 and the world only acknowledged it sixteen years later. I watched my sister wither away for sixteen years until when she was clinically dead. I hope you are all happy to have been accomplices to a murder. Aunt Betty, I am sorry the system did not spare you either," and she deliberately dropped the mic on the ground, creating echoes and feedback from the speakers.

During all this spectacle, Aunt Betty had not moved from her seat and with the way her face was always expressionless, it was hard to tell what she was going through. The Moyo uncles were in a little circle that looked like a caucus meeting. Everyone else from the Gatsi side was either silent in their little corners or in groups of three or four murmuring. Adam had tried to silence Natasha, but she shot him with a 'dare me' look which he immediately covered up by taking their mother to the car. In the car, MaNdlovu was weeping, beside herself with grief, pain and embarrassment. She cried for all the things she had lost in her life; her parents at a render age, her husband who left without a word, her daughter she had not been able to save from the claws of a vile culture, her other daughter who had turned her back on her only to come back and embarrass her, hell she even cried for her dog that had been hit by a refuse collection truck a few days before the ceremony. She blamed herself for letting Natasha be in charge of the tombstone designing and erection. Why had her intuition not told her that this was too good to be true? She should have known that her feisty daughter was going to pounce, and pounce hard she did. Alas, she was just a mother who was happy her daughter was now talking to her. The unveiling arrangements also gave her the excuse to randomly call her daughter in the pretence of planning, then she would steal a moment to have conversation with her child and they had grown closer. Who could blame her? So, while she had not expected the events of the last couple of minutes, she could not find herself mad at Natasha, she was rather proud that eventually someone had spoken up, regardless of the circumstances. In her heart of hearts, she was a proud mother.

With the world at her feet, Natasha did a catwalk to her car by the parking area, like one who had just been crowned Miss Universe. She made sure not to turn or miss a step though, tripping and falling was not how she wanted to end her five minutes of fame. The five minutes in which she had reclaimed her power, reclaimed her sister's voice and place. The five minutes in which she had written her name in the books of history.

With loud music blasting from her yellow Mazda 6, she drove away from the drama she had started!

Naila

The man from whose loin I came,
It took me a long time to find a proper way to address you. Political correctness was not my issue though – I do not owe you that. I am just going to say what I feel and think about you not because I want a response or reaction. I have gone this long without it anyway but sometimes things need to be said and I am going to say them. Sometimes I wish you and mum had never met. Mother, being the only person who knows you more than I do seems to not have any good memories of you. No single good word about you either. Perhaps the bad times erased the good times you ever shared. But if fate and destiny are to be believed in, then if you two had not met, the twins and I would not have been born. So, I guess my feelings about that will remain an oxymoron.

My heart sank each time other children talked about their fathers. It always felt like they were bragging or making all those things up just to hurt me. Angela used to wait by the gate for her dad to come back from work every day, and I waited with her. It was their little tradition and they never broke it for anything. The look on his face was priceless when he saw her. She would run into his open arms as fast as she could, and he would pick her up and give her warm hugs and kisses on the forehead. Little fatherless me then walked besides them, third wheeling. Once in a while he would give me a pat on the head just to make me feel included.

While waiting with Angela, I secretly waited for you also. I hoped you would come home so we could have our own magical moment. The first few weeks after your departure were the worst, because with no clear explanation of your whereabouts I stayed in the hope and belief that you would one day walk through the door and we would continue with life. Five-year-old me could not read the clock, but she knew time. She knew when her father ought to come home so she could sit on his lap. Yet I never got another glimpse of you.

I remember debating, back in high school, that there should be a law that binds men to be present in their children's lives beyond financial maintenance, which most – including yourself, did not even cover. I had my 'facts' right; "every child deserves present parents no matter the circumstance", I argued. I maintained that for every child a man has, adequate time should be allocated for him to be with that child. Every child is conceived by two people for a reason, because that is the number of parents one needs to have. I was so sure of my standing and was hoping they would one day become the law so that I could also have 'my dad stories', I won the debate but not the case. I often laugh at that young teenage me, and how that line of thinking that people are liable to you more than they want to be, messed up how I viewed relationships too. I am glad I know better now.

I could write a book but here's the thing, I made peace with your abandoning us as a family. After being angry most of the time, pushing people away, bleeding on the people who did not hurt me; I healed. It helped build my character and life expectations. More than anything I am writing to tell you to never try making contact with me. I know Uncle Tom gave you our contact details, the same way he gave us yours and he might even push for reconciliation…please DO NOT!!! They say 'when the past calls don't answer, unless you have a pension plan' no one needs any pension from you so I will not be taking any calls. Needless to say, everyone at home considers you dead, and we find it easier to cope that way. Do not expect me or anyone else at your funeral or death bed either. That is reserved for close friends and family; we are neither.

I hate how I had to sneak out to go to the library lest mother be triggered. Most of my classmates thought I lived with grandma since she attended to all of my and the twins' school business. She was all I talked about when we were talking about our mothers. Consultations, prize giving days even school meetings it was all grandma. I was crashed every time I brought my report book home and my own mother was not as thrilled as my class teacher or grandma. Even though the twins are two years older than me, I had to mother them from as early as the age of twelve, cooking for them and ironing their uniforms when mother was not in the mood and could not be bothered. I resent how those days tore me apart, and that is all on you! I hope it makes you proud of yourself.

Now that I have academic pursuits of my own, it puzzles me how pursuing your academic enquiry was the reason you left your family. Was that really the reason? Now I have mother to deal with, always indirectly telling me not to be 'too academic' as she puts it. She does not talk much yet the moment I mention attaining a PhD she becomes the most vocal person ever. Whatever good and revolutionary developments education does for individuals and their communities, she could never acknowledge it. For her it always boils down to it destroying lives. I have to defend my academic life on a daily basis, thanks to you. The worst is how that part of me reminds her of you, that could explain why she and I were never close, you made me fix something I did not break!

I have no idea how to sign this off, so here it is…

Writing this letter proved more gruelling than I had predicted. A lot of emotions were in the room, yet I had to compose myself and say my truth. I also struggled with whether or not I wanted to see him again and if denying him access to me meant that I hadn't forgiven. Thankfully, I had learnt along the way that forgiving and forgetting does not necessarily mean letting someone back in your life. It is perfectly fine to love people from afar. After another long debate with myself over either sending the letter or burning it, I sent it. A response did come, but I did not read it. I did not want to. After a life of being kind and treading carefully around my mother, it felt good being self-centred. Doing that which only served for a change was needed. The blissful moment of burning that sealed letter was bonus therapy.

Next letter was to my mother. It felt uncanny writing to someone who was in the next room but I had found my salvation in writing and so I was going to harness that command as much as I could. This time it was different though, I had to be careful with what I wrote. Further breaking her was not part of the plan, I loved her, adored her too much to do that. I was only attempting to pave the way for a better relationship and express the countless things that were heavy on my heart for the longest time. Not forgetting that I was still living in her house, so I had to tread carefully if I wanted to keep the roof over my head.

Dear mother.

I love you! Phew, you have no idea how much I have yearned to say this to you in person, yet opportunity never avails itself. Between affection not being a norm in our culture and us being two strangers living under the same roof, 'I love you' did not find itself in the few conversations we have had. I find it odd how love has to be constantly inferred than deliberately expressed and verbalised. I am so relieved to have finally said it and I hope to hear it back. In our coexistence of less talk and presence, I understand and appreciate what you have done for us as a family, parts of you that you had to give up just so we could be.

I am sorry for the pain you have endured in life. Raising three children on your own could not have been easy. Explaining yourself when people asked about your marital status, which our society sadly places so much significance on must have been no easy feat. I cannot imagine how painful that must have been for you, reliving the abandonment and betrayal all over again. I am sorry you didn't have a support system to help you through the pain. I so wish we could offer each other more comfort than just 'be strong, you will be fine with time' as a people.

I wish you and I could talk more. I hope it's not too late for that because I would love to be able to have 'I can't wait to tell mother about this' moments like my friends do. Surely, I cannot miss out on those and daddy stories too, with you at least, we can still amend that part. Having to tell grandma I had period cramps so she could tell you and you would in turn buy me painkillers and place them on my dressing table is not exactly the kind of story I want to tell my children about my own mother or the memories of you I want to have. Or how I had better relations with my childhood nanny than with you. Please understand me here, I am not trying to trivialise what you have been through that hardened you and confined you to your cocoon. I only wish you the courage and strength to work through it and experience life to its full. To be able to get over the past hurt and look forward to tomorrow. I have not seen that glow of life in your eyes for the longest time and that tears my heart apart. Nothing seems to move you anymore, whether in the positive or the negative and that breaks me. I have gone on for too long thinking I am strong enough and can survive without a stronger bond with you, but a girl will always need her mother. I yearn for deep conversations with you, evening conversations by the veranda while eating frozen yoghurt, talking about everything and anything.

I wait for that day when we can finally sit and talk. Embrace and weep in each other's arms and allow ourselves to be vulnerable. For when I can bring my children here and they have fun times with their grandmother. Again, I love you and thank you for all the sacrifices you have made for us, even though it meant sacrificing yourself in the process.

Joanne

Again, I battled with whether or not to slide it under her door, put it on the table with the other mail or simply tear it up and consider having written it down as therapy enough. But she mattered more to me than her former husband and she needed to hear me, even if it was through a letter. I wanted to be heard but more importantly to get through to her and have a relationship with her. I was just twenty-two years old at that time, trying to figure myself out and definitely not ready to move out. What if she had got angry and kicked me out of her house? Stopped paying my university tuition? A picture would constantly play in my head of her saying something along the lines of the little attachment salary I was getting made me feel like an adult. I didn't rule out being snubbed either, it was possible for her to just read and pretend like nothing had happened and my already fragile heart was not ready for that. So, it took me over a week to decide, I drew strength from the fact that I had gone for so long in silence so I could survive it again. But the unpredictability of life and death is the one that made me slide it under her bedroom door one morning as we left for work. Took her three whole days to knock on my door and hug me soon as I opened the door. The three days were torturous though. The awkward silences every moment we were in the same space, I was even considering taking the bus to work just to have less encounters with my own mother. Hence that deep embrace by the door meant the world to me, and I later learnt to her too.

The walls of Jericho did tumble down on that day.

We talked! And it felt so surreal! I had no recollection of mother sitting on my bed like this before this day. Actually, it had been years since she had been in my room, and the times I remember she had been there to make sure I was keeping it clean or telling me to keep the noise down. Hell, the woman did not even help me with packing when I was going away to boarding school or university! So, you can imagine what this day meant for me. Of course, it was not on some autopilot smooth sail. This was an uncharted territory, so we took it a day at a time. It however gave me more reason to write to my future daughter because I did not want this awkward situation. I did not want to meet my daughter when she was twenty-two yet we were staying under the same roof.

P.S. We did get to share frozen yoghurt by the veranda, and we both savoured every moment.

***

I had often wondered how I would fare as a parent and not having had the best of parents did not make it any easier. My dad was the first man to abandon and walk out on me at the age of five, not an easy thing to forget, considering the countless months I spent hoping he would somehow show up and everything would be normal again; him, mother, my twin brothers and I. Our perfect little family. Well, he never showed up; leaving me with my now angry and bitter mother. A mother whose view on relationships was always some version of 'it will end in tears'. She lost so much faith in human relationships and general decency. A mother who was so sceptical of anyone showing her affection, even us her children.

If my culture believed in mental health conditions prior to the state of being labelled a mad man or woman, I am sure she would have been clinically diagnosed with a couple of them, but she was given the 'it will pass' line as comfort and that was it. Mother would always lament that it would have been better if her man had left her for ten other women than books. It remained unconceivable for her how she had failed as a woman to make a man lose interest in women and turn to academics. She blamed herself for it. Refused to admit how she had noticed how withdrawn and unattached to everyday life and companionship. But she disregarded that because he was a nice guy and she felt she was getting past her prime years and the biological clock was not on her side. She got a nice husband, he remained nice but grew unhappy each day he spent confined to family life. Each day he spent away from digging up old bones and carbon dating them, he resented us!

So, with such parentage you can imagine how sceptical I was about the kind of mother I would be. While I did not want to give someone else the kind of childhood I had, I had no idea what an ideal one would be like. The only other family setting I knew, besides the neighbours, was at grandma's where we used to go during school holidays. She became the closest person I had to a mother while Mike and Brandon, my older twin brothers, had male figures in my uncles. They made sure to make up for the absence of our father as did grandma with me. All this, however, came to a halt when uncle Prince was arrested for selling alcohol without a licence and mother stopped us from visiting grandma.

In her defence, mother said she had enough to deal with than have us stay with a lawbreaker and adopt his bad ways. We once again were confined to our little home in a quiet low-density suburb of Burnside where we only watched news and gospel channels because everything else was going to distract us and bring the demons of our father upon us. Mike and Brandon had each other for company and I was left to find solace in books. You can imagine what that did to my mother! I read everything that was in sight and with that I grew to love words. How they could create an entire world from nothingness, how they could express things from the heart of hearts! Perhaps if I had a sister or mother to talk to, then the words would not have been piling up in my head as they did. I had so much to say with no one to say it to. My home life also made me withdraw from people, so it took me a very long while before I could have real close friends.

The thought of being a good mother kept bothering me though, I kept having scenarios in my head of how it would be like to be someone's mother, especially to a daughter. Was I going to be emotionally available to her? How was I to know I was doing the right thing? What would happen if I failed her? What if I ended up as one of those mothers who are labelled as toxic or undeserving of any children? While burying myself in books I stumbled upon numerous series of 'letter to my younger or older self'. The idea fascinated me and that is when I decided to write to my daughter. If I never got to have one, then hopefully some lucky girl somewhere would stumble upon my journal and harvest from it. I had found a way to take someone else through my life step by step; my triumphs, mistakes, crushes, successes, first heartbreak, whore phase, dates; you name it. Not in any particular order of course, life is not that mechanical. Before I could be a mother to you though, I needed to address my own parents. I had to deal with what they put me through, let them know how I felt. This might as well serve as my first advice to you, address things that bother you, whatever the source.

To my sweet little mini me.

I do not know when you will come into my world, but I promise that when you do, I will be the best possible mother to you and I cannot wait for that day. I am writing you this letter and hope it will be one of your most treasured possessions. This is my way of sharing my views and experiences with you, to tell you things I wish I had known earlier on in life, so we could call this giving you a head start. It is my desire that by so doing, you can avoid the wrong turns I took in life myself. Though of course, you are entitled to your own fair share of mistakes, as I believe you can only learn so much from other people's mistakes, than your own. I might mumble and my words be jumbled up here and there, but I hope you get the gist of it, and feel the love with which I wrote it. I will love you like you are all I have. I will give you warm hugs and kisses as often as I can. I promise to always be there for you, even at 3 am when you don't feel like sleeping.

In a world where you can be anything; choose to be kind, be polite, be courteous, be generous and all the nice gestures that spice up and sweeten life. Help that old granny carry her groceries to her house or the taxi. Don't listen to toothpaste commercials, the best smile comes from deep within you as an extension of your heart to the receiver. Give, not because you have too much or are no longer in need of something, but because the next person needs it more. Respect everyone and approach them as equals. Respect those in authority. Greet the janitor, the fuel attendant, the person sitting next to you on the bus; courtesy should not be a rare sight. Take some time to give back. Volunteer at a home or organisation that speaks to your heart. Make dinner for an old couple down the street once in a while and just spend time with them. Take up some girls under your wing and mentor them. These things may seem small or futile but trust me when I say they go a long way in making the world a better place.

Punctuality shows respect for time, self and others; so does keeping promises.

I reckon it is best you hear this from me, darling, you will get heartbroken a couple of times in your lifetime and that is an inevitable part of life. I will hold your hand through it and buy you a tub of ice cream, hoping you will not be lactose intolerant. Your first crush might not notice you and you will feel like the world is ending-normal feeling, but it will only be getting started. That boy who gives you butterflies in the stomach will kiss another girl and crash your world. No need to rush getting into the dating pool, it can be a bit too intricate for your gentle soul. But when you do start dating, love whoever you're with for who they are not what they are or have. When you genuinely love and care for someone you argue peacefully, you do not get to throw ugly words at each other because your concern is to be heard and find a solution than winning the fight. And this will also influence you not airing your dirty laundry after a break up because even if the relationship did not work out, you still have some form of respect for each other. Enter a relationship as a complete person seeking companionship not completion. Have your own set of principles and beliefs and not be defined by every relationship you have been in. Coming in as a whole being means you are not a chameleon, changing colour with every relationship as you let it define you.

While we are on that topic, getting attention from older men in your teenage years does not make you special or hot. Even in your adulthood why should you be with a man who felt the pinch of Zimbabwe's bearer's cheques era? It simply means they are predators and you are their prey. They are weak predators who want you to feed their egos and make them feel special. They are too shallow to be suitors for their age mates, so they prey on impressionable young girls who are still finding their feet in the world. Girls whose belief system hasn't solidified and are bound to believe anything, and in this case; that women are subservient to men and anything else that suits their needs. They cannot stand a chance with women in their age range because they lack depth, which any woman should seek in a man. Stay away from them. They will try and lure you with material things, and whatever is fashionable during your time. While feeding your pretty young mind with their delusional ideas of the world which your innocent mind may want to take as gospel truth. These are the men who do not want to see their daughters dating anyone because they think every man is like them and it sends shivers up their spines. They would kill anyone they think is doing the evil they do to other people's daughters. Be wary of such evil men.

Career path is an important part of your adult life and I will let you decide on your own. This does not mean I do not have dreams for you, but it is the field of work you will be stuck with for the rest of your life and I would not have you going to a job you hate every day until you are 65, simply because that's what I, or someone else, wanted. It is therefore my wish that you will choose a career that is fulfilling and rewarding. The kind of job that will have you look forward to Monday on a Friday evening. A place where you can put your passion into and enjoy every moment of it. And it is my prayer that you may excel in it and surpass my and anyone's expectations. I will do my utmost in nurturing the talents I see in you, but if it suffocates you please communicate, and I will stop because this is about you not me. I am only here to be your mother and guide you through life but not live vicariously through you. You are your own person, daughter dearest.

That being said, I will make you read! From a very early age too. I will make it look like the coolest thing on earth and you will love it. That is one of the many things my grandmother taught me well and it unfortunately drove a wedge between my mother and I. We were already distant, so I do not regret my insatiable love for books, it took me through my darkest hours. Grandma was so gentle and simplistic in her teaching, it became the one thing I held on to when all else was falling apart. Reading will open up the world of possibilities for you and broaden your imagination. It will take you to places some think are impossible. You will gain different perspectives in life as you will be seeing the world through other people's eyes and experiences. I always say, 'travel as much as you can but if you can't afford it, books will take you there'. Books will teach you about other cultures and religions which will help influence your life and most importantly make you impartial and open minded. It will remind you that diversity makes the world beautiful and that if you want to be understood and accepted you should also be ready to extend the same. On that note, I have started a mini library for you; from nursery picture books to texts that have influenced and inspired my very being.

Allow me to talk about this controversial one; whore phase. Well this is defined and viewed differently depending on the individual and their life orientation. While some people paint it badly and take it as a time where one sleeps around with multiple partners and just being promiscuous, the enlightened, understand that it is a time set aside for exploring the dating pool with no commitments. This is not exactly part of conventional mother-daughter conversations, but I feel it should be talked about, so I will. I see it as a time when one is on an experimental journey on the dating scene. This obviously implies you will not be in any committed relationship. It is so important that both those who do not go through it and those who do it wrong have sob stories. It is not mechanical and so I cannot say at what stage it will happen to you, what is important though is to do it right. Consciously getting into a whore phase means you prepare yourself mentally. Not all dates or casual relationships should result in sex, but if and when they do, be wise and safe! Explore contraception and find one that works for you. You certainly do not want to have a child with a guy whose last name you do not know. Or contract an STI when you were 'just having fun'. Wise ladies come out of the whore phase clearer on the kind of man they want, what turns them on in bed, the things they are willing to put up with and their deal breakers. I cannot possibly exhaust the benefits, but the important point is; go through it with an informed mind. If you don't, you might spend the rest of your life wondering what you missed out and you could have struck a better deal out there if you had given it a try.

Reflect! Practice reflecting on your daily activities. That way you can account for how you used your time and help you to prioritise the important things in life. Reflect on your day, week, month, year and so forth. When you regularly go through self-reflection you become more self-aware and self-regulatory. When you are self-aware you will be on your road to emotional intelligence and understanding the important facets of your life like your strengths, weaknesses, goals, values, principles and what drives you. That then helps you to be in control of your actions, behaviours, emotions and impulses. You might as well add meditation to your daily routines, its fruits are countless. Make working out part of your daily routine too. Not only does it have mass benefits for your body, but it will make you feel good about yourself and give you a good nights' sleep. Do it with friends whenever possible, life is more fun that way and they will also serve as your accountability partners.

One thing I learnt late in life; like-minded female friends rock! I did not know this for a while myself but when I did, my life was completely changed. From hanging out with the boys to 'I can do anything for my newfound sisters'. They become exactly that, sisters you choose for yourself. My female friends helped me through my darkest days by just being there and saying all the right things – or laughing away things together. Because your life experiences are similar it is easier for you to connect and go through life together. They will be a fortress you can always run to, more so concerning women specific issues. Your male friends might be great, but do not think they will give up male privileges that come with patriarchy for you. But your sisters who have long suffered at the hands of patriarchy will be right by your side. One of my few regrets was giving my time and attention to friendships with people I did not see with in the future, sadly I was just filling a void then.

It is perfectly ok to be hated for the things you believe in and you should own it. If you challenge a status quo, those who believe and benefit from it will not take it lying low. They will fight you tooth and nail, and you should be ready. People have been fighting for some causes from before I was born, and they are still at it and the lesson is; change does not always come easy but that is not reason enough to stop fighting. For centuries and decades people have emerged to fight patriarchy, racism, tribalism, homophobia, sexism, abuse of women and children among a whole lot of other causes. If they had given up because they did not instantly get the change they were seeking, then the world would have been a chaos. But with every victory, the fight continues. Bear that in mind and hold on till the very end. Put on your armour, give your best and avoid regrets of missed chances and opportunities. Be ready to get your hands dirty to get to where you want to because no change ever came from a place of comfort.

Life will not be all rosy, but even roses have thorns so that should be your first lesson. Things, people and seasons change for a reason, we cannot grow unless we are tried. If you see yourself getting up and continuing on a path after a fall, then that is your path. You will face hate, betrayal, opposition, setbacks and best believe everyone has their own portion of those. Some days will just be unexplainably gloomy while others will be sunshine and roses. All you have to do is navigate through them. Even I may not be the best mother at times. I will do and say things that will break your heart, not because I hate you but because we see things differently. Life's dark side has nothing to do with your deserving it, it is just nature striking its balance. But whatever life throws at you, strike back with thrice the energy and emerge even stronger.

The first men to say they love you will be your father and brothers. I will make it family tradition that they pull your chair, open doors for you and extend all gentlemanly courtesy and treatment as humanly, fatherly and brotherly as possible. That way you won't think a man opening a door for you makes him your soulmate but rather a decent human being. You will not be blown away by simple gestures because you will be standing on a stable and firm foundation from which that is just bare minimum. More importantly, I want you to be surrounded by men who respect women so that when you go out there you will not settle for less.

You will be fully aware of what a decent man is capable of, in whatever relations, meaning you will know when you are not being treated well, and how to act accordingly. With your brothers and father showing you so much love and respect, telling you how much they love you; a 'I love you beautiful' from a boy will not give you wobbly knees. My having sons and a husband who respect women will not only serve us, but the entire gender as well. In my pursuits for women to be born into a beautiful world that is safe for them, I have to help build the ideal men whenever and whenever I can. Speaking of siblings, I will take utmost caution to do away with favouritism and comparing, I have seen it break the strongest of people and I would not want to do that to any of my children.

Never assume or act like you are better than the next person because you are not, we are just different pieces to the same puzzle. The world has developed a quota system and women are made to compete to fight for a quota which is not even a quarter of anything. In a bid to fulfil that quota we are bound to try and trample on others and think we are better than the next person, because we made it into the quota. Wherever life takes you though, always remember that as many as we are in the world, we all need each other to have a contribution to make, hence none is better than the other. The world does not know how to deal with women as a united force and so it has always been trying to divide us. Driving wedges between us so that they will not have to fight us much but watch from the terraces as we tear each other apart. Be wary of people and systems that promote that; fight to stay away from them. Your job is to help your sisters up when they are down, help them clean up after they pass through muddy waters and fix their crowns. We are better off united than acting like alpha females. Be a sister's keeper!

Guard yourself jealously. That includes the kind of friends you surround yourself with as they will have an influence on how you see the world and what you do on a daily basis. Always be alert on the literature and media you consume, they also have an impact on your mind and attitude towards life. If it is not positive or constructive then maybe you should not be saying it! Words have the power to make or break both the hearer and the utterer; trust me when I say, there is no joy in spoiling someone's moment or life with words you should not even be thinking about. And your habitual thinking patterns forms a large part of who you are, including the energies and people you attract in your life. There are few books on the power of attraction and thinking patterns in your library, make use of them.

I cannot cover all the areas of life, can I? But when they do arise along the way I will be here, ready to put on my supermom suit. I will be there when you need me. I wish you the best life can offer. I promise to love you with my all and always be there for you. Live your life to the full without hurting others. A mind that questions things has room for growth and innovation.

P.S. Remind me to give you the missing page on your 20th birthday, wink wink.

I love you, always

Your super-mummy

***

It took me close to three years to finish writing this letter. Sometimes I would go for months on end without writing anything. Next thing I would be on a writing spree, for weeks, inspiration does that. Of course, a lot was deleted and edited along the way, I also had to make peace with the fact that I could never be exhaustive. The page on whore phase was withheld for a while, even though our sex education talks started when she was twelve. It certainly is not the kind of content to give to a girl on her 16th birthday, lest she misquotes me. I had the pleasure to discuss some of the topics with my mother, usually during our regular frozen yoghurt chill outs.

Exactly three weeks after signing off this letter, I held perfection in my own hands. The product of my love with my college sweetheart. My little girl with ten fingers and ten toes, that one person I was willing to do anything for…

Naila – the successful one.

Finally, I cried

I did not cry when my mother died! Whenever I say this, I feel myself sounding like Tambu from Tsitsi Dangarembwa's Nervous Conditions and that makes me feel guilty. "I was not sorry when my brother died," she says. But of course, we are different. Tambu lost her eldest brother, Nhamo, with whom she was estranged, long before his untimely death. Nhamo, was the kind of character one would love to hate-hate, a chauvinist who looked down on women, with an exaggerated ego; to be honest, there is nothing positive to say about him. So, when he died of mumps, Tambu clearly states how she was not sorry he had died. Instead, Tambu was sorry for her mother who was devastated by losing a son, and was not shy to own up to her callousness. The last part should inform you why I feel guilty for saying I did not cry when my mother died, because she was nothing like Nhamo. My mother remains one of the gentlest souls I will ever know; kind, true and wise. While Tambu was not sorry, I just did not cry. I acknowledged that I had lost a mother, I just failed to weep as expected. At the tender age of eleven I understood death and its implications, understood how life was to change after the funeral, but I just did not bring myself to break a tear. Being the youngest child; family and neighbours were worried about me and kept checking on me to see if I was 'fine', whatever their definition of fine was.

Distinctly, the day before her burial stands out the most for me, being the last time mum's body was to spend the night at home. It is a teary moment at every funeral as everything draws closer to the final day and the ultimate reality kicks in. So here we were, standing by the gate as the hearse brought her body in. Word had already arrived that the hearse was almost home, a few minutes away. In that moment, everything came to a halt as everyone including the community, friends and family stood by the gate in wait. It was almost theatrical, if you ask me. Now that I think of it, I wonder how word had reached us at home that the hearse was minutes away. Back in the day mobile phones, or should I say phones in general were for the elite few, but either way the coordination still happened. Everyone left what they were doing and waited. At the sight of the hearse, people broke into tears. I remember my siblings sobbing as pain overtook them. They each had someone holding them, as I was also in the embrace of a cousin sister I had only met during the funeral. Best believe she had fortified herself for my sobbing or even fainting, grief does that to other people. But there I was in the hands of one who was a stranger days ago, the stranger waiting for my emotional breakdown that did not come. I watched as events unfolded like a fly on the wall, untouched by the situation. I would later often think of what was going through my cousin sister's mind in that very moment, when I did not weep or throw myself to the ground. Something was not right, but again, one should not confuse embracing the deceased's children for fifteen minutes for care. I do not quite remember if she sat with me through the evening church service.

One thing I do remember is that I was never hungry throughout the wake. Somehow people made sure my siblings and I were well fed. I was asked if I had eaten much more than how I was doing. Culturally, food plays a significant role in bringing people together and there are a couple of proverbs that speak to that. In this instance, I assumed it worked as comfort eating. *Make sure her children eat enough so they will not have to think of their dead mother much, so that it lessens the anguish they're going through.* There is a saying, about how a child never goes hungry during their mother's funeral, *nherera inoguta musi wafa mai vayo*, which is open to interpretation. While some use it to refer to how mourners keep the children fed, others translate it to mean how the welfare of the children is obscure as the mother who had been keeping the household together is gone. Whatever the choice of interpretation one adopts, they all lead to a toxic cultural trait with little to no provision for children who just lost a parent. There is so much done to make them forget or ignore their pain and sudden reality altogether.

This is by no means a blame game either. Grief is never an easy subject to deal with, and it is a delicate subject especially when children are involved. People grieve differently and in grief they usually project their experiences to the next person. If I had cried uncontrollably my cousin sister would have probably said something along the lines of 'do not cry, she is in a better place now'. Others say something similar, 'stop crying so much or else the deceased's spirit will not be at rest'. I have never understood the reasoning behind such a statement, and the worst is it has been used on me before on a different occasion, but as a child still. Looking back, I do not remember my own father talking to me about mum's passing away. I am not sure what I wanted him to say or if there was anything to say either, but I believe it was difficult for him too to talk about it and he also had no idea how to, so after the funeral we just 'went back to normal' minus mum. He must have operated on the basis that the children knew their mother was gone and talking about it would not change anything. Subsequently, I slowly withdrew from social circles and was eventually closed in a cocoon, constantly building the Great Wall of China around myself, which only a few managed to get past. The underlying fact I had to face and accept later in life was that my subconscious mind did not trust anyone to stay long enough, and the most dangerous thought pattern I developed over the years was that, if I had managed to live without my mother, then I could do without people. From a loud, happy and welcoming little girl I turned into a quiet, shy, rude and lonely child; but who was watching?

***

The night my mother died haunted my childhood. One moment we were going to sleep, and everyone was in good health; well to an extent at least, then in the dead of the night I was woken up to go and sleep in a wooden cabin that was detached from the house. The adults had to 'protect' me from what had just happened and the events that soon followed. I do not remember being told straight up that my mother had passed on, I just inferred it until the next morning. The way the elders present who included my grandmother, sisters, my father and a cousin sister; were all over the place as soon as they realised mum was gone. Being a light sleeper, I was up already and heard enough to convince me something was wrong. After spending two years of my young life watching my mother battling with a cardiovascular disease, the worst registered in my mind, but I quickly went into denial. Given the number of times she had been admitted into hospital and still managed to come back home, I grew hopeful she would live long enough to see my children. Each time she emerged stronger, so did my faith in understanding that she was a fighter and would make it and live longer. In that moment between her passing and my being removed from the scene, so many scenarios had played in my head, but I still refused to accept my fate. In the wooden cabin I stayed awake for as long as I could, trying to decipher the events around me yet one thing was central; denial. I kept convincing myself that she was still alive, and I remember even praying that God keeps her alive; but I was too late.

In the two years between her diagnosis and passing away, life had been a rollercoaster ride. She would fall ill to the point of being admitted in hospital. The first hospital admission took its toll on me. With each passing day and the whole family avoiding talking about her illness, I had prepared myself for the worst. I was prepared to receive the bad news at every waking moment. Every day I walked home from school expecting to find the customary red cloth tied to the gate. Sometimes I imagined the red cloth flying past our gate, to mock our loss. But for two years it never came. For two years the family's and her life changed, those two years however gave me confidence that one day she would stop the hospital consultations and admissions and be my lively and bubbly mother. As her medical condition advanced, she had a special diet which required her to consume the least possible oil and salt in her food, and that changed my life for good also. Between sympathising with mummy dearest and wanting to enjoy what I deemed privileges at the time, my brother and I joined her in her diet. To date, I still use very little salt and oil in my cooking. 'Salt killed my mother' I often said. Bad days were a different story, not caring about what I ate, stating how special diets failed to save my mother. After calming down, I would go back to the diet. It meant more than just watching my diet, because with diet change mum and I bonded. My holding on to it meant keeping a part of her with me, staying true to our special little tradition.

In her two years of being ill, mum would recover and take up her role of the invincible woman she was; keeping the household together, plaiting African threading on my hair every other weekend, attending school prize giving days where I always scooped prizes and watched her beam with pride. The last prize giving day, I received a prize that was a few weeks before her passing away when we closed schools for the August school holidays. Fortunately, it was a small ceremony of names being called out during assembly and being handed our tokens with no parents' present. That meant I did not feel the void created by her absence. I recall not showing her my report book because for the first time in my five years of primary school, I had taken position three in my class. I made up a story of why I had not been given the report card with the others knowing fully well that I had hidden it among my books. I could not let my mother see my failure and break her heart; I had no clue that this would be my last time in the top three until I redeemed myself at the final grade seven exam, only to relapse again.

The mind is a dangerous place, and grief worsens the situation. Life would have been better if I was good at expressing the grief, but vulnerability was not part of my DNA. My mum's passing away was not the first death in the family, because we had lost my younger sister a year earlier. My recollection of those events is vague, which one might attribute to the denial and shock we have established as a coping mechanism for loss. It is funny how I only remember when the wounds were healing as a family. We calculated my sister's age to have been one year two months two weeks and two days, and we somehow managed to make jokes around that. And that it was the month of August. And a year later the same month claimed my mother. Your guess is right, I developed deep seated trepidation for the month of August. Again, we fooled around about who would die the next August. I was not sure about the others, but thoughts of a possible death stayed with and petrified me. I could not bear the thought of losing anyone else. It undeniably heightened as we approached the following August. With no family member ill at the time, scenarios kept playing in my head of what could possibly happen and to who. That is an eventuality I was never ready for, and in my fear of going through more grief I would foolishly pray that if it were a family plague then rather it be me, because the family still needed everyone else. Thankfully, August turned out to be a mere coincidence and we were all safe; but the thoughts would sometimes visit me, since misery loves company. In all that grief, I still did not shed a tear.

***

The day I eventually cried was no different from any other, but one can only bottle up such strong feelings for so long. I was a mobile ticking bomb and it took one of the most unexpected events to make me explode. Before that day, I had pushed away people I should have drawn closer. I had bled on countless people who had not hurt me. I had shunned away commitment and happiness as my heart kept reminding me how people would eventually leave. After breeding all these unhealthy and self-destructive traits over many years, I eventually gave in during a rehearsal. Yes, a theatre play rehearsal during my second year of my undergraduate studies, but it was not as dramatic as you might want to think. Let me let you in on a secret.

Screen and stage performers have a couple of techniques to summon emotions and feelings, and since I was doing theatre studies, I had some up my sleeves. Emotional memory is my favourite of them all for its practicality, authenticity and because it led me to my salvation. Emotional memory is when a performer draws emotions from a past similar event or one that evoked the required memory. So here I was playing the bereaved girlfriend whose boyfriend committed suicide while they were not on speaking terms. The mixture of guilt and grief makes her whimper uncontrollably by his grave. In the first stages of rehearsal I would playfully promise that when the time was right, I would summon my crying skills, which I frankly did not possess, but no one knew that. Anyone who has undertaken acting knows how no two rehearsals or performances are the same, and shockingly how some of the best performances will not make it out of the rehearsal room. So was the case with my crying.

On this day, I was in a very good mood and felt energetic. I had promised myself to give my all. As a co-writer, co-director and co-producer I had to execute my part and lead by example so that I may demand the same from the others. I looked for emotions from all of life's pitfalls and none matched the scene intensity. The one matching memory I did not want to temper with was the only one that was going to get me there. So, I played with the memories through the happy times, the fights and the mourning scene awaited. With some time to myself backstage while another scene was taking place, I bravely allowed myself to soak in the memories of eleven years back. The thoughts came streaming like fresh ones and suddenly the grief and tears came. When it was time for me to get on stage, I was ready for the performance. I dragged myself from the tabs to where the grave was set and the atmosphere had changed, it was electrifying. From the playful and never serious Natsai that everyone was used to during rehearsal, to this deranged girl that could draw any audience member to jump on stage and console her.

With a combination of what ifs and memories of yesteryear, the emotions escalated. From 'I need this to pass my module', to picturing my mother in her coffin and how peaceful she had looked and the thoughts of the loss I had consequently incurred. I was already in tears when I eventually got to the wooden cross that signified the grave. Real emotions can be felt in the atmosphere and the other cast and crew members fell silent. I got to the grave, knelt and wept my heart out. The weeping that had been expected of me the day before and during my mother's burial happened on that wooden floored stage to a smaller crowd. I even cried for not crying during my mother's funeral. On that day, I set free the eleven-year-old me that had bottled up her emotions all those years ago. She made peace with her fate and allowed herself to be vulnerable. After what seemed like an eternity, I calmed myself down as the character I was playing was expected to and left the stage. My friends were both amazed and amused, with no understanding of what had just taken place. On enquiry of how I had transformed like that, my reply was 'emotional memory' without divulging more. Rehearsal was done, but I was not.

We said our goodbyes and walked to our different hostels to retire for the day. Upon getting to my room I put my stuff away, washed off the rehearsal sweat and continued where I had left off. Suffice to say I woke up on a wet pillow and with a confused roommate. I went through all the memories of the two years succeeding mum's death, acknowledged and bemoaned them. I also wept for the moments when I had missed her but was unable to tell anyone about it. For the times I had wished she had been alive to hold my hand, to assure me tomorrow would be a brighter day, to randomly tell me I was beautiful. I wailed for the words I wished I had heard from her than anyone else, because some things would have sounded better if she had

been the one saying them. The thoughts of how different life w
ould have been had she been alive to put me to sleep that night, as I let tears roll freely from my eyes onto my fluffy baby blue pillow.

The following day I was a changed person, I felt indestructible. A weight of eleven years had been lifted off my shoulders, one I had carried for half my life. My mind and my heart saw the world differently and clearer. I accepted how expecting everyone to leave was only destroying me and hindering me from experiencing life in its fullest. In that moment, I acknowledged how in my hurt I had hurt others, so I promised myself to work it. That morning I reminded myself of the good woman mum was and how she would have wanted me to turn out to be. I also made peace with the fact that at times the pain is bound to hit differently and that it was okay to grieve in cycles. The important thing was to not lose myself in the sorrow. Sitting in that 12 m² university hostel room, I made a vow to live and be the daughter mum would be proud of, though I was fully aware that becoming half the woman she was, was going to be a huge task.

Spoiler alert: my final performance of the play was not as emotional as that rehearsal night; no two performances are the same, remember!

Edith Virima

Edith is a Zimbabwean-born writer and blogger who mostly writes for fun and to appreciate her creativity. She writes in between school runs and chasing after her active toddler. Her fictional story collection is mostly inspired by societal issues and the diversity in people's characters. This is her first published work and definitely not her last.

The promotion

His desk was full of paperwork. He had been faced with a tough decision throughout the week. "Head of Operations!" The title seemed small, but the job carried a heavy responsibility that came with huge benefits.

The banking industry was flourishing and the bank was becoming more profitable. It was imperative that they appoint a Head of Operations who was going to steer the bank to greater heights. Capital Bank had started as a very small bank with a few overseas and local investors. The bank now had six branches across Zimbabwe. Their offices were state of the art, nested at an affluent shopping mall catering for the rich and famous. George, the Chief Executive Officer for Capital Bank for the past ten years, had pondered on who to appoint based on qualifications, but he knew it was going to take more than qualifications. He also needed to consider experience and previous achievements, and above all someone who would not sabotage his plans for the company.

George was in his mid-forties, tall and well built. He was a witty, sharp-minded risk taker who had risen in the ranks. He was also involved in a number of underhand dealings that not only benefitted the bank, but him as well. He had been rather fortunate because no one had suspected him of dodgy dealings as he knew ways of cleaning up the audit trail. His background as an auditor had helped in that regard. On the outside, he was known to be a man of high integrity; and well respected in society where his company was heavily involved in Corporate Social Responsibility projects.

Just as he was thinking on which task to start with on that Friday morning, his phone rang.

"I am coming to your office!" the voice on the other end sounded very worried. "I need to tell you something very important." It was Sheilla, his colleague of many years. Sheilla was a very smart, competent and highly professional woman with many achievements under her belt. However, she was a no nonsense taker whose short stature and beauty fooled a few. She was one of the candidates George had been considering for the job. She had earned the bank an exceptional reputation as Head of Customer Experience by introducing a number of significant innovations. Her drive and resilient approach were qualities that George admired about her.

As he put the phone down, Sheilla flew open the door to George's office. "George, tell me what is this?" Sheilla was holding an A4 paper with a string of transactions trying to be as calm as possible. "How have we been transferring all this money to this unknown account without my knowledge?" She asked with a concerned look on her face. "All these transactions bypassed me. Only you and Keith authorised these transfers. This is a lot of money George. How could I not know anything about this?" Sheilla continued furiously.

She was frantic as she demanded an explanation from George. George paused for a moment. His face looked unsettled, "Listen Sheilla," he paused for a moment, "We did not bypass you on purpose, but we just needed time to make sure the plan we had was going to be successful."

Sheilla was furious. Annoyed and not convinced, Sheilla thought to herself, *Typical! Men can sometimes undermine you in order to get what they want, right or wrong.* Sheilla stared at George, waiting to hear his explanation.

Before George could say anything, the phone rang again. This time it was Keith, George's right hand man. Keith was a shrewd character in his thirties. He not only helped George with his corrupt dealings, but he was known for being sexist undermining women in the work place. George however trusted him because they had been friends before recruiting him to the bank a few years back. "Hi George, we have a problem." Keith sounded tense and in a panic. "I know!" George answered Keith trying to maintain his composure." Come to my office immediately."

Sheilla knew that George and Keith had a close friendship but unbeknown to George, Keith was actually a snake in the grass who could even betray his own friends to get what he wanted. Sheilla's heart was now racing. Whatever explanation George was brewing could never justify what she had stumbled upon. Were they stealing money from the bank or was this a practical joke? Sheilla asked herself. By this time, Sheilla's head was spinning; suddenly she felt an excruciating pain in her stomach. She tried to ignore the pain, but it felt as if a knife was ripping her insides apart. As tears of pain started streaming down her cheeks, she made an effort to hold them back but without much success. She immediately excused herself in a haste to avoid further humiliation. She ran out of the office, passing a puzzled Keith who was standing by the door. This pain was familiar to Sheilla. The doctor had warned her to take it easy. The moment Sheila entered the bathroom, she let out a loud scream and began sobbing uncontrollably. Looking down, she saw droplets of blood on the bathroom floor. She knew too well that she was having a miscarriage AGAIN. Her blood pressure levels had been very high over the past few days, but with the promotion looming, she had decided not to miss work, disregarding her doctor's caution to take some bed rest.

This would be her third miscarriage. Sitting in the bathroom in a pool of blood, she let out an irrepressible cry with a myriad of thoughts racing in through her mind.

Meanwhile, Keith and George sat in the office arguing over the matter of the exposed transactions. "Keith, you were supposed to clean those transactions before anyone found out!" yelled George. "This is a mess, that woman will take us down Keith!" George continued rather miffed. Keith just tapped his pen on the desk, deep in thought. "You know what, I am going to be forced to give Sheilla the promotion with the hope that she will not expose us.

Keith looked at George with a stern face, "Nooo George that is out of the question, Keith fumed. "I risked my reputation to help you siphon that money out of this company, so I deserve this promotion." The room was tense as both men pondered on a possible way out of this mess. It took some time for them to realise that Sheilla had been gone for a while now. George and Keith were the very executives that were at the helm of the company. They prided themselves in securing deals for the bank and growing the company through corrupt dealings which no one had been aware of until now. Now their secret was out. How were they going to get out of this sticky situation? Although he contemplated giving Sheilla the promotion, George knew it was a long shot, given that Sheilla was known for her integrity and clean record.

George paced up and down, and then looked out of his office window, which was on the eighth floor. He loved the beautiful view of the garden because it made him think clearer. He suddenly stopped and looked closely to his right at the parking lot. An ambulance had just parked and paramedics were rushing into the building. "Keith, an ambulance has just parked downstairs, a confused George uttered. They both rushed out of the office, only to realise that Sheilla was on the stretcher bed being rushed to hospital. Fadzai, the receptionist, was standing in the passage looking horrified. "What happened, Keith asked a clearly shocked Fadzai.

"I found Sheilla fainted in the bathroom then I called the ambulance!" Fadzai replied. By this time, most people had stopped working and were standing in the passage trying to make sense of what had happened to Sheilla.

As the ambulance sirened its way to the hospital, a heavy silence surrounded the office with some murmuring what could only be words of prayer for their colleague. Fadzai had called Sheilla's husband and was also on his way to the hospital.

George went back to the office, completed the paperwork for the promotion. He put in Keith's name and forwarded it to HR. Keith cleaned the transactions that had been exposed by Sheilla and made sure there was absolutely no audit trail or any evidence that could implicate them of their schemes. Sheilla had been passed for the promotion though George knew she deserved it more than Keith.

Meanwhile, Sheilla was resuscitated at the hospital. It was confirmed that she had once again had a miscarriage due to Pre-eclampsia. Two weeks passed with Sheilla still battling the loss of her pregnancy. Her pain was unbearable. Her marriage was on the brink of collapse as her husband accused her of putting her job first and not prioritising starting a family.

A month later, a bruised Sheilla returned to the office. Without any doubt, she knew that George had passed her for the promotion and awarded it to Keith. However, she had sacrificed a lot over the past years and was determined not to go down without a fight. Sheilla had contemplated her decision to play dirty too, over and over again. As much as it daunted her, she did not care anymore. It is true what they say, that hell hath no fury like a woman scorned. She sat down and sadly looked at the job title written on the wooden plank on her desk. It had not changed over the last five years no matter how hard she had worked. For how long was she going to allow men to undermine her abilities whilst they used every trick in the book to get ahead? She thought to herself. Her trembling hand picked up the phone and dialled his line.

"George, may you please come to my office if you have a minute?" She asked.

"Sure, no problem!" a self-assured George answered from the other end. As she heard George's footsteps, she almost changed her mind. An envelope with the pictures was in her hands. She knew this would destroy George, but she convinced herself that she was merely a victim and bearer of the truth. George walked into her office, trying by all means to show sympathy for Sheilla who he was seeing for the first time since breaking the news about the promotion to her. Before he could sit down, Sheilla handed him the envelope. George was a little taken aback. He thought Sheilla had kept records of their transactions but he was confident they were not enough to implicate them in any way. He opened the envelope in a huff. Nothing could have prepared him for what he saw. His face turned blue as he flipped through the collection of pictures. Were his eyes deceiving him? He wondered. He felt a lump in his throat as his anger and disgust was flaring up. Perhaps he was dreaming but it was clear, Keith his trusted friend and right hand man was having an affair with his wife. Judging from the pictures, this had been going on for some time.

George did not utter a word, and all his senses numbed. The thought of Keith with his wife sent shivers down his spine. George had always joked with him that his secret affairs would end him in trouble eventually. Sheilla did not know what to say next, and neither did he. George took the envelope in silence and returned to his office. He looked out of his office window, where the serenity of the garden beckoned. Convinced he had found the solution to his quandary, George locked his office door then headed straight for the window.

The marriage

Tendai looked again at her sister in awe and asked, "Did you just order a three tier cake for this event Tapi? What will people say? I seriously don't understand this so called modern day. You have already spent too much money on this event and it's not even a wedding!" Tendai was looking at the African themed cake on Tapiwa's phone.

"That may as well pass for a wedding cake." Tendai continued.

"Oh, my dear sister, get with the times, we now call it The Traditional Wedding!" Tapiwa replied with excitement.

"Is that so? What happened to calling it *marooro*? You have spent way too much money on catering, decor, bridesmaids, matching attires, photography, what next...a traditional honeymoon? You kids are too much!" Tendai retorted.

"That wouldn't be a bad idea actually." Tapiwa chuckled.

"A traditional honeymoon." Tapiwa repeated to herself, not minding her sister's concerns.

"I hope your fiancée is paying for this." Tendai said looking at her sister more seriously.

"No Tendy, I can't trouble him with all of this, after all it has nothing to do with him. My family should take care of all the expenses. Anyway you should not worry; bae has got more than enough for *roora*, so we can get some extra cash after the event, Tapiwa replied.

"I hope you are right, I would hate to see all this going to waste," Tendai snarled.

"You worry too much Tendai, things have changed since the time you got married," Tapiwa argued. Tendai looked around her mother's lounge area. It was over-decorated in her opinion, with the climbing flower that she always begged her mother to remove.

Tapiwa imagined how it would feel living away from her parents. Much as she knew she would miss them, she was very excited to begin her new life with Sam.

In a family of three, Tendai was the eldest, Tonderai the second and Tapiwa the last. Tapiwa and Tendai were chalk and cheese, with Tapiwa being the outgoing extrovert and Tendai more reserved. Tendai was in her mid-thirties and had been married for five years. She was excited to see her young sister getting married too, and hoped Sam was the right person for Tapiwa.

They had all grown up with their parents in the leafy suburbs of Harare. Tapiwa and her siblings had had a pleasant childhood attending the best schools and not lacking much, as their father worked hard to give his children the best. Tapiwa was more than confident that Sam would be a good father to her children too. She and Sam had been dating for the past year and the proposal had taken family by surprise. Samuel seemed to be a very honest boy who was very much in love with Tapiwa. Her parents' worry was that they had only known each other for a year and now they were already getting married. Neither of the two wanted to listen to any reason so the family simply let them be. Tapiwa had just finished college and was working as an accountant at a small firm in town. No one seemed to know exactly what Sam did for a living, but he clearly had more than most people his age. Tapiwa maintained that Sam was an IT professional who did freelancing jobs for several clients around the city. Whenever that argument came up, Tapiwa shut it down by saying what Samuel did was not anyone's concern as long as he paid the bills.

Tapiwa had organised the function to the last tee, regardless of her clashes with her mother and sister who argued that the *roora* be done in the traditional way. The traditional ceremony as the elders knew it was an exchange of cultures where the groom's family would come and pay the bride price according to the in-laws' demands. However through negotiations, they would finally settle the bride price. Afterwards the bride's family would invite the groom's family for a meal whilst family members were introduced. However, the new trend was to have a traditional African wedding, with a traditional cake, African attires and elaborate decor. A photographer and sometimes a videographer would be present to capture the moments of the day. They lost the argument of course, Tapiwa being the head strong person she was.

The day was filled with excitement and laughter. The aunts as usual presented a bustle of noise in the sitting room whilst the men deliberated on the amount of money the soon to be son in law was to be charged. Tapiwa was busy trying to coordinate the event together. She had become very edgy because her bridesmaids were running late. Her tailor had not finished her outfit up until the previous night. It was an African print fitted skirt of a vibrant yellow and red pattern with a plain white blouse carefully lined with buttons matching the skirt. Her bridesmaids would be wearing the same print only this time in wavy dresses. Tapiwa was so proud of her carefully thought out designs. The tailor had sewn them to perfection. The cake in the shape of a *hari*, an African traditional pot, was also adorned by ribbon to match her dresses. Her brother Tonde had promised to pick it up on his way from their farm a few kilometres out of Harare where he always went every Saturday morning. She hoped it would be just as lovely as the picture she had shown the baker.

Meanwhile, Tendai was trying to run after her toddler son who seemed to get himself into trouble every time she turned her back. Tapiwa was starting to get irritated because she felt no one was helping her.

"Tendai!" she screamed, "Can you stop running after Chiko and help me? I thought Ben was watching him today."

Tendai posed before she could answer. Ben was Tendai's husband. He had promised to watch Chiko but as usual, something had come up in the last minute. Tendai never knew what always kept Ben busy away from his family.

"You know Ben is always busy Tapi and besides you know mum never gets to see Chiko as often so at least she gets to see him all day today," Tendai replied rather annoyed too.

"Oh, I wish you could give me some help instead of always babysitting," Tapiwa complained. "I promise you as soon as I have kids I will have a full time nanny," Tapiwa laughed.

Tendai was deep in thought, and did not reply. Ever since she got married five years ago, she had never known happiness, but she tried to hide it as much as possible. She only prayed that her sister would have a much better marriage than her.

"Guess who I saw?" screamed a voice from the kitchen door. It was Tonderai.
"The man of the moment, SAM...I almost felt sorry for the poor guy. He was carrying two sacks of potatoes. Tapiwa, how can you ask the poor guy to buy potatoes?" Tapiwa looked at her brother and replied, "Trust me, I had nothing to do with that grocery list, ask your mother."

"Well, you surely know how to make a brother sweat!" he chuckled again. It was Shona tradition that the future son in law would buy a list of groceries, as ordered by his in-laws as a way of honouring the bride's family, as part of the *roora* process.

Tonderai and Samuel had become friends since being introduced to each other. It surprised Tapiwa though, who thought they had nothing in common. Tonderai had never been known to make friends easily, but for some reason he seemed to have clicked with Samuel when they had been introduced. It worked to Tapiwa's advantage because she was always using Tonderai to sneak out and meet with Samuel. Tapiwa would ask Tonderai to tell their parents that he was going out with her.

It was almost midday, everything was coming together. The weather was beautiful that day. There were fears that it was going to rain as it had been raining the past few days but luckily the sun was out that day and the garden looked beautiful. The Gardener, Jimmy had been put to task to make sure the lawn was impeccable. The rains had helped brighten the garden. The photographer had arrived and was busy taking photos of the family members. Tapiwa looked very elegant in her dress. It fit her so well, she could not help but admire herself. She had several photos taken in different parts of the garden. The only photos that she still needed were that of her and her future husband and one with her maid of honour. She wondered where she could be up to this time. Memory, Tapiwa's maid of honour had promised her that she would be the first person at her house. Tapiwa was more worried about Samuel and his relatives. It was almost lunchtime and they were running late.

Memory and Tapiwa had practically grown up together. Tapiwa had gone to the same school with Memory since preschool. They had attended the same university and were inseparable.

"Tapi, look who is here!" Tendai shouted from outside. Memory had finally arrived. Tapiwa breathed a sigh of relief. At least someone who she could trust to take care of things was now here. Immediately she put Memory to task, briefed her on the details that needed to be attended to before they proceeded to get their photos taken. Tendai was also happy that Memory had come because she adored Chiko and could babysit him more than anybody else. She could at least relax and do other things.

"Memo, please put on your *dhuku* when you are serving food, that weave of yours is too long," Tapiwa's mother shouted. Memo looked down and whispered to Tapiwa, "Eish, I forgot it at home."

"Don't worry about it; you can just tie your hair. Besides you are still single, so perhaps this is your lucky day. Sam has good looking friends you know, go ahead and flaunt it!" Tapiwa laughed.

"I tell you if Samuel does not get here this minute, I am going to cry and spoil my makeup!" Tapiwa screamed. She went out to look for Tonde.

"Tonde, where is your friend?" she yelled.

"Easy tiger!" Tonde replied trying to calm her sister whose nerves had clearly sky rocketed.

"I am sure he is in a queue somewhere trying to buy sugar," Tonde joked.

"It's not funny Tonde," Tapiwa was close to bursting into tears.

Just as she turned her back to go and call Sam, someone shouted, "They are here!" Tapiwa was about to cause a world war three so it was good timing. The hustle and bustle started. Each person was busy with one thing or the other. Ben came just around that time too. It was really a happy day. The caterer had done a splendid job. The food looked colourful and mouth-watering. All the kinds of meat Tapiwa had requested were on the menu. She had included some traditional foods too. Tendai had laughed when she saw chicken feet and cow's feet on the menu and joked about having an animal feet parade. The decor looked exquisite. The white table cloths blended well with the African print on the centrepieces and the napkins.

"Oh wow girls, u really did an excellent job!" exclaimed Tapiwa's aunt. "I should hire you when Rudo gets married *mwana wehandzvadzi yangu*. This is really exceptional, a far cry from our disorderly traditions!" Tete exclaimed.

There were several ululations in the house, which meant the lobola money was flowing without any hiccups or negotiations to lower the price. The guests were happy and excited for the new couple. "This is the happiest day of my life!" Tapiwa exclaimed as she came into the kitchen where her sister Tendai was.

"I am so tired. I need to send a photo to my friend in the UK, she has serious FOMO," Tapiwa laughed.

"Where is my iPhone anyway?" Tapiwa asked.

"Why can't you just say Phone?" Tendai always never seemed to understand her sister and brother's obsession with the latest iPhone. She picked up the phone and handed it to her sister.

"Let's go outside and breathe some fresh air," an exhausted Tendai said to Tapiwa. The two sisters hand in hand went outside. Let's hide in Ben's car and catch up on some social media. Ben almost never locked his car, so the two sisters went in to relax for a while. Just as they relaxed, each on their phone, Tapiwa realised that Tendai had handed her Tonde's phone instead of hers. Well, she decided this was a good time to sneakily find out her brother's girlfriend who he never showed his sisters. Tendai was busy on her phone as well. As Tapi browsed through the photos, she let out a scream and dropped the phone in shock. She almost fainted as she tried to turn to her sister. With her mouth still open failing to say any words, she looked at an equally shocked Tendai who was holding a scarf that clearly belonged to Memo. At that moment both their worlds were shattered.

YES....both sisters never in a million years imagined what they realised at that very moment. Tapiwa had just seen a photo of her brother and her fiancée enjoying a romantic sunset cruise in Kariba. She clearly remembered that weekend. Sam had told her he was being introduced to new clients by a friend of his in Kariba. Tonderai had asked Sam if he could tag along as he needed a breather away from the city.

On the other hand, Tendai realised who had been keeping Ben busy almost every other weekend. Sometimes he would even take their son Chiko. She always wondered how Chiko was always clean and fresh every time he came back home with his father. Memo had been playing weekend Mum all this time. It was now clear why Chiko loved being with Memo and how he never refused to go to her.

Love literally makes the world go round! As Tendai and Tapiwa's heads were spinning at a rate faster than the earth could orbit the sun, they looked at each other with eyes that screamed, "What NOW?"

The secret

Theresa didn't like hospitals. She only went there when it was really necessary. Nevertheless, this time around, she had to go. The situation with her father had become serious.

Theresa was an only child. She had grown up in the most loving of homes. Her parents adored her. She always asked them why they never had more children. Her mother told her how she had suffered some complications soon after her birth so she had to have her uterus removed. At 34 years of age, Theresa was a beautiful young woman and had not found anyone she wished to settle with. Her father always joked with her about how he wanted to enjoy his grandchildren before his bones failed him. Theresa's father was in his late sixties but he had been as fit as a fiddle. He had however suffered a broken knee after falling in his backyard whilst tending to his plants. The doctors were worried that his leg would never be strong enough to stand on its own and that he might have to use a crutch or a wheelchair for the rest of his life. This was a bitter pill to swallow for Mr. Nyathi. He slumped into a depressive state. Mrs. Nyathi, a bubbly and cheerful woman tried by all means to encourage her husband. She didn't know what else to do to get him out of this negative depressing mood. She tried by all means to stay positive and encourage him to be grateful that he still could live his life as much as before, but Mr. Nyathi was not convinced. She was a retired nurse who had witnessed how a positive attitude had helped even in cases where doctors had no hope. She had worked for one of the biggest government hospitals in the country but took an early retirement package to get into the private sector. She however never talked much about her stint in the public hospital but no one really bothered her about it.

Theresa would go to the hospital several times a day. It worried her that her father failed to be positive and lift himself out of this slump. After all, the doctor had said, with the right attitude and a good diet, he may be able to walk unassisted. Before he was discharged, the doctor asked if he could see Theresa privately. Theresa wondered why the doctor had requested to see her without her mother.

It was 2pm, three hours before her appointment, Theresa was a bit anxious. Was it something to do with his condition she pondered? She would find out soon enough anyway. She was positive that a change of environment will help her father recover. As she got ready to leave the office to make her way to the hospital, her phone rang. It was the hospital. The doctor who had consulted her father was asking to postpone the meeting to the following day. Theresa was terribly annoyed. She decided to go to the hospital anyway.

Theresa found her mother there. They laughed about how they had both bought guava juice for Mr. Nyathi. To say Mr. Nyathi liked guava juice was an understatement. He drank it for breakfast, lunch and supper. "Where did you find guava juice mummy. I was almost giving up when I tried the little supermarket across the street," asked Theresa.

"I had to send your uncle to buy it when he went to Botswana last week. Of all juices, your father had to like this one. Moreover, he does not drink any other juice." Mrs. Nyathi replied.

On that day, Mr. Nyathi seemed to be in a much better mood than the previous days. "Are you here to take me home you two? I am tired of this hospital bed," complained Mr. Nyathi. "The doctor still needs to run some more tests, maybe tomorrow," replied Mrs Nyathi.

"How convenient, as if they haven't kept me long enough. My dogs must be starving back at home," retorted Mr. Nyathi.

Everybody laughed so hard. "Daddy, are you seriously worried about Bingo and Rex? Those dogs can even feed on the neighbour's chickens if they don't get their food," Theresa chuckled.

"Where is that doctor anyway?" Mr. Nyathi asked.

"I am told he went for an emergency operation, but we can see him tomorrow," Mrs. Nyathi replied to her rather impatient husband. By the time visiting hours were over, everyone was happy that Mr. Nyathi was handling the situation better than most days.

The following day, Theresa called the doctor's office to confirm their appointment and once she had the new meeting time, she soon hurried with her work and headed to the hospital. She was ushered to the doctor's office as soon as she announced her arrival. As she entered the doctor's office, being an interior decorator, she couldn't help but mentally organise his office space. As she was doing so, her eyes landed on a carton of guava juices in the corner of the office. She almost laughed but held it back. The doctor, noticed her stifled laugh. "Sorry, excuse my rather untidy office, I was trying to create space for my new fridge," said the doctor looking a bit embarrassed. The doctor, a rather short, untidy in appearance man, was however very friendly which immediately put Theresa at ease.

"This fridge will do for my juices," the doctor seemed relaxed. He took a box of guava juice and said, "Can you believe that this is the only connection I have to my biological father?" he laughed. The only two things that my mother had told me before she passed on were that I have a twin sister and that my father was addicted to guava juice."

At that moment, Theresa noticed the large birthmark on the doctor's arm that looked just like hers. Could this be her twin brother ... but how? She asked herself. As she was immersed in deep thought, the doctor continued, "Well Theresa, the reason I asked you to meet me was that as I went through your father's blood tests, oddly enough he has one of the least common blood types which is exactly like mine. This prompted me to ask him for a blood donation but he refused any of that. I was hoping you could help me by donating blood if your blood type matches your father's. I know it's a rare request but sometimes we really face difficulties when we have patients with our blood type." Theresa did not hear a single word the doctor had said. She was trying to figure out in her head, so if this was her twin brother, who was her real mother?

Gwadamirai Majange

Gwadamirai Majange, born Gwadamirai Nhamo, is an aspiring author who has spent most of her young life working as a development communications professional. She is passionate about contributing positively to the world but also to change the narrative of how the world perceives women and Africa. She is inspired by a firm desire to ensure that her children will be able to get more literature that speaks to their reality so that their world is opened to possibilities. Gwada is married and is a mother of three.

Her dilemma

"Hallo Mrs. Dee, are you able to pop in when you get back? I just want to update you on how your son is doing," teacher Mary wrote on a WhatsApp message. Teacher Mary was an exceptional teacher who loved what she did so much that she paid special attention to each child. She would tell parents at the beginning of each term that if there were any changes at home, they must let her know so that she knew how to manage the situation with the children.

She had got used to Mrs. Dee's regular absence and would tell her funny stories of some of the things the kids said and did when she was away, which convinced Teacher Mary that they missed their parents a lot. She would also give Mrs. Dee tips and hints on how to make up for the time she was away and how to make them miss her less. This was especially important for Mrs. Dee because she had no idea at all how to manage this situation.

Her young family had moved across the border to South Africa from Zimbabwe a few years back after getting exciting opportunities that looked like they could change their lives. At that point, it was just Mr. and Mrs. Dee and the world felt like their oyster. They could be anything they wanted to be and go wherever they wished to go. South Africa did not feel like their final destination; they wanted to see more of the world and fate seemed to have that lined up in their paths. Their jobs consisted of living out of suitcases, often meeting at their small two-bedroom apartment to chuck clothes in the washer while packing the next batch of clothes for the next trip. Mr. Dee worked in Marketing for a huge multinational company that sold canned organic food. He had to travel to meet clients and open up new markets for the company across the African continent. When he got his contract, it stated that there would be 75% travel and to that they celebrated. This had always been the game plan; they were going to see the world and it was great that Mr. Dee's world was opening up so fast.

Mrs. Dee worked for a technology company's Corporate Responsibility wing, and her function was to introduce technology to informally employed women in marginalised communities through hosting workshops and training on the different tools on phones that would help them improve their businesses. The training was usually followed by yearlong support as well as donations of phones that were compatible with the tools that were introduced. She found her work very fulfilling especially when they went back to monitor the impact the tools had on the women's businesses. Her initial projects had been in two countries which she now knew extensively because, like Mr. Dee, her contract also said 50% of her time should be spent in the field engaging with the beneficiaries.

"When I grow up, I want to fly around the world and work for an important organisation," Mrs. Dee recalled herself saying as a child. In those days, it had seemed like a distant and almost impossible dream. Besides her father who had been on an aeroplane for business, she did not know a lot of people in her community who had flown. It was after a business trip in which her father described the interior of an aeroplane to her that she made the decision that she too would one day fly. She remembered how her father described the interior of the aeroplane, "It is like the interior of a fine porcelain teapot," he said, making her even more curious of what that looked like from within. Her mother would often shout at her whenever she found her looking inside the teapot while doing her household chores. She could never understand why her daughter found this so fascinating.

She finally managed to see the inside of an aeroplane, and it did not disappoint her. It was like nothing she had ever seen and on her first flight, she wondered if this was really how it felt like to be inside a porcelain teapot. The message from teacher Mary however brought her back to her new reality. Unlike in the beginning where she owned her time and could visit three countries in one week her life had changed a lot. After a few years, she had given birth to twins and suddenly so much had changed in her life and not much in Mr. Dee's. She suddenly had these young souls who seemed to need her so much more than anything else. But Mrs. Dee did not let this weigh her down, opting to take only six weeks maternity leave because she noticed how her boss kept emphasizing how the deliverables would be delayed because she had to take a break. She hated the way her boss, who was also a woman and a mother of four, kept bringing up her pregnancy in team meetings. So, when she filed for only six weeks leave, the boss looked surprised but did not object.

"Are you sure you will be ok? You know, you younger generation are not as strong as we are. We would give birth and still do a lot of physical work. But your folk, I see from my daughter, you guys I think it is the food. So, you think you will be able to handle it?" she asked.

"Yes ma'am, if I can't I will let you know." Mrs. Dee said and left.

So, from the day the twins were born, Mrs. Dee created a network of support and found an amazing helper who when she went home for her vacations the twins would cry immensely. She had become like part of the family even though they also really enjoyed having their mum around.

Auntie Sue was their other mum. Mrs. Dee did not mind initially because this helped her to navigate and chase her own dreams. She genuinely wanted the best of both worlds. She wanted it all, to be a successful career woman, a mother and a wife and until these last few days, she thought it was possible and that there was enough balance in her life.

The message from teacher Mary, however, gave her the chills because she instinctively knew there was a problem. Mrs. Dee had been so busy at work and living out of her suitcase for the better half of the quarter. She had missed quite a huge chunk of her children's lives, even though Auntie Sue seemed to be doing well. Mrs. Dee loved being a mum and spending time with the family, and because the twins were now four years old and asked so many questions whenever she had to leave home, she felt a certain kind of sadness. Teacher Mary's message came in when she was checking in her luggage and getting ready to go back home from close to two weeks in Tanzania. She was so excited to see the kids again and had brought a lot of goodies for them. She tended to overcompensate when she came back home with so many toys and gifts, because she believed that would show the children she had been thinking of them.

When she finally boarded, she immediately fell asleep. It had become a habit of hers to fall asleep as soon as she got onto the flight, so she would be fresh when she got home. Unlike other trips, it was not a peaceful sleep. She dreamt something horrible had happened to her kids and everyone kept looking at her and saying it was all her fault for being so irresponsible as a mother. So bad were these dreams that she kept waking up and each time she fell asleep they would come and haunt her again.

When this trip came up to travel once again to Tanzania for a few weeks, she did not hesitate to begin packing. She had so much she needed to do there to conclude her projects and she planned on hitting the ground running. Her performance indicators were good but the team on the ground had been waiting for her to come back for a while. Events that happened the evening before her departure, however, convinced her that something was very wrong, and the kids were not happy with this trip. Initially, being a bit superstitious she thought something terrible was going to happen. When she was packing one of the twins, Rudo, came into her room and sat on the bed.

"Are you travelling again?" she asked.

"Yes, my baby I am. But I will be back before you even realise that I was gone," she said trying to comfort her.

"You always say that, but you go away for long. Is it something we do to you that makes you want to leave?" Rudo asked.

"No, you know I would not go away if I didn't have to, right?" she said to her but not really looking at her.

Rudo's mumbling was interrupted by loud sobs. Mrs. Dee froze and was unsure if she wanted to understand why the kid was crying, as she did not think she would have an answer.

"Why are you crying?" Mrs. Dee asked

"Because I don't want you to go," Rudo said. Mrs. Dee put her packing aside and spent a good hour soothing and assuring Rudo that she was going to make sure they had a great time when she came back. However, at the back of her head, this was concerning. She called in auntie Sue and asked her if all was well. Auntie Sue assured Mrs. Dee that there had not been any challenges at home, but she did note that the kids were generally more subdued when she was away. Bath times were particularly difficult as the twins kept asking multiple questions about when their parents would be back home. She also explained how Rudo seemed to have more temper tantrums of late whilst Rufaro the boy had developed a strop.

"But I guess it's because they miss you guys." Auntie Sue concluded.

This was a difficult issue to deal with and Mrs. Dee felt very embarrassed that auntie Sue seemed to know the kids so well that she would also pick out the changes in their attitudes, something she had never paid attention to.

"Ok, thank you so much auntie Sue." Mrs. Dee said handing Rudo over to her to put to bed. She was lagging behind time as she needed to finish packing, then review an urgent report before she could sleep for a few hours and leave the following morning. To comfort herself, she told herself that she did not have a choice. She had a good work ethic and could not make up some story of why she could not go for this trip. She did, however, say a lot of silent prayers that everything on her path would be ok. So, it was during her return from this trip that teacher Mary was summoning Mrs. Dee to pay her a visit.

When she finally got home, the kids were asleep. There had been some delays with her luggage and the traffic congestion from the airport meant even though she arrived an hour before their bedtime, by the time she got home they were fast asleep. She wished she had managed to fall asleep, but she spent a good two hours tossing and turning thinking about what she would say in her and Mr. Dee's defense when she met with teacher Mary the next day. She woke up at 1am and spent some time finishing off some outstanding tasks needed done for work. She looked at the clock and time seemed to have stood still. It was only 3am and despite the very hectic days she had just endured away from home, she still could not sleep.

"Hey hun, you awake?" She sent a WhatsApp message to Mr. Dee.

"Was about to check if you had travelled safely - you know the time difference. I could not wait up for you. How is the crew that side?" he asked.

"They are fine, but remember that issue I told you about Rudo's tantrum before I left. Well, teacher Mary has asked me to come in and I think we have problems at school." Mrs. Dee said.

"Well, I told you these kids are spoilt. You need to be firmer with them. Who can survive without working? I think you need to come up with a plan to firm them up. When we were growing up, we were not spoilt and never acted up because our parents were traveling." He said.

Mrs. Dee read the message over and over again. She wondered where in Mr. Dee's young life he had gone for months on end not seeing his parents. If he did, he had never shared it with her.

"Look, I have to go, leaving Cote D'Ivore for Senegal today, then off to Egypt, so I have to finalise a few things. I am so happy things are going well here. I will be home on Saturday next week. Please can you make time to buy me three grey shirts from that shop as I leave on Monday morning for Egypt. Also remember to get the dogs vaccinated. Did the plumber guy you mentioned manage to fix that leak in the ceiling?" he asked.

"Yes, everything is fine. Ok, I will get the shirts." Mrs. Dee replied.

"Great, have to rush. Have a good one!" he said and went offline.

Mrs. Dee had lied; she had not had the time to ask the plumber to come. She had even forgotten about the leak in all the running around she needed to do. Her thoughts immediately came back to the twins. A part of her wanted to be angry at them for being spoilt to not understanding why she and Mr. Dee had to work so hard for them. Did they not realise this was what paid the bills, the Friday night pizzas, the movie tickets, and the very basics like the food they ate? Did they not realise that unlike her counterparts at work, if an engagement ended at 4pm and there was a 5pm flight out of that country, she would be on it so she would make it home in time for the weekend, or to watch them performing at a school event, or just so that instead of them going another day without her, she would be home by the time they woke up? The most regular conversations she had with colleagues from other offices were usually;

"So, have you been here before?"

"No, this is actually my first time," she would respond.

"Oh, that's awesome, I hope you have taken a couple of days after your engagements to check the city out." This would usually be followed by narrations of some of the iconic places in these cities that she should see before she left.

Her usual response was to thank them heartily for all their help and try to use the evenings to run around and at least see one of these great places. She did not find the after-work tours exciting, as she was usually tired, but she did them to tick off her bucket list. It made her mad to think that after all the sacrifices she was making to be at home as much as possible, it was not enough.

As she pondered on, her mind took her back to 1992, a very terrible year for her. She was 10 years old and lived with her parents and siblings. Her mum dedicated most of her time to taking care of them when we were younger. She worked from home as a tailor and Mrs. Dee did not remember ever getting home after school and not finding her mother home with a hot plate of food ready. She did not enjoy food much as a child, but there was always something so soothing about that aroma of freshly cooked food that greeted them as they entered the yard.

1992 however, made her appreciate her mother more and somehow at this moment helped her understand why her kids were struggling with her hectic work life and her seemingly never-ending absence. You see, 1992 was a terrible year for her family because there was so much death around. It was what felt to her as a young child the peak of the Aids pandemic, as so many relatives succumbed to the disease. She remembered how she began to really hate that loud ringing of the landline which was strategically placed on a side table next to her father's favorite chair, because in 1992 it felt like each time it rang, it meant her parents more so her mother, would have to leave them for three to four days to even a week at a time, to go and bury yet another relative who had passed away.

She remembered how miserable she felt when she had to be brave for her little sister who was eight at the time and tended, like her daughter, to cry a lot when her mother was away. She immediately recalled having to check on her at break time at school, when often she found her crying and would lie to her that mum had called and promised she would be home by that evening just so she would stop crying. Even though a helper or cousin who was asked to stay over with them made sure they had freshly made meals whenever they got home, the food did not really taste the same. There was just something missing because it was not mum who had made it.

As her parents attended more and more funerals, she also began to worry about them. Each night she would pray they would not die too, because she did not know how their lives would turn out if they stopped coming home at all. This memory of 1992 helped her to appreciate and understand why it was so difficult for her kids when she was away. But it did not give her much consolation or a solution on how she was going to solve this huge challenge that lay before her.

She continued to toss and turn, then eventually fell asleep. Next, she was awoken from deep slumber by loud screams and little bodies jumping on to her bed. There was so much joy in their voices and somehow, she understood them. It took her back to 1992 and how happy she had felt when she saw her parents enter the yard. It always felt like a heavy cloud had been lifted and somehow all the things that had worried her when they were away disappeared. When they came back, she knew she did not have to check on her young sister anymore at school. You would not believe it was the same child, the way she would spend her break time running around and practically ignoring her.

She held the children one on each side but unlike other times did not ask them how they were when she was away, because she knew it would come up soon anyway. She just relaxed and enjoyed the moment as they got ready for school. As they drove to school, she felt nervous. You know that feeling you get in your tummy when the headmaster calls you to his office, well that was exactly how she felt. They had to arrive at the school a lot earlier because the teacher wanted to meet with her before school started. She left the kids playing at the playground and found her way to their classroom.

"Welcome back! I hope you travelled safely." Teacher Mary said with a smile.

"Yes, I did thank you. How have you been?" Mrs. Dee asked.

"Very well my dear but I think we might have a problem. This week Rudo and Rufaro did not really have a good time at school. Rudo cried a lot, almost every day she cried, and, on some days, she even cried twice or thrice. Rufaro has been fighting a lot too. They are both very quiet, even Rudo the chatterbox seems to have lost her voice during class activities." She said.

The conversation was worse than Mrs. Dee had imagined. She sat there looking at the teacher wondering where she was going with this issue. For a moment her mind went back to 1992. You see, she went to a school where corporal punishment was the main method of disciplining a child. There was a lot of disciplining in those days because it felt a lot like whenever one's behavior was a bit off the mark the teacher's solution was not to ask what was wrong but to give the child a beating. This kind of attitude toughened us up and somehow, we knew not to take our issues to the classroom. This was so true, for even though my young sister cried during breaktime in 1992, she was a standard student during lesson time and just toughened up and did her work. So as teacher Mary went on with this conversation, Mrs. Dee wondered if maybe that was what the kids needed. A tough approach that showed them it was this way or the highway and reminded them to get over themselves.

As she continued thinking about it, she realised 1992 was one of her worst performing years at school. She was an above average student who always got a book prize for some subject at school, but in 1992 because of her parents' horrible absence that seemed to turn her life upside down, she hardly got any recognition. Until this point, she had not in any way linked her limited success in 1992 to her mother's absence.

"What do you reckon we must do about this?" Mrs. Dee asked teacher Mary.

"Well…" she was about to say when one of the school kids walked in with tears streaming down their cheeks and a very bloody forehead.

"I bumped my head! Help me, I bumped my head!" he was screaming as he walked towards teacher Mary who was now wearing a first aider hat. I observed her comfort the child and press down the wound with a piece of cotton wool to try and stop the bleeding. It seemed the cut was deep, as each time she tried to stop the bleeding, more and more blood gushed out.

"How can I help you?" Mrs. Dee asked.

"Please rush to the principal's office and get her here. This boy is also anaemic, and I don't like the way things are going," she said in a panicked voice.

Mrs. Dee rushed to call the principal who came through and agreed that this was an emergency. She called the boy's mum who was already at work. They agreed that the principal would drive the boy with another colleague to the nearest emergency room and the boy's mum would meet them there, as waiting for an ambulance might have been catastrophic.

By the time the commotion was over, the school bell rang, and teacher Mary apologised frantically for not being able to finish their conversation. She requested that they set another appointment for the following morning if Mrs. Dee was available. Teacher Mary insisted on a morning because she knew Mrs. Dee never had afternoons free. They bade each other goodbye and Mrs. Dee walked back to the carpark in deep thought. She wondered what would happen if one of her kids was injured while she was away at work. She remembered the fear on the little boy's face and how he looked so much calmer when they told him they would meet his mum at the hospital.

There were so many things, good and bad that she had been missing in the children's lives due to her competing commitments, even though she was trying hard to be there. She remembered how she had once got a speeding ticket as she raced to make the time for the kid's year end Christmas concert. It was such a big deal because according to the teacher, they had spent most of the year rehearsing for this grand event. She had been so held up in meetings and could only leave just when the concert was starting. She had also forgotten to get one of her relatives or friends to attend the event. The preschool was small, and a child would definitely notice the absence of their parents.

As she walked into the small auditorium that day, she noticed that the twins' class was the one performing on the stage. She had hardly caught her breadth but immediately noticed that her kids were not singing at all. They kept looking around into the audience. She knew immediately that they were looking for her. They had not seen her before the concert started like other kids had. Because they were on the lit stage and the parents were in the dark, they did not know if she had made it or not. She knew she could not allow them to finish the concert like this. She had to think on her feet.

She went to the side of the small stage where they were standing and yelled, "*Nhanha! Nhanha!*" This seemed to work as they immediately turned to look her way. "*Nhanha,* mama is here my babies!" she screamed. This seemed to do the trick because the moment they heard her voice, even though they could not see her, they came to life and began to sing with so much energy and joy. It felt as if they had done this year long rehearsal for her alone and when they thought she was not there; had decided there was no need for them to perform anymore. The rest of the concert was smooth sailing, and they each recited their poem lines perfectly. She wondered what would have happened if they had not managed to make the concert at all.

She wondered if the problem might have been how she was raising the kids. If this were 1992, the teachers would have reprimanded her rather firmly for drifting and looking around during the concert. But then again, although 1992 saw her mum being away quite a bit, she never missed any of her school activities. She therefore did not quite understand what that moment felt like for Rudo and Rufaro, when their concert started and their turn came up, when she wasn't around.

Mrs. Dee eventually came back down to earth and drove home. She had taken the day off, as had become tradition after spending time away from home. She got home and made the children their favorite homemade pizza. She dashed off to the shops and bought them some ice cream and sweets and whatever else she could find to show them that she cared.

As she did all this, she also thought a lot about how she was going to try and be there more. In the next few months, she was going to turn down more, if not all travel requests. She also remembered that she rarely took time off for long periods of time. This post travel day off was the most she ever took off work. Over the years, she had accumulated so many leave days because there was never really a right time to take time off. She was only off work when the office was closed during the Christmas break and those were free days. As she kneaded through the pizza dough, she promised herself that on the next day when she got into the office, she would apply for some time off to be more present at home. She committed to taking time off, where she would switch off her work gadgets and completely focus on her family.

She took out her phone and sent a message to teacher Mary. She let her know that she did not think there was any need for another meeting and was making arrangements at work to take some time off so she could focus on the kids. She told her she understood the impact her absence was having on the kids and would try to make things work. Teacher Mary responded with a lot of excitement and said she was sure this would make life easier for the kids.

The rest of the day was spent having a lot of fun with the kids. She did not give them a chance to talk about her absence, because she did not want to know more about how she was failing them. She just wanted the day to be perfect and for her to feel like she was a great mum like her mother had been. She wanted them to walk into the yard to the smell of freshly cooked food made with her own bare hands and feel like everything was falling back into place. She did not want them to feel the way she felt on those grey days in 1992 any longer.

The home was finally quiet after she had put the kids to bed. She kept thinking she could get used to this kind of life, being there for them all the time. Fatigue and exhaustion were taking a toll on her. As she settled into bed, all she wanted to do was finally rest. She believed she would sleep like a child. She had managed to solve the crisis that had kept her awake the night before.

At 9pm, just as she was about to switch off her phone to call it a night, a WhatsApp message came through from her boss. Her boss was a lot like her and tended to work around the clock. Mrs. Dee did not want to read the message till the morning, just in case it contained information that would make her take out her computer and start working. She decided to read it in case there was an emergency.

"Hi there, great work in Tanzania this week. The team was very happy with everything you delivered. More great news, still awaiting official letter but it has been approved. We have decided to promote you to the role of Regional Program Lead. You have really proven yourself over the years and I think you are ready. You will now take care of southern and eastern Africa. Next couple of months will be a bit travel heavy as we need to induct you into the region and make sure all stakeholders and partners know you well. Anyway, more information in the official email but I just thought to share this well-deserved news. Congratulations!"

She forwarded the message to Mr. Dee just to hear his thoughts around the promotion, especially in light of the challenges the children were having.

"Oh Congratulations, this is awesome. When do you start? You are now in the league with the big boys my dear!"

At 4am, she had hardly slept since reading that message. How could such great news cause so much confusion and sadness. This role was her next big thing. She had wanted it badly for so long and knew she deserved it. But how was she going to be in two places at once? Why did things have to be so complicated? Was the universe telling her to choose and why was she the one caught up in this dilemma? Was it her feminine side making her overthink the situation with the children, because Mr. Dee saw no problem with grabbing this opportunity without thinking twice ...?

Looking to the spirit

They say when things are not going as expected, the human mind tends to seek a higher spirit that could help the person to understand and overcome challenges they face. When most Africans go through things they cannot explain, their instinct is to look to the spirit and try to get a higher understanding of the adversity. It is something that helps us to get by, believing that at some point soon, we will be ok.

Spirituality can take different forms, but Fari had been born into the Christian faith. It was this faith that had somehow kept her afloat and believing that maybe something would give and help her overcome her challenges. She had not always been like this. She had been very pragmatic before, looking at practical solutions to whatever came her way. Her friends often called her "madam practical". But the way things had been going made her think there must have been a higher force.

It was her birthday and not just any ordinary birthday. This year marked her 40th year on earth. The first 40 had been a rollercoaster to say the least. They had started so well. She was the star student from the word go. Doing so well, even at the age of three years when she went to preschool at the school her mother taught. It had been one of the first early childhood development programmes introduced in Mucheke Township of Masvingo where she and her parents lived. Her mother noticing how bored she was, managed to get her into the programme with classmates aged five years old. She had done so well, but the school had advised her parents to let her repeat the programme for another year and if she did well again would go to primary school at the age of five. She did and it was clear from that moment she was very gifted.

So great were her academic conquests that she had been handpicked into numerous leadership roles throughout primary school and high school. Her final high school results were exceptional and guaranteed her an unconditional offer at a reputable university. She remembered her days at university and her graduation, but at this point it did not matter anymore. Her father had thrown her the biggest party anyone had ever seen in their neighborhood. That, according to the stories doing the rounds was where the problem began. People talked about how she had been bewitched at that party by jealous neighbours or relatives, because from that point on, her story became a dark hole of nothingness.

Her father had slaughtered a cow and invited everyone to come and celebrate his oldest daughter's success. She was the first in her whole clan to go to university, most of her older cousins and family members were mainly teachers and nurses. She was also a leader pacesetter in her neighbourhood as the street had also not yet recorded a university entry most of the kids had gone to the local polytechnical college.

Sadly, nothing else had come out of her life from the day she got that certificate. In her current situation, it no longer mattered that she had been such an amazing student, because it seemed that was all she was good at, being a student. Perhaps she should have chased academia and succeeded as a professor, but it felt too late.

"Happy birthday Fari!" the messages and phone calls kept coming on her phone, and she ingested them with difficulty. The excitement everyone seemed to have about her birthday made her question what it was about her 40th that drove them crazy. The messages seemed tainted with reminders of what was wrong with her life.

Cousin Roja: "Wish you many more cousin, but I think it is time you settled down."

Ruva: "As you turn 40, I pray that your life takes a real 360 and begins to change. I mean cousin, you got a degree before all of us, but it seems you just drift and have nothing to show for all those years of seeking an education."

Auntie Suzzie: "How much longer must I wait for my nieces and nephews, make a plan – happy birthday Fari my girl!"

Bernard: "You know I loved you then, I still love you now. You can come and become my third wife; I will take care of you. Happy birthday sweetheart. Please don't reply after 6pm, the Mrs. will be around, and it can cause drama!"

Nattie: "My prayer for you is that you heal from all the things you have been carrying. You do not have to keep apologising. It has all been forgiven. Happy birthday beautiful soul."

Unlike other years where the jokes about marriage and settling down had been funny, this particular year they were hugged by a bitter hue. She had spent the whole month praying and fasting, asking for a special kind of blessing, something to at least remind her that the last 40 years had not been a waste. So much had gone wrong, to a point that some woman had told her people would understand if she just gave up. It was her neighbour, Mai Mupa. Fari had been born and raised in the same house she now lived at 40. Mai Mupa was known in those parts for her rather vile tongue, and she often said things a lot of people thought of but never said. Fari had met Mai Mupa at their local store and when she greeted her, Mai Mupa smothered her with a scan from head to toe. Only this time, her familiar arrogant judgmental look had turned into a gaze of pity.

"We would all understand if you gave up. Life is really throwing you serious curve balls. But I do not think you should. Our church will be having a revival in a day, and you should come. Many lives have been transformed there," she said, in an unconvincing tone.

"What is it about me that makes you feel sorry for me?" Fari asked.

"Well, I mean look at you. All our children wanted to be you. You were a shining example of what a successful young woman should be growing up. But since you graduated, all you have done is stay at your parents' house. Were you not among some of the first people to get that prestigious degree; must have been Medical Laboratory Scientist. You even refused to do Medicine proper, but the university had offered it to you, right? I think that was when your parents should have picked up that something was going wrong. Who goes to medical school for a few months and decides to change programmes to a lesser course? I told your parents that this business of parading the streets with your results would not end well. People are evil Fari, but they never listened. Now look how disappointed they both were when they died, but refused to look outside your denomination for answers. Your mother would wear that black and white Dutch Reformed Church uniform religiously and say God will hear us in the right time. But look where it has brought you. 40 years and you are still wearing black and white girls fellowship uniform religiously. Come on, open your eyes!" Mai Mupa exclaimed.

"But the economy is in a bad place…"

"Don't give me that rubbish about the economy. All my children who graduated 5 years after you got jobs, either here or overseas. Your own siblings, all younger than you found their feet. Why are you struggling so much? I think it is time you took issues to another level. I mean look at you. You look almost my age and I am over 65. Are you not just 40? Look at the way you dress. You seem to have already given up." She said looking at her.

"I will come and collect you tomorrow at 6pm. Something bigger than the economy is wrong with you." She said as she walked away.

After this intense verbal undressing, Fari forgot why she was even at the shops. Somehow it felt like everyone was looking at her and feeling sorry for her. She ran most of the way home, holding back her tears. As she got to the gate, her right ankle failed and sent her flying to land on her abdomen. A sharp rock penetrated her knee and sliced it open, causing blood to gush out of the open wound. Her skirt had been ripped and as she looked around, she noticed her phone a few metres away from her; its screen had cracked and as she reached out to pick it up, she realised that it was practically a write off. An expense she had absolutely no capacity for.

"Where are you?" she screamed, looking up into the sky.

"I have called on you, pleaded with you to tell me what I did wrong and how I should make it right, but you don't seem to hear me. God, where are you?" she yelled gasping for air in between sobs.

As if possessed, she scooped the soil around her with her bare hands and poured it on her nearly bald head. She rolled in the gravel that now made up most of the road where the Tarmac used to be. "What did I ever do to you, why have you shamed me so? Today, I want you to tell me the answer. Enough is enough, today you will tell me!" she continued weeping bitterly.

Mai Mupa, who had started this turmoil rushed up the road. In her rage, Fari had run past her without noticing her. Mai Mupa eventually caught up with her and held her close to her chest the way her mother used to.

"Fari, He has heard you." Mai Mupa paused to inspect Fari's face for a sign of hope. "I will come and get you tomorrow at 6pm and you will get your deliverance," she said, helping Fari to stand up. She did not want to stand up. Fari wanted to stay there and ask this higher force why her path had been so twisted and messed up. What was wrong with her?

After Fari graduated, she had started applying for jobs like everyone else. She had done this from the comfort of her parents' home. They were happy to have her at home as she was very helpful, not only around the house, but with her siblings and at the small plot her parents had managed to obtain under the land reform programme in Zimbabwe. The programme had commenced on the eve of her going to university and securing the land was a big deal for her father who was an agriculture teacher at a mission school just outside Masvingo. It was a 3-hectare plot where her father grew vegetables, reared chickens and grew maize for mealie meal. The project did well and somehow kept Fari terribly busy while she waited for her opportunity to come up. They supplied the local TM Supermarket with vegetables and her father had managed to secure a deal to also supply the local Polytechnical College with vegetables.

The few months, however, became years of not getting that job she had hoped for and when her parents died one after the other, six years after she graduated, the family agreed that Fari could continue staying in the family home to keep it maintained. Her siblings were amazing souls; the monthly allowance they had given their parents would secretly be passed on to Fari. They also agreed that as the underdog, Fari could take over her parents' small agricultural project, but the land would remain family property. Fari had inherited all her mother's clothes, which explained why she looked Mai Mupa's age. They said it was their way of thanking her for taking care of her parents to the extent that she bathed them, and her mother even passed on in her arms.

As she sat in that soil, she remembered her mother's last words. How she had thanked her for everything she had done for her over the years and how she spoke her blessing into her life. "It will be well for you Farirai. All your problems will go away and you, like a bamboo will grow taller than all the others." Her mother had said the day before she passed.

This had given her so much hope, but it had been five years and still nothing. She suddenly noticed for the first time that she had torn the green pleated skirt; one of her favorite skirts from her mother's inheritance. She loved it because her mum had worn it all the time, but it seemed to never age. Now an unexpected fall had ruined her moss crepe skirt, which was notorious for fraying if not mended properly. As she looked at it, she realised it would be difficult to repair, because it had torn against the grain and she would have to let it go. A dark cloud seemed to follow her, and she was tired of being the underdog. Just looking at the skirt made her more agitated. She pushed Mai Mupa away and once again began rolling in the soil and demanding answers from that higher force. She did not want to be calmed. Inheriting a 68-year-old woman's clothes had allowed the world to calm her. Her patience and acceptance of situations had seen her living off handouts from her family, but she wanted a new beginning. A chapter that no longer settled.

As she continued weeping, she noticed that a small crowd had gathered, made up of the elderly women residents on her street. They had bought their homes as young civil servants, mainly schoolteachers and were now retired and enjoying staying at home. As she paused to take a breath, she overheard one of the old women saying,

"I always knew she was cursed…"

Could it be possible that she was cursed? The first year after she took over the agricultural project, she had lost so many of the chickens and goats that got sick and perished mysteriously. It was also a drought year, so the fields did not yield as much as they used to, and she lost the supermarket deal. She had had to look once again to her siblings for help to get by. The strange thing was she was not lazy at all. She spent all her days on the plot working hard and only getting into the house at supper time. So even when her siblings called or asked the neighbours, they always heard of how hard she worked. But somehow, all the work seemed to be going into a deep dark hole.

"Mupa, Mupa! Come here with Gibson!" Mai Mupa shouted into her yard, calling her grandson Mupa Jnr who was visiting her for the holidays. Gibson was her gardener who had lived with her for many years. She did not see them coming; and all she recalled was that they lifted her and took her into her parents' house. Mai Mupa led the way holding Fari's cellphone and house keys and the one American dollar she had carried with her to the shops to make her purchase. Fari heard Mai Mupa telling the other women that they could leave and because Mai Mupa was an opinion leader in the street, the other women left. When they eventually got into the house, Mai Mupa broke into a worship song. She sang and sang and as she did, they made her want to cry even more. Fari just rolled onto the old maroon carpet that covered the living room floor.

As her face landed on that carpet, she remembered how happy she had been as a child sitting on that carpet. Her mother never allowed children to sit on the couches, so this was a very familiar space. But being there lying on the same floor, knowing she has been unable for over 20 years to change that carpet, lying to herself that replacing it would have taken away the memories that the carpet represented made it worse. There were parts of it that were now torn and all she could do was mend it with small pieces of different colored carpets she had taken when the neighbors had renovated their homes.

These thoughts brought in a new wave of pain. It was as if she was possessed, and she did not understand what was going on. She just felt like letting it all out and cry. Mai Mupa then stopped singing and broke into serious prayer. She prayed for what felt like an eternity. Fari did not listen to the words and kept crying, screaming and protesting against this unknown higher force. She had been fasting, so she had not eaten for a while and suddenly felt very weak. She realised that she had used up most of her energy and strength, so she lay on the carpet sobbing quietly. Mai Mupa came close to her and asked if she was ok.

"I am fine, thank you so much," she said.

"I will check on you again later."

"No, I am fine mama." Fari said

"So, I will see you tomorrow at 6pm." She said walking out.

"Please lock the screen door and the gate padlock as you go out." Fari told Mai Mupa.

That was the last thing she recalled from that day. As soon as Mai Mupa left, she fell into a deep sleep. She was not sure how long she had slept but she was startled by a huge bang on the kitchen door. She thought she had been sleeping for a few minutes but when she sat up and looked at Mupa Jnr banging the door, she realised there was a problem.

"It's ok, she just woke up!" Mupa shouted to someone at the gate.

"Oh, thank God!" she heard several voices say from the gate.

She stood up and unlocked the screen door. As she did so, there was a sharp pain on her knee. That was when she remembered that horrible fall. She gave the boy the key to open the gate. And looked at the clock. 2.45pm. How could this be possible, she thought she had slept for an exceptionally long time, but it seemed the time had not moved at all. She moved closer to the clock to check if the clock was working, and as she got closer, the minute hand moved.

"Fari, oh my child. Thank God you are ok," Mai Mupa said as she walked in accompanied by Maiguru, Fari's maternal aunt, her mother's older sister.

"Fari have you gone mad? Why do you have all this soil all over your body?" Maiguru said as she embraced her.

"Have you been sleeping all this time?" Mai Mupa asked. "You do realise that it's already the next day, did you sleep for a whole day?"

Fari said nothing. She just stood there looking at them. Could it be true that she had gone into a 24-hour nap?

"I was so worried I ended up calling your aunt and asking my nephew to jump over and see what was going on. When I left you yesterday you were such a mess, so I was worried. I thought something had happened to you. I gave Mupa the truck and he drove to Gutu to collect your aunt because I was so worried and confused.

Fari's heart leapt with joy when she saw her aunt. "Thank you for coming mama." She said embracing her.

"Mai Mupa, thank you my dear. Let me talk to this child and then we can discuss your suggestion and see what to do." Maiguru said as she beckoned Mai Mupa to leave.

"What's wrong Fari? Why are you so angry? Do you know that there are homeless and destitute people out there, but they never lose hope? Why do you act like the family has neglected you? Why are you acting like you have no money? Do you know there are people who have gone for days without food?" Maiguru said.

"It's not enough. No one else with the same qualifications as I do lives like me. It's not enough mama, and I am not happy. I am the scum of the earth," she said, about to start weeping again.

"We need to fix your leg before it gets septic. Let us go and bath and see how we can fix that leg." Maiguru who was a retired nurse said.

"I don't care if my leg gets septic. This is the problem with my life. Everyone just looks for ways to patch me up. She does not have a job, give her a few dollars. She does not have shelter, give her her parents' house. She does not have clothes – wait a minute there are trunks full of clothes that belonged to a 60-year-old woman who passed years ago, give them to her. I am tired of being everyone's patch project. Everyone just bringing bits and pieces to create the impression that I am alive when in reality – I am not." Fari said sobbing.

"Oh, my goodness, life is always changing Fari. Don't despise days of small beginnings." Maiguru said

"I am 40 years and a day today. What beginning is this, retirement is almost here, and you are telling me about beginnings. I have read all those stories of the late bloomers, but I also know millions of stillborn children, so all I am saying is I am mad mama. I am tired of waiting, tired of trying to breakthrough but nothing ever really happening.

Look in that corner, there are Tupperware brochures, and over there some Aloe brochures. Over here some forex thing I have tried, and in those trays are things from when I tried cake baking. In that small pile are secondhand clothes I have been buying in Mozambique to sell. There at that desk I teach extra maths, physics and science classes. There in that small room are my harvests from the plot. I sell them. But you know what, people do not pay their debts. Others just ignore me. After all this effort, I still wear secondhand underwear. What did I do wrong?" Fari began to weep again.

"I hear you my dear. We all know and agree that laziness is not the reason why you are in the situation you are in. It is a pity that good guy you had found ended up not marrying you. That could have been your saving grace. Now that I am seeing your situation, through your eyes, I think I agree with Mai Mupa. Something is wrong somewhere."

"Tonight, there is going to be a crusade on the dusty open piece of land in front of the shopping center. It does not make sense why this church has chosen this spot because it is generally a nosy space busy with cars and pedestrians going up and about to buy different things from the shopping center. But they have chosen it. Isn't there a bottle store behind the shops? Anyway, Mai Mupa says it has helped people with different challenges to overcome. Apparently, the preacher is a powerful man of God. Maybe you should consider joining them for the next five days. At this point, we don't know where your breakthrough is going to come from." Maiguru said.

So began Fari's quest to find an answer to her problems, beyond the Tupperware and secondhand clothes and pyramid schemes. For five days, she had gone to the crusade and listened to the preacher. She was unsure what exactly she was going there for, which particular component of her life she wanted to evolve, but she went there anyway. Desperate for some good news. Maiguru and Mai Mupa begged Fari to take a bath to wash away the soil and the blood or at least change out of her clothes that made her look like a mad woman. To this she remarked.

"But this is way better than what I feel inside. It's a mess…" as she walked out of the house for the last day of the crusade.

She was hopeful that this crusade would transform her story because night after night, she had listened to various people giving their testimonies about how prayer had changed their lives. The other night a woman who was barren had confessed that she now had a child. Some man talked about getting a job after years of struggle. There was a woman who had got healed of some terminal disease and was now fit as a fiddle. Every night they went up there and every night she held her breath and prayed that maybe one day this too would be her story.

The church had set up a big stage where the preacher and the praise and worship team sat and stood to sing and share the word of God at various intervals. They always came so well dressed, wearing their beautiful matching outfits. Each day they would wear a different type of outfit and they would sing their hearts out. So powerful and deep were the songs they sang, that they often left the audience in tears. As they transitioned from the praise songs which usually saw a cloud of dust covering the whole area because they all stood up and danced as if in dancing the doors of heaven would open. People's moods would quickly shift from the praise songs to the worship moods which would change from the happy "I am a winner" to a more "Oh, I am so broken" type of mood. The sad mood would seem to continue throughout the service and each time she lifted her head someone was weeping and just asking for that special kind of miracle.

On this night, her mind had drifted in and out of the actual service. She still had not bathed and could now smell her own body odor, because it was a hot summer, and she was always sweating. It had been five days and she just did not know if the breakthrough would happen this time around. She was anxious that all this prayer and fasting would be another false start to her next 40. Unlike the previous days where she had attended the service as if in a trance, on this specific day she had suddenly become conscious of her surroundings. In this crowd, so many people had brought so many of their burdens, and like her they were also looking for that breakthrough. Maybe God thought their issues were more important than hers…The worship team broke into another song,

"*Tumirai Mweya, Mutsvene nemoto,*
Kana tonamata, munamato wedu usvike!
Send your holy spirit and a fire oh Lord,
So that when we pray our prayers may be heard!"

The worshipers kept repeating. As this song began, Fari felt the urge to weep. Why had He turned a blind ear to all her pleas? It had been years. Years of being honest and ensuring that she followed all the commandments and yet there seemed to be a dark cloud that not only followed her, but always found a way into her life. She began to look around the audience as she was crying and praying. There was so much pain on this open piece of land. Although it was summer, it had not rained in a while and the dust seemed to make everything look even more barren as the sun was setting. Even the shopping center looked so neglected and old. She suddenly noticed that the huge shop that had once stood out with its bright yellow paint now looked dull and some of the paint was peeling off.

Opposite the shopping center there were some vegetable stalls where women and men sold fruits and vegetables. They appeared neglected because almost all the vendors who usually manned these stalls had used their proximity to the church place to secure themselves almost front row seats.

Her attention then came to the people who sat near and around her. Until now, she had never noticed them. For five days she just came focused on her one issue. Tonight, they had told them was the 'Night of Deliverance' and being a practical person, she began to wonder what the probability of her getting her miracle would be with all these people present.

On her left was a man who seemed to have something growing from his forehead. He had it covered in what used to be a white bandage but now looked brown and foul. Judging from the clothes he was wearing, he had lost a lot of weight because his clothes appeared oversized. He looked fragile as he raised his hands in worship. She could hear him weeping rather loudly, "I am back again today Lord, won't you hear my plea?" He seemed to be saying. So deep and intense was his plea that it added to her grief. She found herself praying for him too. Maybe maiguru was right, there were people who had much bigger problems than she did. At least she still had her health.

She turned to her right and there too was a young man who was kneeling in prayer. He had his hands on the benches that had been provided and what drew her attention was the rope running through the belt loops around his trouser. It was made of plastic insulated electricity codes exposing the earth, live, neutral colors intertwined to strengthen it. They say a man's belt and shoes will tell you his story and she did not need any further narration of the journey this young man had travelled. Although he was wearing formal clothes, he was also wearing a pair of plastic flip flops. The bright yellow footwear was in sharp contrast with the rest of his clothes, exposing unmoisturised cracked heels. The young man had evidently bathed, because the smell of cheap soap lingered on his dry flaky skin. His oversized formal shirt and pants explained why he needed to use that 'belt'. She wondered if his shirt had been tucked in as a form of respect for the 'house' of the Lord.

There were two women directly in front of her. One was on her knees holding a pair of baby booties. She held them up, silently weeping without saying much. There were people in wheelchairs and on crutches. There were people who looked too fragile to stand up. She wondered if these people had been waiting for their deliverance for all the five days she had been going too, or they knew that today was going to be a big day.

The service began and the preacher took the microphone.

"Today I am not going to preach, but we are going to talk to God to deliver us. Are you ready people of God to receive your miracles?" he said with excitement.

"YES!" many people shouted, some jumping up.

"And you," the preacher said, "Why are you not excited?" he suddenly said pointing in Fari's direction. She panicked for a bit, "I mean that young lady with short hair and a green top." He said describing her. "Come forward, today the Lord says it's enough!!" he said as ushers made their way towards her to take her to the front. She walked with a limp and hoped the man of God would not assume she was there because of the limp.

As she found her way to the front, others cheered her on and encouraged her. Mai Mupa moved towards her and said, "I knew you would get your breakthrough this week." Fari's heart beat fast and she was afraid. Her doubts began overwhelming her. Why would God choose to hear her prayers and not that man with the growth or the weeping woman with the baby boots.

"Come forward, come forward! Receive it, receive it!" he said as she continued to walk towards the front.

Suddenly her phone rang, she could not see who it was because the screen was broken, and she decided to pick up the call. After all, her phone had not rung in an awfully long time. Meanwhile the audience was getting more and more excited. Fari suddenly noticed a path on her left that would lead her out of the service. Without thinking twice, she briskly walked out of the gathering and picked up the call.

"Hallo!" Fari shouted so that the caller could hear her. "Let me just move away. I am in a noisy place!" she said once again

"Ok," the caller said faintly.

Fari walked to the back of the vegetable stalls, it was quieter there.

"Hallo!" she shouted

"Oh, hallo, is this Farirai Shoko?" the caller asked in a polished British accent.

"Yes, this is Farirai Shoko." She responded.

"Oh, thank goodness, I have been sending you countless emails and getting no responses. You applied to the School of Science a while back. We had some funding challenges so had to freeze that postgraduate programme. But we just got good funding for it and we went back to old applications and really like yours. I am not saying you have secured the scholarship yet, because we will have to reassess you, specifically because you have been out of school for a while now. If you pass the assessment, then we will take you on…"

Fari could not believe what she was hearing. This was the first response she had got for anything she had applied for since she left college. Could it be that the revival had brought her deliverance? Could it be that her anger and fasting and praying had led to the breaking of the curse? Or could it be that her mother's last blessing on her was starting to manifest? Or was it just her time for things to start happening…?

She was not my type

"Sister Jane?" the Uber driver asked as he pulled up in front of her.

"Yes, do you mind if I sit in front? I am a bit motion sick."

"Absolutely sis. Your ride, your choice of seat!" he said.

She opened the door and sat next to him. Her reasons for choosing the front seat were beyond the motion sickness. Jane was a Zimbabwean living in South Africa. She had moved to South Africa at the peak of one of the most horrifying xenophobic violence to affect the country in 2008. She had not only seen in the news the images of the 'burning man' Ernesto Alfabeto Nhamuave, but she had had her fair share of experiences of xenophobia, though not violent. So, she made a conscious decision to at least always sit in front when she used transport like this, so that she knew what was going on with the driver and have a bit of control should things go south.

The driver looked like a young man, in his early 30s. He seemed a bit short because of how his seat was pulled so closely to the steering wheel. He had a very pleasant smile and seemed like one of those guys one would call a *skhothane*. These young people, born in post-independent South Africa were easily identifiable by the expensive clothes they wore. They liked letting people know how much they spent on these clothes, because it was a sign of their level of success.

Jane was not very streetwise, but she could tell from this young man's demeanor that he really believed he was a force to reckon with. His clothes were loud with a lot of yellow and red. He wore expensive perfume and kept looking at his wristwatch, which Jane assumed must have also cost him an arm and a leg. The Uber taxi drivers used smartphones for business and this young man had the latest iPhone as his business phone.

"Is there a route you prefer to get you home sis?" he said with a smile, and Jane immediately noticed his gold teeth. The man, Nqobile, as the Uber App showed, had several gold teeth. After he smiled, he made a strange sucking sound which made Jane think it was the effect of having all that metal in his mouth.

"I will direct you, but I don't think your GPS would take you too far off," she responded and smiled back.

"Do you want air conditioning, and which radio station do you prefer?" He asked once again.

"I am ok with the current condition for both thank you Nqobile," she responded.

"It's so hot, would you like some bottled water or juice?" He asked.

"No thank you, I am fine. You are far too kind." Jane responded.

This was the longest question and answer Jane had had before a ride commenced since she started using this mobile transport application. None of the drivers had ever offered her something to drink before. So, she was convinced that this was going to be a remarkably interesting ride. She was also in the mood for a fun chat, and Nqobile looked like a nice young man, so she relaxed and absorbed the mood.

As the ride began, the DJ on the radio asked an interesting question.

What is the one thing you have done which is out of your character? Send us your voice note on 334400 or call us on 100-650-184. We want to hear from you!

Nqobile immediately interjected whilst Jane was still focusing on the question. "Sisters, what would your response to this one be? If you don't mind that is." He said and immediately sucked at his teeth again.

Jane wanted to tell him to stop that strange sucking and that she preferred to listen to the radio station than to share her own stories, but she realised that Nqobile's question was driven by his desire to tell her his story.

"Aaargh look Nqobile, I am an extremely boring person – a creature of habit I would say, so not much to share. What of you?" Jane asked

"I thought you would never ask sisters!" he said, sounding extremely excited and ready to tell his story.

Jane was sure it was going to be larger than life, with some serious exaggerations, judging from what Nqobile's personality had shown thus far.

"Sisters, mine is a long story I tell you, but I hope after this story, you will also give me some advice on what I should do.

So, as you can see, I am quite a prolific person. If you visit my neighborhood in Voslorus and just ask for Nqo, even a small baby will show you where I live. I have my things in order. This Uber business is just a side hustle I do to keep myself busy, but my core business is that I throw these huge socials in my township. You should come through some time. They are so great, and I have gained popularity over the years. I am selling out events now and you know when I thought to go into this business, I was like let me just buy these cars cash and diversify my portfolio you know." He said.

Jane smiled and said, "Wow, I would have never guessed you were such an entrepreneur!" This story did not really excite her. She had hoped Nqo would share a more elaborate story demonstrating he had acted out of character.

But that he does socials wasn't really something that excited Jane.

"Anyway sisters, I am the kind of guy who has dated supermodels, slay queens, and I have won girls who billionaires wanted but I came up tops you know. If I wanted you, I am so convinced that I have the capacity and resources to sweep you off your feet, because I am charming and I know how to treat a woman right. Once I wanted this girl from Pretoria. For Valentine's Day, I flew her to Mauritius and let's just say the rest is history. When I want her, I get her no matter what. But I'm generally a player and I easily get bored with women and just move on.

So anyway, this other day we were chilling at a hot spot in my hood. You know, where the who-is-who go to chill, and this girl came in a car with a man I assumed was her blesser. She did not leave the car; the man just got out of the car and went to buy some take away. I asked my friends who that girl was because we know the man. I later learnt it was his daughter, a very uptight girl who was a bit of a nerd. Look, she wasn't even beautiful, and she just looked plain, but somehow I just really wanted to see if I could charm such a girl.

I went up to the father's car and greeted her and asked for her number. She spoke in an accent like these people you know *ama*Zimbabwe. It was strange because her father was one of us, so I did not understand how she sounded so Mugabe. Ha ha ha ha!! I later learnt that her mother was a Zimbabwean and had at some point left the country with her as a baby after they had challenges with the father. She had only come back to South Africa when she was going to college, but somehow that Mugabe accent had refused to leave her.

Anyway, she gave me her number and we began chatting on the phone. She was doing her master's degree at that time in financial management and you know what, I had never had such intelligent conversations with anyone in my life before. By the time we went for our first date, she was teaching me things about life and managing my finances.

I won't lie sisters; I make a lot of money. I have deals which I will not talk about here, but somehow before I met this girl, I never had any savings. I stayed in a rented house and owed hundreds of thousands in credit cards, traffic fines, and other credit. She went on a journey with me and helped me clean up my act. It's been 3 years now and I have a house to my name, I have this thriving Uber business – I have seven cars under my belt – I am almost done with my credit card debts and I even have some good savings sisters. This girl is just amazing, it's as if she has a magic wand which just put my life in order.

My mother loves her, because now I have even managed to renovate my mother's house and she has seen more of my money than she has ever dreamed she would. I am really a better man," he said with a glow in his eyes.

He then shifted and began pulling something out of a compartment under his steering wheel. Jane got into panic mode. She began to imagine the worst-case scenario. Was this man telling her all this to then pull out a gun and rob her or even rape her. She remembered the rape statistics in South Africa; did she not read just the other day that there was an average of 116 reported rapes each day in the country? What of the ones that were not reported? We all know people don't always go the police when such things happen. She put her hand in her handbag and gently started fiddling to find the pepper spray her cousin had recently given her after she was also nearly raped. She also checked the doors and was relieved that they were unlocked, so she could find a way to escape somehow.

Nqo seemed to have sensed her anxiety and as he was about to pull out whatever he was looking for in the compartment, he asked if she was ok. Jane responded that she was fine, just the motion sickness getting the best of her.

"*Eish*, sorry sisters. You need to come to Voslorus and see mama Mnemo, she is really good with herbal remedies for different things. She might be able to assist you because imagine if you buy a Ferrari; how will you even enjoy the speed if you always get motion sick in moving cars?" he asked looking very concerned and sucking at his teeth as he looked at Jane, waiting for her response. Jane just smiled but did not respond. She was calming down now when she realised he had pulled out a small black suede box and not a gun.

"Tonight sisters, I am going to ask her to marry me." He said opening a box with a very expensive looking ring. It was the kind of ring Jane expected from someone with this guy's personality. Something anyone could see from far off.

"But my boys don't understand why I am with someone like her. She was not my type at all sisters. I mean she is a good girl, a church girl. She doesn't even own a Brazilian weave and won't allow me to buy her one. She is obsessed with this natural hair business and sometimes she can even come to one of my big parties in cornrows. She drives some cheap Chinese car no one even knows except her, even though she can afford a much better car and frankly sisters, she is not beautiful. She is dark and a bit on the chubby side. Like when I introduced her to my boys, no one understood, and they didn't think she and I would last you know. I usually go for yellow bones, but there I was with this black number.

But now they love her. She is wise and she updates us on so many important things happening in the world. But even on social media, it took me a while to get the courage to post a picture of us together and when I did my DM was flooded with messages. Some of my exes laughed that I must have hit hard times and could no longer afford to keep my woman. The strange thing though is that the more they DMed the more I wanted to show her off and all she has done for me. I mean now my social media has also changed a lot since I met her. I used to post about clothes and parties mainly but now I am also talking about current affairs. Sisters, I even read the news now!" Nqo chuckled.

"Tell me though Nqo, do you think marrying someone you say is not your type is the best thing to do? I mean what happens when you wake up one day and realise you miss the slay queens and yellow bones?" Jane asked him, with concern.

"I am 47 years old sisters. For 44 years I was having a blast and just living in the moment. I had nothing to my name except clothes and stamps in my passport as well as a huge social media following and lots of pictures at parties. If I wake up one day and think I miss the last 44 years, then I will lock myself up and revisit the last three years and remind myself of all the gains I have made, and I am so sure more awaits.

What I forgot to tell you is that I now love her so much. You said she is not my type, but I say she was not my type, but now I think she is. She is an awesome person and even though a lot of the messages I get on social media imply that she is lucky to catch a big shark like me, I know personally that I am the lucky one.

Would you believe that since I met her, she has never demanded all these expensive things other women demanded from me. For the first time ever, a woman bought me a well thought out gift which she actually paid for herself. When I wanted to take her on a vacation, she first asked me if I had saved for it or was using my credit card. When I tried to defend myself and tell her that it was the same anyway because I would just repay it, she told me to wait. We eventually went when I could prove that we were spending money I had earned not just swiping my credit card." He said.

"I must say, you look a lot younger than your actual age. I would never think you were almost 50. I honestly thought you were in your 30s. So, does she know that she was not your typical type of girlfriend?" Jane asked.

"Ha ha ha! You are not the first person to say this. Even when I met my woman's family, they did not believe I was such an old man. But I think it's also because I dress so well and I eat healthy, I go to the gym every day. Thank you for the compliment by the way.

About the girlfriend, a lot of people have told her that over the years. Some of my ex-girlfriends have even got in touch with her to annoy her and push her away from me by telling her all sorts of things, mostly true about me and them and how I am obsessed with how a woman looks, and hence they did not understand how on earth she ended up with me. The weirdest thing about her though is that she is so confident in her own skin. She really can't be bothered. She turned me into a sapiophile." Nqobile concluded as he stopped the car suddenly. There was a car parked in front of them that had hazards on. Nqo could not use the other lane because there was also another car on that side.

He hooted and hooted, but neither of the cars were moving. As he attempted to reverse, a third car drove and parked behind them. Nqo seemed panicked and whispered, "Relax sisters, I will try to handle this."

"Eita," a guy said as he walked up to Nqo's side of the car. Another walked to Jane's side and signaled that the window be opened.

As soon as the window opened the guy on Jane's side held her hand so tight, she nearly screamed.

"We have been tracking this car the whole day. You have something that belongs to us." The guy standing next to Nqo said. "Give it to us or we will take your girl."

"You can't take the girl and I don't know what you are talking about." Nqo said

Jane's heart was racing. She did not understand what was going on and she felt very confused.

"We will strip this car if we have to, that ring is worth millions of dollars. We know Zack sold it to you, how much did you pay for it?" the man shouted.

"No, my guy, I did not know it was hot property, Zack made me pay R70,000 for it. He said it was his mother's ring and he had inherited it upon her passing." Nqo said. Jane couldn't help but note how genuine he sounded. She noticed that the man next to Zack also picked up on his sincerity.

"That ring is worth millions and that is why we have a tracker in the box you bought it in. We know it's in your car. So, do you want us to do this the hard way, i.e. my guy there takes your girl and we do what we want with her until you give us the ring or will you just give us the damn ring?" he said.

Jane was now shaking and crying. This felt like something she saw only in the movies.

"Please leave the girl out of this. She is just my client! I operate a transport service and I only just met her. You can search her and just let her go. It's me you want. She is a clever girl and will not tell anyone about what happened." Nqo said.

"Stop it, just give us the ring and we will let both of you go. You know where to find Zack; he will give you your money back Nqo." The guy said.

Nqo looked at Jane. He looked very sad that this was happening.

"It's in the glove compartment, let me take it out." Nqo said.

"No, allow us!" the guy said quickly opening the door on Jane's side and opening the glove compartment. He pulled out the box, took out the ring and as quickly as they had arrived, they disappeared. All three cars drove off so fast and Nqo began apologizing frantically.

"Sisters I am so sorry about what just happened there. I swear I did not know that Zack had sold me stolen goods. I am so sorry. Are you ok?" Nqo asked frantically.

Jane could not say much; she just sat there sobbing from the aftermath of a very horrifying incident. Her palms were sweating and her whole body was shaking.

"I am so glad they did not do anything to you. I swear if they had tried, I would have died fighting them off. Yobe sisi. Yobe!" Nqo kept saying until Jane was calm.

"Please, I will save your number and see what I can do for you to make up for this horrible incident. I hate people who treat women like objects. What was the link between the ring he wanted from me and taking advantage of you? It's disgusting and I am taking my friend, who is a policeman, to the place Zack hangs out soon after this. He has to pay for what he has done."

Jane did not hear much of what Nqo had said. She looked up and realized that they were a few meters from where she lived. She opened the car door and ran out as fast as she could, forgetting her computer bag. She ran into the complex, barely greeting the security guards.

She tried to relive everything that had happened from the moment the cars stopped and wondered if sitting in the front seat had actually increased her vulnerability, because those guys had assumed she had a connection with the driver. *Would they have treated her differently if she was sitting in the back seat,* she thought? She felt so dirty and could still feel that man whose face she could not even remember, holding her upper arm so tight. She suddenly realised there was some pain where he held her and looked at it. He had held her so tight that his hand had left deep painful bruises.

Jane ran a bath and just sat there, trying to recount the events around the day. She was still in the bath when her phone rang. It was the security guards telling her she had a guest. She was not expecting anyone when they told her it was a man called Nqo.

"I am coming down." Jane said and dressed up quickly to find out why this guy was back. The guards told him to drive in and park near the security post. When she got there, Nqo handed her the computer bag, Jane had not even realised she had left it behind until that moment. It would have been a disaster if she had lost it as it contained a very expensive computer she had ordered recently at work. Her boss would have killed her. Nqo also handed her an orchid in a cute flowerpot and without saying a word started reversing out of the parking lot.

"Nqo! What of the ring and the proposal?" Jane shouted.

"It's still going down sisters. But this time I went to a shopping mall for the ring. It is going down tonight still!" he said laughing so hard.

"Nqo, thank you!" Jane said.

"*Sho!*" He said, winking and showing off his gold teeth.

Jane walked back to her apartment and as soon as she settled, she read the little card Nqo had placed in the flowerpot.

"Not all of us are bad sisters! I am so sorry about what happened today. Yobe! Nqo."

Oh, my goodness, this has got to be one of the craziest days I have had in a while. Jane thought as she fell asleep, silently thanking Nqo for defending her in the moment of danger. She realised that had the guys not threatened to take her, he would have made an effort to fight.

Panashe Mawoneke

Panashe is a young talented and upcoming female author, born and raised in Chimanimani, Zimbabwe. Her thirst is for writing stories based on community and everyday lives of different people and cultures. She wrote two short stories about her personal experience during the Cyclone Idai disaster and the Coronavirus pandemic. She is a TV Presenter in the making and enjoys watching documentaries and TV Shows.

Cyclone Idai

"Panashe!" my mom called. My intuition always sensed the urgency in my mom's voice when she wanted me immediately. She asked me to attend to a knock at the door. It was a soft but demanding knock, and I was curious to know who it could be. To my surprise, I found a good-looking tall white man standing outside.

"Hi, may I see Willis?" he asked in his American accent. He introduced himself as John.

"Hello John, you're welcome!" I greeted him with confidence and the courteous beam of a local resident who rarely interacted with white people. I ushered him in, then called my uncle Willis. After a few minutes of John and Uncle Willis chatting, I offered our visitor a drink. Whilst serving him, my curious ears overheard information which stole my attention.

The white man was telling my uncle that he intended to leave Chimanimani as soon as possible. This was because a tropical cyclone had been forecast, and it was expected to hit Chimanimani, Chipinge and other parts of Zimbabwe imminently.

The word 'cyclone' struck my core like an electric shock. After John announced this concerning prediction, no one in my family knew what to do next. John had come to Chimanimani to tour our beautiful attractions – the Outward Bound, Bridal Veil Falls, and the Pork Pie Mountains among others. When he left, we had so many unanswered questions. I quietly wondered if we would survive the unlikely prophecy.

We found it easier to ignore the warning and continued with our chores as normal. None of us believed the cyclone would affect us. The day carried on as it usually did, and by the time we went to bed, John's forecast had proven false. However, I sensed some truth in what he had told us.

14th of March 2019 presented a fine morning. I woke up early and said my morning prayers, asking God to have mercy and save us, because what was ahead of us was unknown. Following my prayers, I did all my chores. The weather was perfect, as usual. A sunny sky graced us with comfortable heat, and there was not a single sign of danger in the atmosphere. I decided to stroll around our neighbourhood to assess the situation and to find out what others knew. News had spread that Cyclone Idai was travelling from Mozambique and on its way to hit Chimanimani and Chipinge. Nobody thought anything disastrous would result from the predicted cyclone.

"*Hesi* Panashe!" my paternal aunt Naomi greeted me. She was a cousin to my father. I was deep in thought and had unconsciously arrived at our main shopping centre, Chimanimani Village.

"*Hesi Tete, munofara here?*" I greeted her back. "*Mwanangu,* have you heard of the cyclone that everyone is talking about?"

"Yes *tete,* I wonder what God has in store for us." I replied.

"Do not fear my dear, we are safe here and nothing will happen to us," Aunt Naomi said to me with assured confidence. As I walked around, I decided to approach a woman at the same marketplace. I asked her if she knew about the Cyclone, and she had not heard the news, which she dismissed as rumours.

"Child, are you insane?" she walked away as she waved off my claims as nonsense. Another onlooker, a pregnant woman who was also at the market could not believe the cyclone predictions. Feeling confused by the conflict between my reality and intuition, I bought my tomatoes and left the market.

As I walked back home, I lapsed into deep thought, worrying about the safety of my dad who was in Tarka Forest. He was working there as a Forester. There was a phone network problem in Tarka and I did not have any means of communication to warn him about the Cyclone. My gut nagged me to take cover, but as I scanned the horizon in search of signs of danger, everything seemed normal. I observed that everyone went about their business, nonchalantly like any other day.

Later that afternoon, around 3:30pm, there was a sudden cloud cover. The glorious sun that had kissed our fontanelles earlier vanished, as cumulonimbus clouds spread rapidly over the sky to displace the glorious weather. People started talking about the predicted Cyclone Idai again.

As the day progressed, I felt immense fear of the unknown, but was so helpless, as one would when faced with the prospect of death.

Heavy winds waltzed into the atmosphere and soon became harsh, then light raindrops began to fall. Tree leaves detached from weak branches as they clumsily broke off big trees that were buying time but would undoubtedly eventually uproot. Weak rooftops were extremely compromised by the merciless winds. I began to notice early dismissal of personnel from banks and other businesses. Most families rushed back into their homes to cook early supper and stay put, to avoid exposing themselves to danger. That evening, at around 7:00pm the raindrops thickened and were now accompanied by mist and heavier wind. Suddenly, there was a power cut, and the cell phone network signal was immediately lost. Radio station signals were also lost. In that moment of dark silence, I sensed looming danger.

This was one of the worst nights of my life. My mom and I were restless and terrified. Each time I lapsed into sleep, my mom woke me up to check that my siblings and I were okay, and to pray. Uncle Willis also stayed up in our sitting room, confused and helpless. We had celebrated his birthday the previous week when he turned 48.

My sister's children, Tadiwa and Yolanda who were five and seven years old respectively, had gone to bed because due to their ignorance of the situation, they were fearless and indifferent. All they talked about was how they were going to spend their day the following day. Heavy rain continued to fall, accompanied by heavy winds. I finally fell asleep around 4:00am, then suddenly woke up around 6:00am to face the worst nightmare of my life.

15th of March 2019 was a Friday. The storm had not subsided from the previous night. There was still no electricity, so I went to Ngangu mountain to fetch wood to make a fire. What shocked me was that I found no one at the mountain for the same mission as mine. I quickly returned home because it was very scary to be alone there. When I arrived home, the firewood was wet; so it took me more than an hour to make the fire. When I finally got the fire going, I made porridge for Tadiwa, Yolanda and my mother. As it was end of week, I anticipated the return of my dad from Tarka for the weekend. I prayed for his safe travel and hoped he would soon arrive.

Heavy downpours of rain and harsh winds continued that morning. I thought of walking around again to check on our neighbours. Trees were still being uprooted by winds and falling down. Children and workers stayed home.

Everyone sensed that the rain was not normal rain. Deep in my heart, I could feel God telling me that something terrible was about to happen. There were vast bodies of water everywhere! Houses were immersed in water. There was no sign of clouds clearing. In fact, the clouds seemed to be multiplying. There was no electricity and businesses had been brought to a sudden halt. A few shops were open, but no one could have known or predicted what would happen next.

News had already been circulating on Social Media, WhatsApp and Facebook, about Cyclone Idai, which was said to be on its way.

God answered my prayer that afternoon when my dad arrived safe and sound!

"Did you know about the cyclone? Did you have any idea about the news?" My mom asked my dad.

"I had no idea about all this! Even the people down in Tarka are not aware of the cyclone!" I empathised with the people in Tarka and said a little prayer to God, to save and protect their souls.

That evening, the rainfall intensified, and the winds' viciousness increased. We were in no doubt that the predicted cyclone was approaching. Boisterous winds blew from the East to West and vice versa. At around 9:00pm when heavy downpours of water continued to cause offence, that is when I believed that Idai was real. It continued to rain incessantly for three consecutive hours. We could not see anything since there was a thick darkness. We all packed ourselves in the sitting room which we thought was the safest, and danger free zone.

Eating *sadza* suddenly seemed like a luxury one would only enjoy when happy and content. On this unforgettable day, we all went to sleep on empty stomachs due to worry which had robbed our appetites. Mom gave the young ones some groundnuts to enable them to sleep well. The thick darkness was terrifying, and the sound of rain downpours felt like a horror movie. We all went to sleep with immense fear tormenting our minds.

In the middle of the night, I was awoken suddenly by a dreadful sound which sounded like a *gonyeti*, a heavy haulage truck, driving through strong wind. I soon found that the racket was due to collapsing houses and mudslides from nearby mountains. Humongous trees crushed down, floods burst through our neighbourhood, carrying unravelled rocks rolling from beneath the ground. Mud relentlessly trespassed people's homes, leaving their possessions slushed beyond repair. Heavy winds destroyed house roofs, which were carried away in floods. Downpours of rain freely flooded the roofless houses, weakening walls and foundations, and finally bringing the houses down.

I heard cries for help from our neighbours as their houses were washed away by the floods. There was lightning but not the usual lightning we know. Massive boulders tumbled carelessly, crushing upon each other to produce sparks which resembled lightning and tremors like those of an earthquake. I felt my bed shaking. It was a miracle that we all woke up safe the next morning around 4:00am, but all our hope was lost.

Rescuers from homes which had remained intact began helping victims, retrieving dead bodies from the mud and under rocks, those who were trapped indoors and the injured. Corpses and the injured people were carried to nearby churches. It was traumatic to watch! The feeling of not knowing if our relatives or neighbours were alive was the worst feeling I had ever felt. People were caught unaware and unprepared by Idai. Some were already asleep, some were bathing, some cooking after a long day at work, some were even travelling back to their families, when the cyclone struck.

As the deadly winds began to calm down, we went outside to quickly inspect our house exterior, and we found it intact. However, there was severe disorder in our garden as the trees surrounding our yard had broken and continued to fall down. My mother called us back inside our house to say another prayer, and I personally prayed for everyone around Chimanimani to be safe in God's hands.

We could not go back to sleep, so we switched our phones on, even though there was no cellular network. I went outside to see if I could find cell phone reception to make a few calls. Unfortunately, my battery suddenly went off and I was not able to make any calls.

On Saturday the 16th of March, when the cyclone stopped, that is when I noticed the damage that Cyclone Idai had done to our Community. *Makoti* Anesu came home with bad news that many people had died in Ngangu. Anesu was my cousin brother's wife. She told us a list of the people she knew were already dead and whose houses had been swept away. I was shocked to learn that *Amainini* Linnet was dead too. Linnet was my mother's younger sister, but not from the same parents. I was deeply hurt to learn about her death.

When Uncle Willis switched on his phone and found cell phone reception, the effects of Cyclone Idai were all over Social Media. We read about the misery at St. Charles Lwanga Boys High School and the bad news in Koppa too. At St. Charles Lwanga Secondary school, the rainstorm had destroyed the boarding school. Two students and one staff member had died. In Koppa, houses were swept away with people inside. Crops and livestock were all ravaged. I could not believe what I saw on Social Media. Our beautiful tourist locations of Ngangu had been devastated by the Tropical

Cyclone Idai. Some houses had been swept away, leaving very deep gorges and big stones displaced in the area. Hearing all the updates gave me the strength to go out and see the damage for myself. Stanley, my cousin brother, escorted me. We shared the same totem. Outside, there were still rain showers and mist all over. I felt suffocated by pain, as if a massive rock had been placed on my heart. I was deeply shocked that water was capable of causing so much trauma.

My dad received a call from Tarka. His workplace had been destroyed by the cyclone and nothing was left intact. The beautiful forest had vanished. These news reports disturbed our family. Whilst I was preparing tea and yams, Aunt Isabel passed through our home on her way to Ngangu. With Isabel, we were not related but I liked calling her "aunt" because of her talent in giving advice. I wanted to accompany her there to see what really took place in Ngangu the previous night. I quickly put on my coat and boots, in readiness for the investigation. Stanley joined us on the trip on foot. As we approached Ngangu Clinic, I was shocked by the large rock boulders scattered everywhere. I could not help but wonder where such massive stones had emerged from.

Infrastructure, roads, electric wires and poles were destroyed. The Pondo Nyamatanda bridge was destroyed, and all crops near the bridge were washed away. New small temporary rivers and tributaries had formed. A dark cloud of sadness hit me when I saw all this. In Ngangu, everyone was rushing around in confusion. We bumped into my Aunt, *Amai va*Lovemore who happened to be in Ngangu.

"*Amainini* people are dying! The churches are full of injured and dead people!" she said crying her eyes out. She was my father's sister. When we had consoled each other, I increased speed with my brother and Aunt Isa. We met many people carrying their remaining property to safer and upper areas of Chimanimani Village. News had spread that everyone was supposed to move and go to Chimanimani Hotel for it was safer there and it was not known if the devastation had come to an end or not.

As we walked around, I was touched by the way a certain woman was explaining that the previous night, Cyclone Idai had torn into Mozambique first before progressing to Zimbabwe. I then thought to myself how badly it might have destroyed Mozambique where it originated, if it caused so much damage in Zimbabwe. I empathised with Mozambiquans.

Another woman was also wailing, telling people that she had been buried underneath by large rock boulders and her daughter, who she was in bed with, was washed away from her. I felt pity for her and was so touched. Her girl child of seven years old was found dead downstream the following morning. Everywhere I looked, I witnessed people with sad faces who had lost hope. Some men were busy digging for bodies buried underground. Some bodies were still missing. Up to that time, no external aide had arrived, and local people were just helping each other, by carrying the injured to the clinic.

Amidst the confusion and sorrow, the rain continued to fall, and mist remained steadfast. Dead bodies were still being found down streams and were carried to the Roman Catholic Church. A few individuals we recognised had also died the previous night whilst trying to save and help those who were in danger. Mr. Samhiri was one of those individuals who died helping. He owned a Boutique in Chimanimani Village. The last time I had talked to him was when he convinced me to buy new sandals from his store. I was deeply moved by lives lost due to acts of real courage.

As we continued to walk around and observe the situation, I began drowning in mud, an unexpected ordeal I had not anticipated. The Ngangu New Extensions area was heaped with mud and we had found it difficult to move from one place to another. I ended up regretting the tour, as I felt death suddenly approaching. I made a short prayer. I was 21 then and dying at such a young age was the last thing I wanted, because I had a lot of dreams to accomplish before my death. I was in the middle of hipped mud, struggling to pull out of it. Thankfully, my brother Stanley saved me. He pulled me out using a big stick. Aunt Isabel was busy racing up and down expressing her shock. Mud was all over my body, but I did not feel embarrassed because everyone looked the same. I thanked God for saving me. I wanted to continue with my education to University, graduate and relocate to Australia. I wanted to give my parents and future family the best life I could afford, and all these dreams were almost shattered. I thought that returning to safety was the best idea and we started walking back home.

By end of day, more than 150 people were reported dead and many more were still missing. Idai had caused the worst infrastructural damage ever known in Zimbabwe, after houses, roads and bridges were washed away by flash floods and strong winds. An area called Koppa is where the cyclone caused the most damage. Koppa is about 35km away from Ngangu. Houses, livestock and crops were washed away. People were also swept away and most of them were never found nor recovered and were suspected to have been washed into Mozambique. In Mozambique, a large dam had apparently collapsed and destroyed the city of Beira, and most of the cities of Mozambique were destroyed by Cyclone Idai.

Around 3:00pm of the same day, the army started arriving for rescue operations, though it was still raining and no roads were accessible. Air transport was the only means to reach survivors, but because of the mist, it was still very difficult to access. The injured were administered medication, which was at the clinic, whilst waiting for help. Dead bodies were still in piles in churches whilst plans were underway at the District Administrator's offices on how they were going to be buried. Calls for help continued to be made. Since there was still no electricity, the Post Office offered people to charge their cell phones using their generators. Cell phone reception remained intermittent and at most times not available, which meant people could not communicate with their relatives. Communication barriers caused many problems. Several injured victims ended up dying before being attended to. Many people perished and buildings crumbled into rubble. Eventually, rescue teams arrived and began to help.

On Sunday and the days that followed, the seriously injured were airlifted to Chipinge and Mutambara Hospitals for better treatment and medication. I then realised that most victims who survived the disaster had lost everything they owned including clothes and their homes, so they had nowhere to go. They had become homeless in just a matter of hours. My mother's brother, Uncle Tapiwa, who was walking home from Charter also died at Charter Bridge whilst trying to cross the severely flooded river. Charter is about 8 km away from Ngangu. He wanted to check on his family but he was swept away and his body was later discovered in Machongwe, an area 5km away from Charter Bridge.

On Tuesday, the deceased were buried in makeshift coffins, and only if there had been a relative to witness the burial. Roads were not accessible, and many people wished to take their relatives home for burial, but it was not possible. The army and other residents played a pivotal role in helping with the burials and rescuing those who were in need of urgent help. Food aid began arriving, as the news spread all over the world. Countries all over the world came together to offer assistance in cash and kind, mostly with food, clothes and money. Several Non-Governmental Organisations also came in to assist us.

At home, we also helped Granny, Uncle Tapiwa's wife and her two children, Varaidzo and Tanyaradwza who lost their home and father on the worst night of the Cyclone. Our house was not big enough to accommodate 8 people but we had to adapt to the new arrangements. All the girls slept in the sitting room whilst the boys took the girls room. Food became a big challenge. We could eat porridge in the morning and wait for supper. It was hard but I had to adapt, because it was no time for luxury. We stayed with our extended family for two weeks, until the temporary tents for the affected families were ready.

The Cyclone destroyed many schools, health facilities and properties, which affected the day-to-day lives of people and caused traumatic disorders. Local farmers lost all their crops and animals that would have normally fed the community. Churches united in assisting with counselling to the victims. Children became orphans, men became widowers and women became widows within a very short space of time. Many people were never found and are still missing.

May the souls of all who died rest in peace.

Coronavirus

Each day I stepped out to scan the horizon, my eyes were met by painful reminders of the tragic event that had nearly killed us only a year ago. The sight of boulders on roads, broken bridges and remnants of homes that had been washed away tore my heart apart and made me wonder when normalcy would return to our scenic community.

Ngangu village was still recovering from Cyclone Idai, which had devastated parts of Mozambique and Zimbabwe in March 2019. Those who lost their precious homes on that dreadful night were still living in temporary tents that had been set up by the United Nations. The life we had once known was still far from returning to us. Seeing our friends and relatives living in tents was very difficult. A family of eight that had once lived comfortably now shared a single room. Some of them had earned their income from rental properties, but due to the devastation of the Cyclone they were no longer house owners. Poverty was a challenge that now affected even those who had been well to do, and reliance on aide from the Government and Non-Governmental Organisations became their reality.

This wasn't enough for them. I remember this other day when I was in Chimanimani Village, I saw children of about seven years old picking leftovers from the bins, which was heartbreaking. Due to poverty, we witnessed a rise in adolescent pregnancies. Theft became popular in the tents since the shelters lacked a high standard of security. During the rainy season, victims suffered from severe colds due to inadequate insulation in the tents. The spread of diseases like malaria was also a big challenge.

Kelly, my former classmate was in China studying, and she had mentioned the Coronavirus to me whilst we were chatting on WhatsApp. "It has claimed a lot of lives in China apparently" I told my friend Bridget during our daily banter and gossip. "Kelly says they've been staying home for two months now and unnecessary movement is not allowed in China because of the disease. It seems quite serious!" Bridget shrugged, which was her usual sign of apprehension.

I worried about Coronavirus, because I did not want to lose my loved ones to yet another natural disaster.

The following morning, after I prepared breakfast for my parents, I decided to visit Isabel, my friend who lived in Ngangu New Extension area. I met Bridget along the way, and she decided to join me.

"Come in ladies," Isabel ushered us into her room. On her walls were pictures of models and some of her favourite foods that she had torn from glossy magazines. There were also prayers written on the walls which made us feel comfortable. She served us some fresh apples as we caught up on the latest local rumours and movies. After a while, Bridget's face turned more serious then she asked, "Panashe, can you please tell us more about the Covid19 you told me about yesterday?"

I loved it when I got the platform to speak, so I cleared my throat, and began to explain. "Alright girls listen very carefully. Covid19 is a disease caused by the new Coronavirus that emerged last year in China. It is called Covid19 because it appeared in 2019, CO stands for corona, VI for virus and D stands for disease. It appeared in Wuhan, a city in China last year." As I finished the last sentence, I took a final bite of my apple, then savoured the silence that filled the room in that moment. I must have impressed my friends who were clearly waiting for me to tell them more.

Isabel, who could wait no longer asked, "What are the symptoms of this disease?"

When I finished describing the symptoms, which Kelly had told me about in great detail, I added, "You must always monitor your symptoms, and if you become aware of anyone with these symptoms, you must encourage them to seek immediate medical attention. Mind you, this is different from any other sickness which we can nurse from home with our herbs or any other medicines, understood?"

"Yes!" they all responded, although they seemed concerned. Time seemed to fly when I spent time with my friends. It was almost lunch time, so I had to rush home to prepare a meal for my parents.

"Can you wash your hands dear before touching anything!" was my mom's response to my greeting. She was busy knitting her table mats for sale. She took orders every week from local residents and delivered them door to door when the mats were ready. This was also a source of income in my family. The Cyclone Idai had destroyed my father's workplace in Tarka the previous year. Mom had heard on the radio and on social media how the Coronavirus was killing thousands of people worldwide, so she was very serious about following all the recommended measures to stop the disease from getting anywhere near us. After we had eaten lunch and did some chores, mom called me outside to highlight some of the measures to prevent coronavirus. I enjoyed the lesson and looked forward to educating my friends more about the virus.

The month of March seemed to be a cursed month, having lost our friends and relatives to Cyclone Idai in March the previous year. Our family had fully recovered from the physical damage caused by Cyclone Idai but the traumatic memories of the disaster were still fresh in our minds, and we were still trying to heal emotionally from it. So soon after a natural disaster, we were now faced with a pandemic. The feeling of helplessness that had tormented me when Cyclone Idai was forecast, slowly began to eat me up. What could we do except to wait for our fate?

One morning, I was relaxing at home when I received a text message from Isabel. She was suggesting a day trip to Chimanimani Golf course for leisure with our friends. Mom allowed me to go, so I completed my chores swiftly and left before she changed her mind. I met Bridget and Chido at the Jacaranda tree near Tel One residents. This was our usual meeting point. We then started our journey on foot to the Golf Course, which was one kilometer away from our homes. When we got there, Isabel had already arrived and was waiting for us patiently. The golf course was the favourite hang-out place for most teenagers. We started taking selfies and admiring the surroundings. A lot of beautiful Gum and Cyprus trees surrounded the area with well-trimmed hedges. The lawn was evergreen and refreshing, which produced an outstanding appearance.

After a while, we sat down to catch up. We discussed trending hairstyles and fashion. We compared how people used to dress on *lobola* (bride price) ceremonies back then with how they dressed now.

"Have you guys noticed that these days people are dressing perfectly on *lobola* payments ceremonies more than how people dressed before?" Isabel said.

"Yeah! the friends and relatives of the bride now dress in coordinated African outfits with the same design and colours with that of the bride," I responded.

We also talked about men and relationships. Bridget shared her experiences with us on how she felt when she found out that her boyfriend Nick was cheating on her. We sympathised with her.

The looming pandemic must have been lingering on our minds, because we found ourselves continuing our discussion from the previous day. We did a quick recap on what we discussed previously on Covid19, then began discussing the prevention strategies. Bridget went on to give us the information she had gathered on the pandemic. When we had exhausted Coronavirus discussion, we dropped the topic and reverted to talk about more interesting issues. We parted ways when it was time to return home to prepare dinner.

Days turned into weeks, as global news reported about Coronavirus, but no cases had been announced in Zimbabwe by then. There were a lot of false rumours circulating in our community, about ways to cure Coronavirus. The Ngangu Clinic was open but the rumours were spreading like smoke in my Community.

My friends and I decided to meet and discuss the rumours further. On a Saturday morning, we decided to visit Porkpie mountain, to explore our local attractions. We went to the Chimanimani National Parks Office to pay for our permits, then embarked on our journey to the mountain on foot, in order to explore our environment along the way. We had never hiked, so we thought that it would be easy, but it turned out to be quite a challenge. The mountain seemed to be nearby visually, but it was challenging to reach the peak on foot. Our eyes had clearly deceived us. Along the way, we discovered some natural features that had been formed by Cyclone Idai, such as new waterfalls, gorges and craters. I enjoyed taking pictures of the beautiful attractions.

It took us two hours to reach the peak of the mountain, a tiresome but worthy journey. The view at the top was as magnificent as a dream coming true. We managed to have a nice view of beautiful places like Tilbury, Everglades farm and Chimanimani. Mesmerised by the beauty of glorious Chimanimani, we took pictures until our phone batteries ran empty.

"I have heard of theories on cures for this pandemic. The most popular one that I have heard in this community is the lemon and soda solution. But we know there are no herbal remedies that are recommended to cure coronavirus." I found myself resuscitating the burning issue. This time I wanted to bust the myths that surrounded Covid19.

"There is also the garlic theory girls. But there is no evidence confirming foods that should be eaten to cure this pandemic. Eating garlic might cure other sicknesses but not coronavirus," I preached.

"I also heard someone at the market yesterday saying that blacks are not affected by this disease." Chido added. We then had a long debate on the myths and theories surrounding the Coronavirus, until it was time to return home.

When the first case of Coronavirus was reported in Zimbabwe on 21 March, many people began to believe that the pandemic was serious. A famous journalist died from the virus. People in Ngangu began to focus more on protecting themselves after the announcement of the first case. This was followed by the closure of all schools and colleges on 21 March, as a way of reducing transmission of the disease among students.

The President announced 21 days of national lockdown, which began on 30 March 2020. Only seven cases and one death had been recorded by then. Many people in my community were not excited about the lockdown. Even

I thought that 21 days at home without anything else to do was hell on Earth. A few days before the lockdown begun, a lot of people arrived in Chimanimani from different places. The business centres were very busy as many people were buying food stuff for stocking.

My older sister Tatenda also arrived home from Harare. She explained how dangerous the Coronavirus was. I observed a population increase as people arrived at their rural homes for the lockdown. Personally, I thought all these people were bringing Coronavirus to us. My fear was made worse by the announcement from the Ministry of Health Child Care that we had to report any family with a member who had arrived from abroad without being tested. Our neighbour's daughter had arrived from South Africa and a rumour was spreading that she was sick. This was a lie because I saw her daily doing house chores and she was fit and fine. This brought confusion to some of us.

The first two weeks of the lockdown were bearable, and everyone followed the prescribed measures as expected. Everyone stayed home except for those who were going to work, like shop attendants and those in the health sector. Food shops were only allowed to operate from 9am to 3pm. One day I visited the Pondo Supermarket for my shopping. A lot of people were there for shopping too. Social distance was observed. The police were everywhere monitoring all movements. Loitering without good cause was a crime. Everyone wished for the lockdown to come to an end for them to continue with their normal daily routines.

On another day, when I was passing by the vegetable market, I heard voices talking and I got closer to eavesdrop. A police officer was asking an elderly woman why she was selling her tomatoes and disregarding the precautionary measures.

"Why are you not home? You know that you are not allowed to be selling out here," the police officer said at the top of his voice.

"My son, I'm very hungry and my children are hungry at home. I have nothing to give them. I thought that coming here alone to earn some money to buy a bag of mealie meal wouldn't be a problem. This is where my income comes from. Please my son, don't chase me away!" the woman said with teary eyes.

I felt pity for her. Just then, the police officer noticed me and ordered me to go home quickly. I ran back home and lost the chance to find out what happened to the hungry elderly woman.

At home, mom would not allow any of us to go out. She was afraid that if one of us left, they might come back with the disease and spread it to all of us. Being home with not much to do was mundane. I missed my friends and our outings so much, but there was nothing to be done about that. My community felt very different. The usual noise and screams of children playing outside had died down. There were no more cars roaming around. The usual hustle and bustle of our lively community had been brought to a halt. Waking up and going back to sleep again had become the daily routine. I felt as if the world had come to an end.

News all over seemed exclusively about the Coronavirus. The number of deaths in other countries increased day by day. This made me realise that it was worth staying home rather than going out and risk getting the disease.

The lockdown had negative and positive impact in my community. In the recent past, Cyclone Idai had destroyed crops, plantations and a lot of business centres. People had become reliant on charity aid. However, due to the Coronavirus lockdown, some of the non-governmental organisations that had been working in our community had to leave because of the disease. Hunger affected many households. A lot of people relied on informal business as their source of income. Women were especially affected as they were the ones who relied on the market sector. A lot of people's livelihoods came from the day to day sales of their goods, surviving from hand to mouth. Our neighbour told us that they had drastically reduced their daily food intake due to shortage of food. Her husband worked as a driver and she worked at a nearby market, and the lockdown had affected them both.

Due to hunger and poverty many people began engaging in crime and immoral behaviour for survival. Theft cases increased within a short period of time in Ngangu. One morning an unusual theft case was reported. Several car batteries were stolen from different houses during the night. My uncle Matthew was also one of the victims of that theft spree. He was my mother's cousin. The thefts were undetected, and the thieves were never caught. Only a few days after the battery theft, another theft case was reported. This time, thieves had broken into three cell phone shops and helped themselves to money and phones. The stolen goods were never recovered. These thefts resulted in huge financial loss to the shop owners, and since borders were closed, they had no means to restock their businesses. Another theft case involved robbers breaking into a grocery shop by getting into the store through the main door, without breaking it. It was rumoured that spiritual powers may have been employed to carry out the theft. The thefts were being driven by hunger and poverty. We began to see a rise in illegal deals, as a way to survive the lockdown.

Uncle Matthew ran a truck business, where he transported goods like timber, bananas and many other products from Chimanimani to many destinations. Around midnight one day, he was called by an anonymous man who wanted my uncle's service. The man wanted his timber to be transported to Beitbridge. My uncle insisted on doing it during the day, but the anonymous customer refused. He said that the deal was not to be seen by many, especially the police. I advised my uncle not to go, as he may have been tricked into illegal activity. The following morning, when my uncle called back the potential client on the same number, the line was no longer in use. This suggested to us that the potential customer may have been involved in illegal deals.

Girls and women were affected badly by the lockdown. The rising prices of basic needs such as sanitary protection made such items inaccessible. One day as I was queuing up to buy bread, I overheard two girls discussing how prostitution had become the only way to obtain money for basic needs. I turned around to look at them, but they were not ashamed, and my look did not seem to deter their conversation.

"Rudo, pads and many other girly things are now too expensive, but we have a sure way out my dear," one of them said.

"Yes dear, we just need to find a man each and everything will be fine," the other one responded with a mischievous facial expression, and they both giggled.

I was deeply touched by their desperation and I empathised with them. Remembering what Pastor Sithole had spoken about in church, that a lot of adolescent pregnancies in his church belonged to married men, I found myself intruding on their conversation.

"You could engage in income generating projects instead you know, rather than resorting to selling your bodies." They looked at me as if I had lost my mind and chuckled as they walked away from me. Sadly, even parents in our community were succumbing to child marriages, due to hunger and poverty.

The closure of schools due to the lockdown did not help; most kids did not have anything positive and productive to focus on. In schools there had been guidance and counselling, which many kids did not get from home. Due to lack of structure and positive guidance, some ended up resorting to drugs, prostitution and not adhering with the lockdown rules and regulations. Churches were also closed, which led to an increase in immorality. At Church we received healing and deliverance, and although many continued to cultivate their faith at home, many stopped and forgot about the Word. My mom continuously urged my siblings and I to not follow what other youths in the community were doing.

Chimanimani's tourism business was badly affected. Despite being one of the best tourist destinations in Zimbabwe, hotels and lodges had to be shut, and the workers had to go for the lockdown. This meant these areas lacked maintenance and monitoring. Tourist areas of natural beauty deteriorated due to lack of maintenance. International travel was restricted, and as many of the tourists came to Chimanimani from abroad, all local business shut down.

Many local people relied on farming as their main source of income. Farmers usually transported their products to markets, but due to the lockdown, they had nowhere to sell their products. Some ended up selling their produce locally at cheap prices, especially the perishables, and this presented big losses to them. It was challenging to fight against diseases, climate change and severe losses some of which had been triggered by Cyclone Idai. Since workers were on lockdown, farmers lacked manpower especially during the time of harvest, when help was needed most. Some crops ended up rotting in fields.

Movement restrictions caused severe frustration, and the police were everywhere on the road monitoring people's movements. My mom lost her brother who lived in Mutare, but she could not attend his funeral because she failed to obtain a travel permit, which was required to travel out of town. Transportation out of our town was also a major challenge. When one found the means to travel out, they would be asked to pay extortionate amounts of money by the drivers. People had no choice but to pay, because there were not many transport options to reach their destinations. Some people opted to walk very long distances due to a lack of means to fund their travels. Mr. Tinoota who worked in my community also walked from Ngangu to Bumba when his wife was sick in his rural home. Bumba was 60 kilometres away from Ngangu. The journey was worth it because his wife got better a few days after his arrival.

Thankfully, there was only one Coronavirus case recorded in Chimanimani. The health authorities played a pivotal role in educating the community on the dangers of Coronavirus. The police also worked hard and made sure that everyone stayed home or wore face masks in public. The imposition of face masks became the saving grace to some women in our community. Those women made masks for sale and managed to feed their families from the money they got from that business. Many people managed to groom their projects at home. Mr. Penyai, one of my neighbours told me that he managed to write a lot of books at home during the lockdown. My mother also managed to improve her poultry project during the lockdown.

Miss Nancy, a Shop attendant could not hide her happiness whilst explaining, "The lockdown has really improved my quality of life. I used to start work very early and finish late. When my working hours were reduced, I got home early and managed to do some of my duties at home." During the lockdown, a lot of families in my community reunited, as they managed to spend more time together. Children also managed to spend some quality time with their parents who stayed away from work and bars. Many parents were happy to be with their children who had relocated to South Africa and other countries, but fearing the disease they came back home.

This proved that while the lockdown was a major inconvenience for a lot of people, it was a breath of fresh air for others.